TAINTED TREASURE

HAUNTED COAST
BOOK 3

JENNIFER WILLIS

Cover artwork design by Steven Novak.

Author photo by Rachel Hadiashar.

Published by Jennifer Willis

Portland, Oregon

Jennifer-Willis.com

For Suzanne,
who is warm sunshine and gentle rain.

PROLOGUE

They say poison is a woman's weapon. That women like to plan their revenge, and shy away from violence and direct confrontation. That poison is subtle and cunning, and more dangerous than the sharpest blade.

But it is so much more than that.

You have to be sure about your intent. Do you want to kill, or disable? Do you target with compassion? With regret? Should your poison be administered with rage or vengeance? Will you be able to live with yourself once the deed is done?

You have to know what you're doing, too. Some poisons are quick. Some are merciful. Some poisons are hard to detect as they build up in the victim's system. One poison is fast-acting and can mimic a heart attack, if you want to be there to witness the results. Another poison takes its time, bringing illness and death so slowly that when the toxin is at last in full effect, it's too late to apply a remedy. And by that time, the poisoner can be long gone and have a solid alibi to boot.

Researching the right poison for the right application requires patience. It must be a careful pursuit, with no obvious paper or digital trail. If your calculations are off or your agent of choice is *faulty, your poison might incapacitate when you mean to kill. Choosing a poison should be a conscientious and deliberate task.*

Acquiring, blending, and handling the stuff is a tricky business. You must take every precaution to safeguard yourself and innocent others. You don't want to hurt the wrong person, or fall victim to your own mistake.

Then there is the delivery to consider—how, where, and when. Should the poison be baked into a favorite dish or a birthday cake, so the victim can be felled with one last hurrah? Or maybe the poisonous powder can be stirred into a fancy cocktail or a cup of coffee, or added to a prescription pill.

A sharp dagger would be quicker. A blunt object for bludgeoning is sufficient in a pinch. But these are a brute's methods. Poison requires knowledge and finesse. Poison is the lethal choice of an educated mind, and it can be prepared and served with simple elegance or sophisticated artistry.

Poison is also a foolish way to kill a friend.

CHAPTER ONE

February at the Oregon Coast is a chilly and wet experience. The gray soup in the sky likes to surprise those of us on the ground. Sometimes with heavy, ice-cold rain that finds the gap between your collar and neck and runs down your back, inside your clothes. Sometimes with sleet. Sometimes with hail. Or all of the above.

Then there are the rare days that lure you outdoors with the promise of sun, only to engulf you in freezing fog a few minutes later—like this morning, when I'd gotten the brilliant idea to walk into town from my cottage on the sandy point where the Pacific Ocean meets Naghatune Bay.

It's possible the winter beach weather wasn't gloomy or objectionable at all, and I was just in a bad mood. It didn't help that the freezing fog turned to hard rain halfway on my trek to town.

I pulled open the door to the teahouse side of the Tea Reader —my half-bookshop/half-teahouse establishment on Main Street in the small coastal town of Grady. My clothes and hair were damp from the rain. Chilled to the bone and with an ugly migraine throbbing at my right temple, I bypassed the line of customers and trudged right up to the barista counter.

The place should have been packed, especially on such a chilly day, but half the tables sat empty. I pretended not to notice.

"Suri!" Audrey's voice was as bright and cheerful as my mood was dark. The part-time witch and full-time barista had become my closest friend in the roughly six months since she'd moved to town. "You look like you need some warming up. Is it always like this?"

She pulled a ginormous, thirty-two-ounce insulated mug off a shelf and went to work building my favorite tea beverage. The Simply Suri was her own invention, a comforting blend of English breakfast tea, brown sugar, vanilla nut milk, and a dash of cinnamon. It was warm perfection in a mug and precisely what I needed.

"Winter at the coast, yes," I replied. "Pretty much gray and dark and wet from now until spring. But once you adjust, it's kind of relaxing, I guess. Quiet. Cozy, even."

I smiled, feeling my spirits lifting. I'd forgotten the upside to winter. This was the season for nestling in, maybe even hibernating.

"*Hygge*, right? Congenial comfort," Audrey said. "I get it."

Audrey handed over the mug, and I took a big gulp of tea, fully expecting it to burn the roof of my mouth. But it was perfect, just as Audrey was perfect but not in an annoying way that made me want to throttle her. Not often. She was relentless in her enthusiasm for life and its many mysteries—especially the weird magick that pervaded our little town of Grady and Naghatune Bay in general.

I don't enjoy being cantankerous, though I have a stubborn reputation as the town's resident curmudgeon. Chronic headaches plus natural introversion will do that. I know it's a major bummer to be around someone who has a headache every day. I try not to draw attention to the pain, but I can't always grit my way through it. Sometimes the sheer persistence of pain wears me down, and I get cranky. At least no one had called me "Surly" yet this morning.

But then someone's close, loud laughter made my headache screech, and I ducked through the pass-through doors that connect the bookshop to the teahouse. I closed the door behind me and went about the business of opening up the bookshop, without turning the lights on.

While the teahouse has become something of a community gathering place—even with the occasional, spontaneous town council meeting among the mismatched antique tables and chairs, because all the council members came in for their morning tea and scones anyway—the bookshop was my domain.

Thanks to my frequent headaches, I kept irregular hours and spent most of my time reading in a cozy chair nestled between bookcases. The bookshop was quiet and didn't get many customers, and that's exactly how I liked it.

I stopped when I spotted the unopened box on the sales counter. Loki had made another of his mystery deliveries, only this box was waiting for me inside the bookshop instead of outside on the porch.

"Hello?" I called to the shadows. Loki was an enigma, and not in an inviting or intriguing way. He dressed all in black like a Goth beatnik, but had the air of an absentminded professor of sinister wizardry. I didn't yet know if he was friend, foe, or mere annoyance, and I didn't want to think about how he'd gotten inside without a key. I still hadn't repaired the security camera on the front porch, but I could probably put off that task until closer to tourist season.

There was no sign that the Vexation in Black was lingering nearby. Neither did a ghostly apparition manifest in the Oregon history section or over by the watercolor postcards near the front door. No unwelcome whispers in my ear or otherworldly breath on my cheek. I exhaled and let my tight shoulders drop.

Another reason I'm sometimes Surly: being a medium is not

my idea of a good time. It used to be the occasional unwelcome spirit with an urgent message of regret for a living loved one, so they could move on to their eternal rest. The last time that happened, the living loved one turned out to be a now middle-aged classmate from middle school geography class who a) didn't remember the decedent, b) called me a scam artist, and c) literally shooed me out with a broom, after I'd driven two hundred miles to deliver the dead man's fervent apology for putting ants in her shoes. Another long-dead ghost promised me the passcode to a lucrative investment account if I would play messenger, but the bank had gone under shortly after her death.

Nowadays, it was mostly murder victims, and I can't say that was an improvement. I came to this tiny hamlet thinking I'd escape big city hauntings, only to land in an area of magickal weirdness and oddly frequent suspicious deaths.

For the moment, however, I was alone.

My boots clunked on the floorboards as I came around the sales counter. I tried to turn on the tablet that served as both cash register and inventory database, but it had been on the fritz for a few days. I picked it up and shook it, which seemed to help, and the curled pages of the wall calendar rustled behind me. I glanced at the dusty photo of an Irish country stream—in Tralee, County Kerry, according to the small print. I'd nailed the calendar to the wall the week I first opened the Tea Reader a few years back, but stopped turning the pages after October.

Ice spattered against the window glass. I put down my tea and turned my attention to Loki's latest delivery. The musty, nostalgic scent of archival newspapers and grandparents' attics wafted out as I cut the string and the box sprang open.

"What did he bring you this time?" Audrey asked, and I jumped. "Sorry! I didn't mean to scare you."

"Just that kind of morning, I guess," I replied. The books and trinkets inside didn't look especially old. Maybe it was the box itself that was ancient and musty. I turned on the little space heater on the floor behind the counter and let it start drying my soggy denim.

"An extra excuse to get cuddling with Colin!" Audrey exclaimed.

"What?" I looked up in confusion, wondering what she had spied in the box that had anything to do with her romance with the assistant deputy sheriff. But she jutted her chin at the murky morning outside the window, then gave me a conspiratorial wink.

"Valentine's is coming," she practically sang. "And bad weather can make for an extra-romantic holiday. Do you have any special plans?"

"No." I started pulling items out of the box. There was a tall, thin volume of *The Illustrated Egyptian Book of the Dead*, a worn paperback copy of Joseph Campbell's *The Power of Myth*, a yellowing copy of *Conspiracy Theory: Vikings in the New World*, a spiral-bound *Binocular Highlights* from *Sky & Telescope Magazine* that was practically falling apart, a brand new edition of *New in Seattle*, and two copies of *Bewitching the Heart: Love Spells for the Modern Age*.

Audrey picked up one of the love spells books. "Not even with Eddie?"

"No. I don't know." I sighed. Where my love life was concerned, Audrey was persistent.

But it was complicated. I mean, there was Jim Vandenhauter, an ex from years ago who was now the deputy sheriff of Naghatune Bay, and who carried a physical scar from our time together. Then there was Eddie Cortés, the fire fighter I'd seen a few times since he rescued me from the blaze at the Grazzini House that launched a literal ghost chase, a foiled kidnapping, and a murder investigation.

"Just allow for the possibility," Audrey said with a shrug.

Deeper in the box, I found a blue and white paper table cover in a snowflake pattern, a miniature green lava lamp, a half-dozen pairs of fuzzy fleece socks in bright colors, and a toner cartridge for a Brother laser printer.

It was an odd assortment, but if I'd learned anything about these strange boxes from Loki, it was that people would soon wander into the store in search of nearly every one of these items. Sometimes there was a dud, like the box of abstract art greeting cards that had been sitting on one of the front tables since Christmas. No one had come for the Tiffany lamp from the same delivery, but it looked nice in the bookshop window. Maybe that one had been for me.

Speaking of which . . . I pulled off my boots and damp socks. Apparently, my rugged footwear had started to leak. The canary yellow fleece socks from the mystery box felt so much better on my chilly feet.

"This will spice up my Valentine's plans, at least." Audrey waggled her eyebrows, then stood up straight as the bell over the bookshop door rang.

Karina Coyle stepped inside from the rain and pulled back the hood of her Burberry coat. Not a strand of her wavy, dark blond hair was wet, much less out of place. Her delicate floral perfume preceded her as her high-heeled boots clicked across the hardwood—she smelled like tea time with the queen, a welcome change from the ocean salt that permeated Naghatune Bay. Karina was roughly my age, but everything about her oozed sophistication and style—so basically the polar opposite of me, and not just because I was standing in my stocking feet, hovering over a space heater to dry my damp trousers.

She was also the new competition in town, having opened up the Tea & Botanicals Dispensary on the other end of Main Street. Her shop's cannabis-infused teas and edibles had taken a big enough bite out of the Tea Reader's profits that the teahouse manager was talking about cutting barista hours. For the first time, the Tea Reader books were in the red.

I had every reason to despise Karina Coyle, but she'd been nothing but friendly and genuine with me.

"Suri! I'm so glad you're here." Karina's voice was like warm honey. "Your shop is so inviting when it's just miserable outside."

Audrey made a scoffing noise deep in her throat. She suspected Karina's every move and word, as though each action or syllable were a poisoned dagger.

I ignored Audrey. "Can I help you with something this soggy morning?"

Karina's laugh sounded like tinkling crystal, because of course it did. "I'm hoping you can help me find a book." She leaned closer, and I sensed a nervous excitement in her. "Because, well, you know Valentine's Day is nearly here."

She laughed again, and I could feel Audrey roll her eyes without looking at her.

"What kind of book?" I asked.

"Well, I already have *books*, you know, but I'm looking for something more specific, something that might help with . . ." Karina glanced down at the second copy of *Bewitching the Heart* on the sales counter. She looked back up at me with a new glint in her eyes. "Oh, Suri! You're a genius! How ever did you know?"

I pushed the book across the counter toward her. Karina picked it up and held it to her heart.

"You know, my assistant manager, Bard, has a thing for magick, too," she said. "But maybe everyone in Grady does?" she giggled, and Audrey groaned. "I should tell him to come by your shop sometime." Then the snowflake table cover caught her eye.

"Take it," I said. "If you can use it."

"I absolutely can!" Karina pulled out a soft leather wallet. If it was a designer knock-off, I couldn't tell the difference.

"No charge," I said, though Audrey looked like her eyes were about to pop out of her head.

"I couldn't. You've been so kind to me since I got here. Not everyone has been as welcoming to a newcomer like me." Karina held my gaze. I wondered how badly she wanted to give Audrey a sideways glance. Karina placed two twenty-dollar bills on the counter. "Thank you so much, Suri! This is just what I needed."

Karina gave Audrey a quick nod before she was out the door again, taking her sparkle with her. The bookshop dimmed in her absence.

Audrey let out a heavy sigh. "Can you *believe* her?"

I slid the money into the cash drawer. Barbara would be happy to see at least one bookshop sale today. "What have you got against Karina?"

"Are you kidding?" Audrey put down the book and lifted a hand to count her grievances. "She swoops in out of nowhere to set up a tea shop just down the street." That counted as two fingers.

"She didn't swoop." I inched away from the space heater, afraid my new socks would melt. "And the TBD is not just a tea shop."

"She steals your customers by getting them high and then, I don't know, like hypnotizing them or something, and now your business is toast." Another two fingers.

"That's not how pot edibles work, and I think you know that." I tilted my head from one side to the other. The headache was losing its edge, and I felt my body start to warm up.

Audrey paused her counting. "You're ruining my fun with this."

"It's fun to hate someone for no logical reason?"

"Absolutely! You should try it some time." She stuck her thumb in the air to emphasize her last and most grievous point. "And she's going after Jim."

"So?" I looked away, pretending I didn't feel even a hint of jealousy.

"Colin says she's been stopping by the station a lot more than remotely necessary. Always bringing them cookies and stuff."

"She's not taking cannabis cookies to the deputy sheriff's

office, is she?" I didn't like the alarm in my voice, but I also didn't like the idea of some out-of-towner with her fancy clothes and trendy business putting Jim's job in jeopardy as well as my own.

"Doubtful. But Colin said she's asked Jim to her place for dinner on February fourteenth."

"You and your boyfriend are gossiping about the deputy sheriff's love life?" I was a lot warmer and more energized now, and it wasn't a cozy feeling. "Don't you have anything more exciting to talk about?"

"Not the deputy sheriff, Suri. *Jim*." She gave me a meaningful look. "Is this what we want for him?"

A stern throat-clearing announced Barbara's appearance in the pass-through doorway. My teahouse manager was in charge of the bookkeeping, budgets, and all employees. She answered only to me, and only sometimes. She gave Audrey a hard look that even I could read. Audrey was supposed to be manning the teahouse counter, not gossiping with the boss.

Audrey glanced at the remaining copy of *Bewitching the Heart* and gave me an inquiring look.

"Take it," I said. "I'm sure not going to use it."

"You never know, Suri." Audrey snapped up the book and went back to work.

And that was the last semi-peaceful moment I had that day.

"HOW HAVE you never tried kombucha before?" Audrey stood at the end of the teahouse counter and poured a tiny glass of amber-colored liquid that was vaguely fizzy on top.

I'd arrived at the Tea Reader barely an hour earlier, and already most of the patrons had moved on. Now only about a quarter of the mismatched antique tables were occupied.

It was normal for things to slow down in the winter, as tourists left for the season. Sightseers who flocked to the coast to watch the winter storms come in off the ocean usually kept to bigger towns like Lincoln and Newport. But this was sparse attendance even for a rainy Monday morning in February.

It had everything to do with Karina's Tea and Botanicals Dispensary—the TBD for short—just down the street. The only reason some customers stopped at the Tea Reader first was that the TBD opened an hour later than we did.

Audrey pushed the glass toward me. She was always experimenting in the kitchen, more typically with baked goods. She had invented a few popular hot tea drinks for the Tea Reader, including the one she named after me.

I normally didn't mind being her taste-tester, but fermented drinks were new to both of us. She'd already discarded three batches of pomegranate, kiwi, and rosemary kombucha before presenting this brew to me.

"Are you sure we don't need a liquor license for this?" I asked. The dark liquid sloshed inside the glass as I took a cautious sniff. It looked like beer. Smelled like it, too.

Audrey smirked and waited for Ravi King's hooting laughter to subside.

"And then you lost your boot in the mud!" Ravi howled. Ravi and his partner in adventure, Bud Barlow, were back from their latest treasure hunt in the hills to the north of Naghatune Bay. Wearing nearly identical outfits of hiking pants and fleece pullovers, they were holding court at the biggest table in the teahouse—two men at a table for eight, with a pair of single-serve teapots, plates of half-eaten scones, and tall, half-empty glasses of spiced cider scattered between them. "But lady luck was on our side! Didn't I tell you? And look at us now!"

"Yeah, you did." Bud grinned back at him, then glanced around the teahouse. "But maybe let's not tell everybody about it?"

Ravi and Bud were two of the many treasure hunters and spiritual seekers who'd found their way to Naghatune Bay in the years since the freak lightning storm, when the weird magick landed in our quiet coastal enclave. The Meridian Retreat on the other side of the Bay did a brisk business in metaphysical seminars and "psychic weekends" for the transcendentally inclined.

Rumors of treasure hidden in the hills abounded, and the promise of *magick treasure* drew at least a half-dozen hearty hopefuls to the area every summer. But here in mid-February, Ravi and Bud were still in residence at Lantz's Boarding House and lingering at the teahouse for a few days every fortnight or so when they returned to town to gather supplies and warm their bones.

Ravi smacked the table with an open hand and threw his head back to laugh. A young couple from California, who'd somehow picked Grady for a romantic getaway, glanced at Ravi and Bud with irritation. Emmaline Kapul, the proprietress of the Knitting Genie across the street, adjusted her earbuds and focused on the large rectangle coming off her needles as she drew fine lavender yarn from a ball in a bag slung over the back of her chair.

"No respect for other people," grumbled Murray Overhill at a table against the far wall. He was nursing a single pot of tea and taking his time with an orange ginger cookie as he paged through a thick hardbound book. He was probably still grumpy about the community library project coming to town and thwarting his paid library-by-mail scheme.

"I'm a barista, not a bartender," Audrey said when Ravi and Bud resumed their indoor voices. "There's a tiny bit of alcohol due to fermentation, but I'm careful to keep it low. Just enough to give the booch a little kick."

"Booch?" I asked.

"Booch. Kombucha." Audrey sighed in perfect imitation of a teenager whose parents were *so not cool* and way out of touch, even though she was in her late 20s and I was only a few years older. "Look, we need something new to compete with the TBD. Why not this?"

At the other end of the teahouse counter, our newest barista Cyndi looked up from rearranging the heart-shaped sugar cookies in the glass pastry case. She offered a quiet shrug, her long earrings swinging in time beneath her short blond bob. Cyndi looked barely old enough to drink, but she was one of Audrey's taste-testers, too, and had apparently survived.

"Dude, it's good stuff," added Taylor, another new barista who'd arrived in Grady from parts unknown. With wavy dark hair that brushed the shoulders of his worn flannel shirt, he looked like a winter beach bum in training. He went back to his conversation with Mildred Moroni, our local grocer, about a ghost hunting show as he wiped down a nearby table.

"Are you going to the ghost conference up in Seaside?" Mildred asked. "J.P. Howarth from *The Ghost Patrol* is a guest speaker!"

Taylor balled the cleaning cloth in his fist and looked like he wanted to spit. "You know they fake all that 'evidence,' right? There was a YouTube channel all about it, 'til it got shut down."

I held the glass up to the light and tried to convince myself that the kombucha—a lemon ginger flavor Audrey had brewed, or fermented, in the Tea Reader's back kitchen—looked more like thick apple cider than a not-legally crafted microbrew.

Audrey wasn't wrong. Ever since the Tea and Botanicals Dispensary had opened down the street, their cannabis-infused teas and shop-baked edibles had lured teahouse patrons away. If something didn't shift soon, the Tea Reader was in trouble.

So, kombucha?

With Audrey's expectant eyes on me, I took a tentative sip. And . . . It wasn't awful? I couldn't help my grimace or my wrinkled nose, though. The stuff made me feel like I needed to sneeze.

"It can't be that bad, Suri," Audrey huffed. "Even Barbara likes it. We just need your final approval."

Barbara rarely requested my approval for anything, which meant this was Audrey's attempt to keep me in the loop regarding my own business.

"No, it's not bad." I coughed and grimaced again. Audrey told me about how kombucha was wildly popular, with fermented teas driving sales through the roof at coffee shops up and down the coast. She swore her "booch" didn't have even a half-a-percent of alcohol in it, but I was having flashbacks to college keggers after a single sip.

"But it's not *good*." Audrey turned the big jug in an absent fashion, but I could see the gears churning in her head about new recipes and the timing of her kombucha batches already on the pantry shelves.

"I'm sure it's fine." I thought about chugging the rest of the glass, maybe four ounces, to make her feel better. But I couldn't do that to myself. There was no telling what might trigger the next migraine, and I had to be careful when I tried anything new. I pushed the glass away. "I'm not your target customer. That's all. If Barbara likes it, if *you* like it and think it will do well, and if you're sure we don't need any special licensing, then we should give it a try."

"Oh, great!" Audrey's face lit up. "Because I've got at least nine other flavors to try, for different seasons and holidays. I'm working on something warming and cinnamon-y for Valentine's Day."

"Thank goodness we're well past Thanksgiving and Christmas," I said. "I don't think I could take any more pumpkin spice right now."

Audrey's eyes widened. "That's a spectacular idea!"

While I worried I'd inspired a kombucha-brewing monster, there came another uproar from Ravi and Bud's table, this time tinged with anger. Ravi pounded the table with his fist as his face reddened. Cyndi slid a clean cloth over the counter as she came closer to huddle with us.

"They've been doing that for the past hour," Cyndi whispered. "Laughing, and then arguing."

Ravi banged the table again and shouted something about a recreational vehicle, a dog, and a book deal before Bud rested a hand on his partner's shoulder and asked him to calm down. Bud gave Cyndi a pleading look, but she shrugged in response.

Instead, Ravi shot to his feet, and his straight-back chair tipped over with a loud bang. "Everybody! Everybody, listen up!" He slapped the table a few times, as if the rest of us in the teahouse weren't already giving him our full attention—except for Emmaline, who kept her eyes on her knitting but removed her earbuds to listen.

"Ravi, sit down!" Bud hissed, then buried his face in his hands. They'd been on the hunt longer than any treasure team I knew about. Maybe their nerves were frayed after adventuring in the hills for so long.

Ravi strode to the center of the room, pulled a leather pouch from a cargo pocket in his trousers, and held it high in triumph. "*There is treasure in the hills!*"

"So you keep saying." Emmaline tugged on her lavender yarn and kept her needles moving, expertly avoiding getting the earbud cord tangled in her knitting. "Is this like when y'all found that 'priceless artifact of cross-cultural significance' in the woods that turned out to be an old Halloween costume?"

Barbara chuckled. Before I'd come to Grady, a hopeful treasure hunter had come across a delicate and decaying mask in the hills, prompting wild speculations about ancient Vikings settlements along the Pacific Northwest Coast. Then a team of graduate students from Pacific College's anthropology program determined the artifact was a homemade balsa wood Snoopy mask, probably forgotten after a Halloween campout.

That's the story I'd heard, gossip that got resurrected for entertainment at parties and around plates of teacakes. I'd had no idea that Ravi and Bud were the disgraced hunters from that story.

Ravi shot Emmaline a hostile scowl, and Bud looked like he wanted to disappear into the floorboards. Murray Overhill, who had put down his book to enjoy the spectacle, laughed and started reading again.

"This is different," Ravi announced with conviction, even as Bud stood and tried to guide Ravi back to their table. But Ravi tucked a strand of stringy black hair behind his ear and punched the air with his fist around the leather pouch. "We've done it this time. We've found treasure! And it's right here!"

That got everyone's attention. What kind of loot could fit in such a small pouch? Gemstones? Pirate coins? For all I knew, Ravi and Bud had come across another old campsite and found a pouch of custom-printed gaming dice.

"It's really nothing, folks." Bud patted at the air and encouraged everyone to ignore the wild-eyed man shouting about treasure in the teahouse. "We're just happy to be warm and inside again."

"*Magick tea!*" Ravi exclaimed with glee as Bud righted his chair and coaxed him to sit.

"Please tell me they didn't add whatever's in that pouch to their teapots," Barbara said.

"He's kind of cute when he gets like this, don't you think?" Cyndi beamed as she watched Ravi. "It can be a bit much, but he's just so *passionate*, you know?"

"You think they really found magick tea?" Audrey asked.

"Unlikely," Barbara replied.

"It's true!" Ravi raised his cup of tea in a toast. "We've found a stash of ancient herbs that will change the world! Thomas Catesby himself is coming to verify our find! We're going to be famous, Bud and me." He smiled at his friend and drank his tea in one victorious gulp. But Bud looked like he was about to be physically ill as he gripped the edge of the table.

"Bud?" I started toward the table as Ravi boasted about how he and Bud were on the verge of making history. I had no idea who Thomas Catesby was, and judging by the facial expressions of those around me, no one else in the teahouse did, either. But it was a Big Deal to Ravi, who continued his ravings to the point that he was starting to froth at the mouth, and ignored the distress of his partner.

"Audrey, call an ambulance, and call Dr. Settle!" I shouted over my shoulder. We didn't have a medical practice in Grady, and Dr. Settle was down the road in Standish Beach. He was a retired gynecologist, but he might get to the teahouse faster than the rescue squad.

I hoped I was overreacting and that Bud was merely embarrassed by Ravi's outbursts or had acid indigestion. I looked forward to apologizing to everyone—Bud, Ravi, the teahouse patrons and staff, even Dr. Settle and the rescue crew. We'd give everyone a round of tea and scones on the house, and the incident would be the scandalous talk of the town for the rest of the week.

But it wasn't Bud who needed the doctor. Ravi's cackling glee was cut short as he hit the floor with a thud. His glassy eyes stared, unblinking, at the ceiling as more foam oozed from his mouth with every wheezing exhale.

Cyndi started screaming. Bud lurched forward, scattering dishes and spilling the tea and cider, then turned to vomit on the floor.

"Ravi!" Audrey sprinted past me and pulled Ravi's head into her lap. "You have to come now!" she shouted into her phone before she threw it to Cyndi with orders to direct the paramedics to the Tea Reader. It gave Cyndi something to do other than stand by in hysterical tears.

I stood frozen in place as Audrey pushed Ravi's long hair out of his face. She told him to hang on, that the ambulance was on its way. His eyes never found her face. His gasping breaths were quick and shallow.

"Ravi." Bud slumped in his chair, chest heaving.

Ravi gave one last guttural moan as his fist opened and the leather pouch rolled out of his fingers.

Ravi King lay dead at my feet.

CHAPTER TWO

The Tea Reader shut down immediately, of course, with Barbara closing the doors to all but emergency personnel and law enforcement before I could even get my thoughts in order.

Ravi King lay dead on the teahouse floor. The paramedics had covered the body with a silver emergency blanket, awaiting transport to the coroner's office in Hattieville.

Both the deputy sheriff and assistant deputy sheriff—Jim and Colin—were on the scene, snapping photos, collecting tea cups and half-eaten scones in evidence bags, and questioning the patrons and baristas who'd witnessed Ravi's sudden death.

There was no sign of Ravi King's ghost. I kept looking for him, hoping he was lingering nearby—in the shadow of the bakery case, or maybe sitting at the table he'd occupied with Bud.

Had Ravi moved on so soon? Maybe he didn't have any unfinished business that caused him to linger, but he'd been plenty worked up in his last moments. Even if his news turned out to be deluded nonsense, it had seemed urgent to him.

Was it a heart attack? An aneurysm? If he could tell me what happened, I'd pass that information to Jim on the sly. Unfortunately, freshly made ghosts weren't the most reliable or lucid sources of information. And what if it wasn't a cardiac event, but something nefarious?

Being interrogated by my ex-boyfriend only added to the stress of the situation, and I said as much to Jim.

"I'm not interrogating you, Suri." Deputy Sheriff Jim Vandenhauter sat across from me at a small table in a back corner of the teahouse. I'd offered hot tea and muffins to him and the other responders, but no one would touch the stuff. Probably no customers would, either, until Ravi's cause of death was determined.

Jim lowered his voice. "Can you . . . *Ask* what happened?"

I gave a tight shake of the head. The people of Grady already knew about me—Surly Mudge, reluctant medium and full-time sourpuss—but I wasn't open for business as an on-demand fortune teller.

"If he's here, I've not seen him," I said. "I don't know what happened." I wiped tears from my eyes and hated Jim's softening features in response. He was doing his job, but I knew his feelings went beyond professional compassion, regardless of how complicated our relationship had been. Or still was.

He'd believed in me from the start, even when I had serious doubts. But I hated being the damsel in distress. I hated that yet another crisis—yet another death—had been deposited literally at my feet, and that Jim as always was swooping in to fix it.

And I hated that I was thinking more about myself than about Ravi King.

"We'll figure out what happened." Jim reached across the table to touch my wrist. I pulled away and clasped my hands together in my lap. My heart sank as Assistant Deputy Sheriff Colin Jung strung yellow "POLICE LINE DO NOT CROSS" tape over the front doors.

I gestured toward the door. "Business was bad enough with the new dispensary down the street. I know we need to be closed to deal with all of this. But it's not like everybody in town doesn't already know what happened. Do you have to advertise that the teahouse might be a crime scene?"

Jim jumped up to have a hushed word with his overzealous underling. Audrey slipped into Jim's seat and placed a brown glass jug of kombucha and a couple of glasses on the table.

"How're you holding up?" She watched Colin as he conferred with Jim. She and Colin had been dating a few months and they had a kitten together, though the little hellion spent as much time at my cottage as either of their places. "I asked him not to do that."

"They're doing their job." I nodded toward the heavy jug. "You're not serving that, are you?"

"I tried. Just to get some more taste-testers, right? But nobody wants any."

I resisted looking at the body on the floor. The silver blanket stood out against the dark hardwood planks and reflected light from the overhead fixtures. I would picture the scene enough in my nightmares as it was. "They'll probably want that as evidence."

Colin headed our way with a plastic box. He looked genuinely pained. "Sorry, Audrey, Suri. But I need to take that. In case it's, you know, poisoned. Tainted."

"Don't let anybody hear you say that." Audrey slumped in her chair and let him box up the brew she'd worked so hard to produce. Because Colin was always thorough, he'd take everything she had fermenting in the back, too, though I didn't think either Ravi or Bud had tasted a drop of the stuff.

Bud was looking better as he huddled under an emergency blanket on the other side of the teahouse. He was pale and trembling, and it would be a while before he could answer Jim's questions, but at least he wasn't dead on the floor. Bud kept glancing at the covered body a few meters from where he sat, then looked away again.

Audrey slid the jug across the table to Colin. "Take it where? Didn't you tell me the county forensics person is out on maternity leave? You don't exactly have a crime lab at the station."

She wasn't wrong. The Naghatune Bay Deputy Sheriff's office was a converted gas station that sat roughly halfway between Grady and Standish Beach. A couple of storage closets doubled as holding cells, and the rest of the space was occupied by a pair of desks, a kitchenette, and a succession of potted palms that kept dying.

Colin offered an apologetic shrug and sealed the jug inside the box. "But we're still on for tonight, right? Spaghetti and *Starship Catan*? Or do you want *Annikai Run* instead?"

It was their Monday-night ritual: comfort food and a board game, or sometimes a puzzle they worked on together. Friday nights were reserved for culinary experimentation and streaming entertainment, preparing dinner together to match the movie they watched. Previous pairings included Chicago hot dogs and home-made Chicago-style pizza for *Ferris Bueller's Day Off*; chicken pot pie and a spiced peach pie to accompany *Waitress*; and portabello mushroom burgers and doughnuts for *NOPE*. Despite Colin being a conservative skeptic and Audrey being a practicing witch—who had been a murder suspect when they met—they were the most adorable couple I'd ever seen.

Audrey nodded and patted his arm. She watched him cart several weeks of her work out the front door into the icy February rain.

While Jim took a seat next to Bud, the unlikely pair of Emmaline Kapul and Murray Overhill had their heads together near the door as they waited their turn to be questioned. Nothing but crumbs remained in the bakery cases—Colin had cleared everything out. At least a dozen townspeople stood outside in the freezing precipitation and fogged up the windows as they peered in, hoping to be the first to glean the salient details of the latest scandal at the Tea Reader. Behind them, sparse morning traffic slowed to a crawl as drivers shouted questions to onlookers about what was happening inside the teahouse.

And, of course, there was still the body on the floor.

Barbara marched out of the back kitchen and headed straight for Audrey. "Your boyfriend boxed up every scrap of food and tea in our inventory."

"They have to take it, Barbara." The words tasted sour in my mouth. It was hard not to think about how much this inopportune death would cost my business, and maybe impact the jobs of my employees. The Tea Reader had already suffered a steep insurance premium hike after an angry poltergeist wrecked the teahouse in full view of the community. Jim's official report chalked up the damage to "vandalism," but that hadn't been a fun conversation with the insurance adjuster.

My body did the worrying my brain refused, and I swallowed hard against bile rising in my throat. "In case it's a poisoning. Which, of course, it's not."

I looked around for Cyndi. She'd plated the scones and muffins for Bud and Ravi, and she'd made their tea. Now she sat on the floor, her face ashen as she stared at the blanket-covered body. Silent tears ran down her cheeks.

"I'll take the doc's first available appointment," Murray shouted into his phone as he stood beside Emmaline, then commented, "Something like this really makes you think."

"Listen, we're probably all in shock," I said to anyone within earshot. "Let's all cooperate with the deputy sheriff, then go home to take care of ourselves. The Tea Reader is closed for the rest of the day."

"But they've absconded with all our tea and baked goods." Barbara watched Colin head into the kitchen with more boxes and a dolly. "How are we supposed to re-open?"

"We have our regular orders arriving this week." Audrey kept her voice light, but I heard the strained edge. "We won't be fully restocked, but it's something."

Barbara turned to Audrey. "How much baking can you do at home tonight?"

"Tonight?" Audrey had plans with Colin. After the day we'd had, she probably needed a night of cuddling under a blanket, plus fantasy world gaming by an open fire while they sipped hot chocolate and watched Simba the kitten knock over the game pieces. At least, that's how I imagined their date nights.

But Audrey didn't blink. "I can make a few batches of cookies, maybe a couple dozen muffins and scones, if I can use Suri's kitchen?" She turned to me. "As soon as they're done with us here, we'll go shopping for ingredients and get to work. Pull an all-nighter if we have to."

"You're changing our plans?" Coming out of the kitchen, Colin gave Audrey a look that was inscrutable to me but easily read by his girlfriend. Audrey hopped up from her seat to smooth things over with him.

"If he pushes back," Barbara called after her, "remind your boyfriend that he's the reason we don't have anything to sell to our customers."

Assuming we'd even have customers. Despite the weather, the crowd on the sidewalk was growing. Twenty or more faces pressed against the windows. Some I recognized as they shielded their eyes to peer inside. Other faces were obscured and distorted by the fogged glass. There would be plenty of foot traffic outside the Tea Reader, but who would come inside for a warming beverage or baked goodies, if not on a dare?

Barbara crossed her arms. "Not to speak ill of the dead, but couldn't Ravi pick somewhere else to croak? Maybe waited 'til he was in his car?"

A gasp followed by a low moan on the other side of the room let us know that Bud had heard her words. Barbara lifted her hands in apology.

"No disrespect," I called to Bud as the paramedics strapped Ravi's body onto a gurney to carry to the waiting ambulance.

"I'm sorry for your loss, Bud. You and Ravi have been good customers, and good members of the community."

I wanted to say more, but the gurney rolling Ravi's body out the door stole everyone's focus—save for Jim, who had made his way over to Murray and Emmaline. Jim didn't look up from his little notebook as he questioned them.

Eddie Cortés caught the door before it closed behind the gurney, and he shook the ice out of his dark hair as he came in from the cold. The man was as tall and broad as an oak tree, and his easy vitality filled the solemn quiet.

"Suri!" Dressed in his Coastal Fire and Rescue uniform, Eddie headed straight for my little table at the back of the teahouse. His face was an open display of worry and relief as he knelt beside my chair and reached for my hands. "I'm glad you're okay. When I heard there'd been a call to the Tea Reader . . ."

He squeezed my fingers and kissed my knuckles. From the kitchen entrance, Audrey waggled her eyebrows at me and went back to her negotiations with her own boyfriend about their evening plans.

Not that Eddie was my boyfriend. I wasn't sure what he was. We'd met two months earlier when I'd gotten caught inside a house fire at a fundraising event, and he saved me from the smoke and flames. He'd been on a mission to woo me ever since. With dark hair and warm eyes, he could have made a handsome living as a cover model for romance novels. He was gallant, too, and all the things little girls are expected to hope for in so many sexist antiquated fantasies—without being sexist or antiquated himself.

As Emmaline gesticulated with her knitting needles to describe Ravi King's last moments, Jim looked up from his notebook and frowned at Eddie making a fuss over me. When he caught me noticing, Jim rolled his eyes and asked Emmaline what she'd ordered from the barista counter.

"I'm fine, Eddie. You didn't need to come all this way." I was about to say that he could have texted me, but I had a habit of not responding and letting his calls go to voice mail.

"It looks like a stroke." Eddie pulled up a chair. "But I heard someone outside say maybe it was poison?" He kept his voice low, but it wasn't like the rumor of the Tea Reader's lethal biscuits hadn't made two full circles around town already.

"They don't know yet. It happened fast. It couldn't have been anything from our kitchen or kettles." I hoped that was true, but my breath caught when I saw that someone—maybe a spectator outside, or a specter inside—had scrawled K-I-L-L-E-R on the foggy window glass.

I remembered the letters in pink spray-paint on the bookshop entrance the previous December. Paired with a stab of anxiety, I felt deep disappointment at the lack of originality in Grady. But I was distracting myself from the fact that someone had died.

Emmaline gave a little shriek at the graffiti in the window condensation. Gasps from the crowd outside were loud enough to alert Colin. Jim rose to his feet and demanded to know who had pulled this prank, but it was doubtful a living culprit would have escaped his detection.

I glanced around the teahouse again, but there remained no sign of Ravi's ghost.

With a deceased customer in an ambulance out front, and "KILLER" in giant letters on the inside of the front window, this wasn't going to help business at all.

I FOLLOWED Audrey through the aisles of Moroni Grocery, pushing the rickety, narrow cart as she guesstimated how many sacks of flour and pounds of sugar we'd need for the night. At the register, Mildred Moroni was monologuing about the morning's "Tea Reader tragedy" to anyone who would listen, and occasionally asked if Audrey and I were permanently traumatized, without pausing for a response. Not that I was saying anything.

With the teahouse closed, I'd locked the doors of the book-shop, too. I needed to get away from Main Street. Despite the weather, it seemed as good a day as any to fulfill my promise to a little ghost.

After a quick stop at my cottage to unload the baking ingre-dients and to pick up the memorial stone I'd ordered, Audrey and I headed up to Grady's historical area, overlooking the Pacific Ocean.

Eddie was leaning on a shovel and waiting for us by his orange SUV in the front of the Grazzini House. It had been at least a month since I'd last come up the hill to visit the historic Queen Anne home and the child ghost haunting the side garden.

Renovation work was underway at the old house, to repair the damage of the fire that had trapped me inside during the recent Christmastime fundraiser soiree, and to prepare the prop-erty to serve as Grady's first community library. I don't know what the library committee had told the construction crews about the side garden, but I was glad to see they had left the hedges and flowerbeds alone.

Eddie smiled as we wheeled the marble block over on a collapsible dolly, but the concern in his eyes was plain. "You sure you want to do this today?"

"I've been putting it off too long, and I need something good to come from this day." I maneuvered the dolly over the transi-tion from pavement to grass, then slowed when the small ghost of Agatha Cooke took shape in the garden. The child of servants in the Grazzini House, she'd been only eight years old when she and her younger brother were murdered by Teddy Grazzini a century before.

"That's a good spot." She pointed at the frosted grass directly in front of me. "People will see it there."

I gestured to the ground for Eddie. "Agatha wants it here."

Like Audrey, Eddie knew I could see and hear ghosts, and they both accepted the fact with ease. It was a nice change not to hide my talent, and not to worry about being asked to perform super-natural favors.

Eddie approached with his shovel, then addressed the space where he assumed Agatha to be. "Just stand back a bit. I don't want to disrupt you with the shovel."

Audrey nudged me with her elbow. "He's even polite to the dead."

The marker wasn't all that heavy, but Eddie insisted on shifting it himself. "No sense in you getting dirty or risking a pulled muscle," he said.

Agatha looked on with approval as Eddie fitted the stone into place. She asked me to read the inscription aloud.

"In memory of Agatha and Adam Cooke," I read. "You are braver than you believe, stronger than you seem, and smarter than you think."

The first week of January, I'd brought dozens of books up to this spot and read to Agatha children's stories, bits of scripture, and snippets of poetry to find the right words for this memorial stone. She'd leaned toward a Shakespeare sonnet until we came across Christopher Robin's words to Winne-the-Pooh in the book by A. A. Milne.

"How does that feel?"

I shouldn't have been surprised to find the ghost of Trey Lindsey materializing next to little Agatha and resting a hand on her shoulder. He wore the same chinos and polo shirt he'd died in the previous October, when an errant curse found him on a boat trip up the coast. Since our confrontation with the resurrected ghost of a serial killer in December, he'd spent more time here at the Grazzini House to keep young Agatha company.

"It feels good." Agatha looked up at Trey. "It's been a long time."

"Too long," he replied.

"Is Trey here, too?" Audrey asked. Though she couldn't see or hear him—most of the time—Audrey had missed Trey's presence at my cottage these last months. "Can he come hang out with us tonight?"

I looked at Trey, and he gave me a tight nod. Things had been chilly between us for a few weeks, since we'd argued back at the cottage about boundaries and privacy. I was still ticked at him, but I missed his snark.

"Will you be all right tonight?" Eddie leaned on the long handle of his shovel. "After everything that's happened today, I could swing by later. Bring you both some soup? Or wine?"

My cheeks warmed at the suggestion, but my heart was still heavy. "Not tonight. We've got a lot of baking to do for the teahouse. Plus, I know you're working a double shift today, and you've already taken time out to help with the marker."

I said goodbye to Agatha and headed toward Audrey's car.

"If you change your mind, I'm just a phone call away," Eddie said as he loaded the shovel into the back of his SUV.

"Valentine's Day," Audrey sang as she started the car.

IF IT HAD BEEN JUST me whipping up multiple batches of cookies and muffins, my kitchen would have looked like a bakery war zone within a matter of minutes. But Audrey was in charge, just like every other time she came to my little cottage to cook or bake, and she ordered me around my own space with easy confidence. Also per usual, her kitten Simba was tearing around the living room, entertaining herself by batting a wadded up piece of paper across the floor.

Audrey had organized the space into various stations. I was at the "dry ingredients" station, where three kinds of flour—all-purpose, cake, and whole wheat—were lined up on the dining table next to a canister of baking powder, an open box of baking soda, a variety of spices, and enough dark brown, light brown, white, and confectioners sugar to make me fear diabetes just by proximity. I sifted cup after cup of all-purpose flour into a large mixing bowl. At my feet sat bags of multi-colored sugar sprinkles and about five pounds of Red Hots.

On the small expanse of counter space by the refrigerator sat blocks of butter, a variety of dairy and nut milks, a half-gallon jug of Madagascar vanilla extract that Colin had given Audrey for Christmas, smaller bottles of mint, orange, and almond extracts, and three bottles of sparkling cider for making champagne cupcakes, alongside other items I hadn't managed to inventory when we unloaded Audrey's supplies and the dozen shopping bags from our trip to Moroni's Grocery on Main Street.

We'd bought the place out of eggs, and now I had an entire farm's worth of cardboard crates stacked inside the refrigerator. It was convenient there hadn't been much in there to begin with.

The aroma of cheese and veggie scones filled the cottage as they browned in the oven. Audrey added butter and granulated sugar to the standing mixer on the breakfast bar. The mixer was an eBay purchase specifically for Audrey to use in my kitchen. She kept an eye on the poppy seeds in the toaster oven, which she'd brought from her apartment to increase our output.

"We could ask Colin to come over to help." I sifted another four cups of all-purpose flour into a fresh metal bowl. "It's not spaghetti and spaceships, but at least he wouldn't be sitting home alone. And we could use the help boxing everything up."

My couch and upholstered chair were stacked with generic snap-lid containers of varying sizes, collected from our own homes and whatever Barbara had in her kitchen. We'd bake all night and transport everything to the Tea Reader first thing in the morning. Assuming Jim cleared the teahouse to open.

"Not going to happen." Audrey set the mixer on a medium-high speed, then flipped through the laminated pages of her green vinyl Master Baking Binder. With its bent corners and tabbed dividers coming loose, Audrey's recipe book carried the mystique of a witch's grimoire, especially when she clutched it to her chest when moving from one surface to another.

"I mean, I asked," she measured vanilla extract into the butter and sugar in the mixing bowl. "And maybe I should ask before inviting people to your house. But he said it would be a conflict of interest. Or would look that way."

"How would it be a conflict of interest to bake cookies with his girlfriend?" I started measuring out cake flour—for orange and vanilla cupcakes, or maybe sugar cookies. I didn't think we had enough room in the pastry cases for everything Audrey had planned for this bake-fest. But she was in charge, though I was her boss.

"It would be a conflict for the assistant deputy sheriff to aid the employee of a business suspected of fatally poisoning one of its customers." Audrey returned the vanilla to its place next to the refrigerator. I didn't know how she kept everything so tidy when I'd lost count of the number of recipes she had going at once.

"We didn't poison anyone!"

"I know that," she replied. "And you know that. I'm pretty sure Colin and Jim know that, too, even when customers add their own flavorings to their teapots."

My jaw dropped. "What?"

"Just the occasional tincture or herbal blend," Audrey waved my concern away. "Gary Spalding likes to add liquid flax seed to his tea, and Mildred Moroni has been known to add a dash of Irish cream when she thinks no one is looking. And you know how I like to experiment. Even Cyndi sprinkles vitamin powder in her tea, same as Bud and Ravi and a few others."

"Vitamin powder?" I asked. "Could that be what killed Ravi?"

"Doubtful," Audrey replied. "Cyndi had some this morning and said Bud and Ravi did, too. And Cyndi and Bud and everybody else are fine. Which is why Jim hasn't shut us down."

"Yet." I sank into the nearest dining chair. Even if the Tea Reader wasn't an official crime scene, who would want to come inside to eat and drink after Ravi's death on the teahouse floor?

While we were baking, Barbara was at home poring over the Tea Reader financials to determine how badly losing our stock plus a day's sales had hurt us, on top of the cannabis-infused competition down the street. For someone without a lick of business sense, I'd done well in hiring Barbara to manage basically everything about the business. Then Barbara hired Audrey as a part-time barista at the end of the previous summer. Now Audrey was the assistant manager, and my best friend.

Solid, reliable connections with other human beings didn't come naturally to me—not since the headaches started. Being visited by ghosts didn't help, either. But as a practicing witch, Audrey didn't mind my paranormal activities.

Speaking of which, we were waiting on Trey to make an appearance. Though he'd been an investment broker in life, as a ghost he'd helped solve a few murders, including his own. I wasn't his favorite person at the moment, but I hoped he'd be willing and able to track down the lingering shade of Ravi King, find out what happened to him, and settle the whole thing before morning.

The oven timer went off. Audrey pulled out a tray of savory scones, adjusted the temperature, and slid two muffin tins into the oven.

"Any clues about that message in the window?" Audrey lifted the golden brown scones onto a cooling rack, a maneuver I always bungled, with at least half the yield ending up either stuck to the tray or shattered on the floor.

"Nothing yet," I replied. Audrey was remarkably unper-turbed, considering it had been mere months since a poltergeist had dragged The Tea Reader's inventory of tea leaves across the floor to spell out "KILL" and "AUDREY" over and over again.

The memory gave me chills. Maybe that was part of the impetus behind her current baking focus.

I went back to measuring flours and sugars into bowls of various sizes.

"But it would help to know what happened to Ravi, and why he left that message in the window." Audrey ran a finger down a laminated page in her recipe binder, then started cutting sticks of soft butter into a spare mixing bowl.

"We don't know that it was a message from Ravi in the window." I shifted the sacks of flour and sugar to make room for my next measuring task. It was a wonder nothing had gotten knocked to the floor. "Someone could have sneaked inside and done it as a mean-spirited prank."

"Jim said no one but emergency workers were coming through the door."

"How do you know?" I asked. But of course she knew. "For someone who insists on doing everything by the book, your boyfriend sure has loose lips."

"He was trying to make me feel better, in case I was worried someone was trying to capitalize on our misfortune. As if any explanation for 'KILLER' in the window could be comforting." Audrey wiped her buttery fingers on a dish towel and reached for a tube of red food coloring. "But, yeah, lips were definitely involved." She added a few drops of color to the mixing bowl. "And your fireman sure didn't waste any time rushing to your side."

Your fireman. I disliked the term, which was why Audrey used it. She enjoyed the romantic fantasy that I was the prize in a love triangle with Jim and Eddie, when I'd been holding Eddie at arm's length and didn't know where I stood with Jim.

I groaned as an ice pick headache sent a bolt of pain through the top of my skull.

"Suri?" Audrey looked up from rolling out red-colored dough

on my floured breakfast bar, with heart-shaped cookie cutters standing by.

"Sorry." I stacked the used bowls, loaded what would fit into the dishwasher, and left the rest in the sink. "Just not in the mood for girl talk."

Audrey made an easy shift to explaining the complex rules of *Annikai Run*, the board game she and Colin had chosen for the evening. She was missing her date night, plus pulling a full night of baking in my kitchen, and I wouldn't even talk about boys with her.

As she described the many clever ways to achieve the goal of the game—which I think involved building a spaceship and then piloting it to an endangered planet in order to steal an ancient alien relic while also ferrying away the planet's inhabitants before the sun went supernova—I gazed out the picture window toward the beach and ocean beyond. In the gathering darkness, a slender figure strolled alone along the shore, heading south toward Grady, though it seemed a long walk through the winter rain. Probably someone new in town, for whom the scenery and the coastal weather were still a novelty. The rolling waves sounded ominous.

"Ravi, what happened to you?" I whispered toward the gray skies.

"Suri?" Audrey asked.

Before I could answer, her toaster oven started sparking. She yanked the electrical cord out of the wall socket, then grabbed a pair of pot holders to slide the hot oven across the counter and into the sink.

"Okay." Audrey blew a strand of curly hair out of her face. "So, no toasted poppy seeds. At least we didn't burn the house down."

It was a small comfort at the end of a tragic day, but I'd take it.

CHAPTER THREE

I'd fallen into bed close to midnight after our baking marathon, though we took breaks to order a pizza and watch a couple of episodes of *The Great British Baking Show* while orange walnut muffins and heart-shaped sugar cookies went into the oven. After all the cookies, scones, muffins, and cupcakes were packed for transport, the kitchen and dining area cleaned, and everything put back where it belonged, we'd been barely able to lift our arms. Audrey crashed on my couch for the night, with little Simba tucked under her chin.

The next morning was gray and dismal. We were up before the sun to load Audrey's car with baked goods. I declined her offer of a ride into town, saying I preferred the crisp air to clear my head on the walk from my cottage.

I regretted the decision almost immediately. Mere minutes after Audrey's departure, cold rain came down. Still, I reached for my boots instead of my car keys. I don't make the best decisions when I'm in pain. My brain was foggy, and I felt the tug of a mounting headache at the base of my skull. I pulled on blue jeans when snow pants and galoshes would have served me better. My jacket hood didn't help much as a stiff wind blew the icy rain into my face like frozen daggers that stung my cheeks.

By the time I arrived at the Tea Reader, I was a shivering, soggy mess for the second morning in a row. At least the crime scene tape had been taken down outside the teahouse. My keys shook in my numb fingers, and I needed three tries to unlock the bookshop's main door. I could have entered through the teahouse and fortified myself with a hot drink and a muffin, but I wanted a few minutes to myself.

I stood in the center of the dark bookshop and tried to sense Ravi's lingering shade before I turned on the lights.

"Ravi?" I whispered. "Are you here? Can you hear me?"

No luck. Why was it that when I wanted a ghost to appear, nothing happened? I resolved to make another attempt later in the teahouse, closer to the spot where he died.

I tried a different tack. "Trey? Are you here?"

The ghost of Trey Lindsey had come to me in a rough state the previous autumn, then he decided to stick around. I'd gotten used to being able to call on Trey for help, but my sarcastic spectral sidekick stood us up last night and was still giving me the cold shoulder today.

I went about setting up the bookshop to welcome customers. If business was as bad as Barbara predicted, every sale on both sides of the Tea Reader mattered. But there wasn't a new box from Loki, and that felt like a bad sign.

It was quiet on the bookshop side of the business any time of year, but the winter gloom outside made the space feel like a mortuary. Lack of adequate lighting didn't help. With the low ceiling of clouds, little natural light came through the windows. Wet denim clung to my chilled legs as I turned on the few lamps around the store—including several Goodwill finds atop the shorter bookcases and tall IKEA standing lamps nestled between the taller bookshelves.

I paused after switching on the Tiffany lamp in the front

window. On the other side of the glass, I spotted Bud Barlow lingering on the pavement just beyond the front door of the teahouse. He wandered a few meters down the street, then stopped and doubled back. Even in the miserable weather, he looked pale and glum. His friend had died right in front of him not twenty-four hours earlier, and I wasn't sure he had anyone to turn to.

My instinct was to dash out the door to invite him inside, so that he could escape the chilly gloom with a cup of hot tea and a plate of savory scones. But that would mean drawing him back to the scene of Ravi's death, and I didn't think that would be a kindness. I turned away from the window.

The headache was present, but manageable, having settled behind my left ear on the cold walk from the cottage. It had been about a month since I'd last taken an adceparin pill, the prescription med that was supposed to help with my head pain but had more likely caused panic attacks. The withdrawal hadn't been bad, and while I still had migraines, they weren't the rebounding thunderclap kind.

If the severity of my headaches was related to a ghost in close proximity—and that was a big if—I felt confident that I was truly alone in the bookshop. Maybe I could carry on a genuine conversation with another human being today, without interruption from pain or poltergeist.

This morning, though, there was no conversation or laughter or even the sharp clang of a dropped fork coming from the teahouse on the other side of the pass-through doors.

Was it disrespectful to open the Tea Reader the day following Ravi's death? Maybe, but we couldn't afford to keep the doors closed, and Audrey had reminded me this morning that the community needed the teahouse as a gathering space—more than ever in the aftermath of such a shocking tragedy. But it sounded like the community had missed that memo.

Audrey unlocked the pass-through to bring me a massive

mug filled to the brim with Simply Suri tea. "I thought this might cheer you up."

Even her outfit was friendliness made manifest. Between my cottage and the teahouse, Audrey must have stopped at home to change and drop off her kitten. Instead of worn jeans crusted with dried batter, she was clad in wool from head to toe to guard against the weather. Her burnt orange sweater was an homage to Star Trek with its pattern of black-and-silver United Federation of Planets symbols. Beneath her short, felted black skirt, pewter-and-plum striped tights disappeared into her cherry red vegan Doc Martens. Topped by her genuine smile and dark curls, the ensemble practically sparkled with energy and hope. Or maybe she'd had more caffeine this morning than I'd had.

"How many customers next-door?" I wrapped my hands around the big mug and edged closer to the space heater behind the counter.

Audrey's smile dimmed. "A few?"

I gave her a look, and she blew out a sigh. "Okay, it's not good," she said. "But it's early yet. Give it some time."

The bookshop door opened, startling me into spilling hot tea on my jeans.

"Oh, Suri!" Karina cried as she swept into the bookshop. She was again an elegant vision of grace, despite the miserable weather. "I had to stop in, of course. It's just awful what's happened." She reached for my elbow across the counter, oblivious to my efforts to blot the tea from my trousers with a cleaning rag.

"How's business at your dispensary?" Audrey asked.

Karina responded with a tight smile. "You're so brave to keep going, especially so soon. Is there anything I can do to help?"

I started to say that I thought we were okay, but Audrey spoke over me with a quip about how Karina could send us our clientele back.

"Of course you're fine," Karina said, ignoring Audrey's

comment. "You're a woman of strength and compassion, Suri Mudge. Don't let anyone tell you any differently."

I didn't think anyone had suggested otherwise. Not to my face, anyway. Before I could ask her what she meant, Karina was out the door again and pulling up her hood against the freezing rain.

"I'm telling you, business will pick up again," Audrey said. "It has to."

"Is that a psychic prediction, or something you read in the *Naghatune Reader* horoscopes?" I asked.

"Neither. Just a feeling." Audrey headed for the pass-through to get back to work in the teahouse. "It just might take a little while."

I decided to wait exactly long enough for my damp jeans to dry from both the rain and the tea spill. Then I'd have to suck it up and confront reality next-door.

∾

THE TEAHOUSE WAS open to serve customers, thanks to Audrey's baking and Barbara's drive up to Seaside in search of loose-leaf tea, but most of our winter regulars were making themselves scarce.

I came over to the teahouse side of the business around midday, hungry and in need of more tea. I was hoping to snag the last of Audrey's cheesy-veggie scones. They went fast in the mornings, along with most everything else in the pastry cases. But with the slow foot traffic on both sides of the Tea Reader, there was a chance I'd have my choice of baked goods.

I needn't have worried. At noon, the Tea Reader's cases remained fully stocked, with sealed containers of more scones and cookies shelved on a standing rack nearby.

I watched Mildred Moroni stare open-mouthed through the glass as she hurried past on the sidewalk. Gary Spalding, in town on his usual errands for his goat farm, paused in front of the main door, then turned and headed up the block. A trio of uneasy-looking teenagers, probably from Standish Beach, stood across the street in the icy rain and gestured toward the Tea Reader in mild alarm.

The Tea Reader had transformed into the Bermuda Triangle of teahouses overnight. The locals were intrigued but afraid to enter.

At least Emmaline Kapul came over from the Knitting Genie, but she didn't bring her knitting project with her. She stood at the counter to receive a to-go cup of hot tea, instead of her usual small pot and plate of biscuits. She seemed more focused on the thrill of being "at the scene of the crime," and her wide-eyed gaze flitted between the table Ravi and Bud had occupied and the spot on the floor where Ravi had breathed his last.

"Good morning, Emmaline!" I forced a friendly smile, despite my irritation and my unrelenting headache. "How are you today?"

Emmaline gave a start, her eyes widening further as she mirrored my pained smile. "Suri! So glad to see that you're all still here."

I increased my wattage of artificial cheer as my temples throbbed. "Still here? Where should we have gone?"

Emmaline hesitated, tension visible in her face. She hadn't draped her coat over a chair to claim her favorite table, as was her habit. She remained bundled up for the cold weather and didn't seem intent on staying.

"Well, I just wanted to stop in and see how things, how you, how everyone is doing." Emmaline raised her cup of tea but stopped before the plastic lid touched her lips. "Okay, then. Take care!" She hurried out the door into the icy rain. Not three steps down the sidewalk, she uncapped her insulated cup and poured the hot tea out onto the pavement. Billows of steam rose around her.

"Third one today," Audrey commented from behind the barista counter. She looked more glum than she had when she'd brought my tea into the bookshop. "It's like we're the town freak show now."

Audrey took my giant mug, gave it a soapy bath, and started making a refill—decaf this time. She knew my routines and my limitations.

With her phone pressed against her ear, Barbara said a polite but firm goodbye to whoever was on the other end of the line, then made a visible effort not to slam the device down on the counter.

"The media keep calling, too." Barbara grimaced. "Reporters wanting to know about the man who dropped dead and whether we think it's responsible to remain open when we might have poisoned our own customer."

"How many is that now? Six?" Audrey filled a stainless steel tea ball with dried rosehips and lemon rind, a combination I didn't think I'd tried before. Audrey never did anything by accident. There was always meaning and purpose behind her brews and baking.

"Seven," Barbara replied. "If you count the international tabloid barking questions about Ravi and Bud's treasure. How they heard about it over in the UK or why they'd be interested in Naghatune Bay is beyond me. One caller even asked if a curse on the treasure killed Ravi."

"Like the mythical curse of Tutankhamun's tomb?" I asked.

"Maybe?" Barbara replied. "At least it might keep more yahoos from running into the woods after buried treasure. For a while, anyway."

"Has anyone checked on Bud?" I asked. "I caught a glimpse of him this morning, and he was looking pretty rough." Audrey and Barbara shrugged, just before the teahouse door burst open.

"I'm telling you, it's the last thing we need!" Murray Overhill exclaimed as he came through the door, while Mayor Phil

Lindquist remained outside on the pavement, peering through the window.

I'd thought surely the mayor would make a show of support for the Tea Reader. Phil was always one of the first to lend a hand to anyone in town, but now he kept his spot on the sidewalk, shifting his weight between his feet in what could have been impatience, cold, or anxiety.

"More treasure seekers will descend if they get a whiff of anything being found here, doesn't matter if it's real treasure or not. Unless maybe there's a curse," Murray announced to no one in particular. At least he looked like he'd come to stay a while, confirmed when he dropped his heavy winter coat over a straight-back chair. Instead of his preferred table close to the pass-through, he chose a spot in the front window, where anyone passing would be sure to see him sipping tea and reading the newspaper.

Murray was one of the more sullen and argumentative residents of Grady, and I was surprised that he would offer this support. My welcoming smile was genuine as he approached the counter.

"Thanks for coming in today, Murray." I tried not to sound too desperate or too grateful. "I hope you'll accept a muffin on the house?"

Barbara sucked in her breath. First came the sales hit with the opening of Karina's Tea and Botanicals Dispensary down the street. Now the teahouse was a figurative ghost town, and I was giving away our perishable inventory. I cocked my head at my manager and she backed off. One muffin wasn't a huge gamble that generous goodwill to the regulars who were willing to come in might pay off.

"No Cyndi today?" Murray looked disappointed.

"She was pretty shaken up," Barbara replied. "And we're not busy, so I gave her the morning off."

"Understandable." Murray surveyed the pastry case. Audrey

had arranged the cookies, scones, and muffins to resemble a cozy cocktail party under glass. Murray tapped on the case to indicate the frosted pink heart cookies. "Two of those, please, as well as a veggie scone, heated. And I'm happy to pay. Feels like I've got a new lease on life." He patted the breast pocket of his wool blazer. "New prescription for heart medicine, filled just this morning, though the damned pills look like candy. Don't want to end up like Ravi, you know." He blew out a sigh. "But poor Cyndi. Especially considering . . ."

Murray looked up and seemed surprised to find us all watching him, including Bobby Jackson of *The Naghatune Reader*, the area's thin, weekly newspaper.

"Especially considering?" Bobby gestured for Murray to continue. I hadn't seen Bobby come in, but it made sense that he'd be lurking, trying to dig up dirt about the town's latest scandal.

"You're not planning to fill your newsletter pages with idle gossip, are you, Bobby?" I asked.

The hyperlocal *Naghatune Reader* distributed a few hundred copies each week via wire baskets at the Tea Reader and the grocery store in Grady, and at fish-n-chips shops over in Standish Beach. Bobby was the editor and sole writer, save for the weekly horoscopes, which were contributed by his mother.

"Just trying to keep my readers informed," Bobby replied without a hint of a smile. He turned back to Murray. "You were saying about Cyndi the barista? Do you think she's feeling guilty or panicked over having poisoned Ravi to death?"

"WHAT?!" Audrey, Murray, and I exclaimed in unison.

Barbara flat-out glared at Bobby. "Cyndi didn't poison anyone."

"I believe that's up to the authorities to decide," Bobby replied. "Why else would she be so broken up?"

"Maybe because that poor girl watched her boyfriend die on

the floor?" Murray spat, before the realization of what he'd said dawned on his face.

The revelation that Cyndi and Ravi had been dating was news to me, and apparently to Bobby, too. The ersatz newsman jumped on Murray like herbed biscuits hot from the oven. He started recording audio on his phone and peppered Murray with increasingly outrageous questions framing poor Cyndi as the town's vengeful "black widow," while Murray tried to place his beverage order with Barbara.

"It was a stroke, or a cardiac event!" Murray erupted after Bobby pushed him too far. "That's what I overheard the rescue squad saying." He patted his breast pocket again.

"Bobby, if you can't leave my customers in peace," I said, "I'll have to ask you to leave the premises."

"What if I bought something?" Bobby turned to Barbara. "Give me the same thing Ravi had, right before he died."

"Out!" I pointed at the door. "Right now."

Bobby smirked as he slipped his phone into his pocket. "Suit yourself. You know I'm just getting started." He made a beeline for the exit.

Audrey handed me a steaming mug of herbal tea. With the first inhalation of its floral aroma, my shoulders relaxed even as determination stirred in my belly.

"Lemon for the sun, and for making a new start," Audrey said. "Rosehips for good fortune. Let it steep for a few minutes."

I had seen Audrey's magick in action. She was an effective witch. I was learning to trust her inspired tea blends, though the locals whispered about them with both awe and disdain.

"Suri!" Mayor Phil came inside at last, followed by a pair of strangers who didn't appear the least concerned about entering the teahouse on a day when most everyone else in town was avoiding us like the plague.

The wintry weather precluded the mayor from modeling a colorful broomstick skirt from his wife's shop, the Chichi

Boutique, as was his habit. But a turquoise and coral silk scarf, probably a new arrival at the shop, peeked over the collar of his heavy coat. His worn cowboy boots were holding up in the wet weather, and a dark gray Stetson kept his balding head dry.

"Phil!" I channeled the lightness of Audrey's lemon and rosehip tea. "Thanks for setting a good example for the town. And for bringing friends!"

I gestured toward the newcomers. One was a middle-age man in a crisp, olive-colored overcoat and matching fedora that repelled the rain as though foul weather didn't exist, while beside him the mayor dripped all over the teahouse floor. The other new face was a younger person bundled up in a forest green puffer jacket, who peered out at me between a thick wool scarf and a tweed hat with a wide brim.

"We have a limited tea menu today, but our bakery case is full." I waved toward the glass cases and awaited an introduction, but the mayor hunched his shoulders and shook his head.

"No, Suri, I'm sorry. We're not here for that." Phil's eyes pleaded with me to understand his meaning without his having to elaborate.

"That's fine," I said, though it wasn't. They weren't here as customers. How could they be, the day after Ravi's death not two meters from where the mayor stood with his guests? "What can I do for you?"

Phil gestured toward the man in olive. "Thomas Catesby. And his assistant, Max Turner. They're here from Cascade State University in Seattle. Ravi King called them in." He paused. "*Before*. About the treasure."

Thomas Catesby grasped my fingers in a courtly fashion and bent over my hand. "Professor Thomas Catesby, at your service." He had an unusual accent, not exactly British but sounding an awful lot like Captain Jean-Luc Picard on the episodes of *Star Trek: The Next Generation* Audrey had gotten me to watch. "Am I to understand you are the proprietress of this quaint establishment, dear lady?"

"Uh, yeah," I replied.

Somewhere behind me, Barbara swallowed a chuckle. Catesby's unwavering smile let me know he'd decided to overlook my lack of sophistication.

"Very good. And this is where the unfortunate fellow met his untimely end, I presume?" Catesby released my hand and looked around the teahouse dining room. He pressed his hand to his chest and wrinkled his nose as if smelling something on the spectrum between interesting and rancid.

Phil stepped over to the spot where Ravi had fallen to the floor. There wasn't a stain or even a stray scratch to mark it, but entire seasons would pass before anyone would forget. "Right about here, Suri?"

"Phil?" My query was more of a demand. "What's going on?"

"Very good," Catesby said again. He snapped his fingers at his companion and barked, "Max! Take this down."

"Yes, sir." Max pulled a clipboard out of a heavy canvas satchel and uncapped a pen. With the thick scarf loosened, I spied pink cheeks against pale skin, and I worried that young Max was close to frozen solid.

"Max, would you like a cup of tea?" I asked. "On the house? To warm you up."

This time, Barbara didn't make a sound or flash a disapproving look at my offer of free goods. Max's eyes lit up, but Catesby gave a dismissive wave and proclaimed they wouldn't be staying and that his assistant was perfectly fine and didn't require "local charity."

Catesby stared at the floor. Even in silence, the man took up more space and oxygen than anyone I'd seen. He wasn't handsome or striking—a bit shorter than average, and a little heavier, though it was difficult to make out his features beneath his coat and hat. But Catesby's presence was magnetic. Even Murray watched him from his seat in the window, his newspaper lying ignored on the table.

Catesby muttered something to Max, who took quick notes, then looked to Phil. "I will of course, Mr. Mayor, require transcripts of all police interviews as well as all documentation they have or will amass."

I frowned. Who spoke like that in real life?

Phil looked puzzled. "I'm sorry, Mr. Catesby, that won't—"

"*Professor* Catesby, if you will," Catesby replied with a patronizing smile. "Or Doctor Catesby, if you must."

Phil coughed. "Okay, *Professor* Catesby, I'm afraid that won't be possible. It's an ongoing investigation and unless you're working directly with law enforcement—"

"My dear man!" Catesby exclaimed. "*Everything* is relevant! If we're to thoroughly explore the origin and significance of the cache in question, there simply can be no question about my access to every artifact and every last shred of information. Especially considering the absolute travesty that we don't have the *in situ* context of the find. *Ipso facto*, no effort can be spared to overcome such an inconvenient deficit." He paused, an imperious expression frozen on his face. "Would you not agree?"

I hadn't seen Phil so flummoxed. He glanced at me for help, but I still didn't understand what was happening. Instead of giving a direct answer, Phil gestured toward the door. "Why don't we get you set up at the dispensary, and then you can direct those questions to the deputy sheriff himself."

Catesby affected an exasperated sigh and swept—there's really no other word to describe it—toward the door, which he got Phil to hold for him.

"The dispensary?" I asked. "Why is Cascade State so keen on Ravi's death? How is the TBD involved?"

Phil's weary glance promised a full explanation later.

Max turned to me. "I apologize, Miss Suri . . . ?"

"Mudge. But Suri is fine," I said.

"Suri," Max repeated. "The professor has a particular way of doing things. He can come off as, um, brusque?"

"Peculiar," Barbara suggested.

"Ostentatious," Audrey said.

"I've heard worse," Max replied. "We were contacted by the late Mr. King to authenticate his find in the hills."

"The treasure?" Murray asked from his seat in the window.

Max nearly laughed. "Okay, yes. The treasure. There's no room at the deputy sheriff's station, and the professor requires a fully equipped kitchen for his work."

"We have a kitchen here," Audrey said, which earned a sharp elbow from Barbara.

"Well, yes," Max replied, then gestured to the infamous spot on the floor and winced. "But since your business is . . ."

"A potential crime scene," I said, finishing the thought.

Max swallowed. "Karina Coyle offered her space at the dispensary, and the professor accepted."

"Hold up." I looked through the window and saw Catesby on the sidewalk gesticulating broadly while Phil tried to get a word in edgewise. "Why do you need a kitchen? What kind of treasure did Ravi and Bud dig up?"

"Tea." Max glanced at the clipboard. "Mr. King and his partner, Bud Barlow, reportedly discovered a very old box containing a leather pouch of tea in the hills of Rock Creek State Park. We don't normally accept requests like this, because of the questionable background of the treasure hunters, and the lack of access to the site they were working. But the professor and I are here to examine and authenticate their find." Max tried to mask a grimace. "It's not a very straightforward case."

"Tea," I repeated. Was this a curse? The Tea Reader, the town's only dedicated teahouse, was losing customers to the new dispensary even before Ravi King's death. Now this tea treasure had been claimed by the competition, too.

CHAPTER FOUR

N ot even two hours later, we closed up the Tea Reader for the day. Murray Overhill was the only paying customer who lingered in the teahouse, though a few curiosity seekers came up from Standish Beach to do as Emmaline Kapul had done— buy some tea and a muffin or cookie, have a look around the "murder teahouse," then dump their purchases in the street as soon as they were out the door. After a full night of baking at the cottage, it was difficult not to take the behavior personally. At least the seagulls and crows were eating well.

I sent Audrey and Barbara home with the promise they'd still get paid for the full day, but the looks on their faces told me they didn't believe that any more than I did. We could survive another couple of weeks like this, but no longer. With our complicated insurance history and now a possible homicide investigation, there was little chance of a bank loan to keep the Tea Reader afloat.

I packed up a hefty selection of scones and cookies to take to the deputy sheriff's office. They say the way to a man's heart is through his stomach, but today I was after information rather than affection.

The rain was letting up, but not enough for me to set out on foot again. Audrey gave me a lift back to the cottage, and I stepped inside only long enough to grab my car keys. I parked my Subaru Outback outside Jim's office and took note of his county-issued SUV, Colin's yellow Ford Focus, and a red sedan with Washington State plates. I sat in my car, massaged my temples, and silently negotiated with my headache to back off.

The Naghatune Bay Sheriff's Office was a single-story, converted gas station located roughly halfway between the quiet town of Grady and its larger and more rambunctious sibling, Standish Beach. While Grady saw a seasonal influx of tourists, magickal seekers, and treasure hunters, Standish Beach was overrun every summer with surfers, vacationing families, and day-trippers from Portland looking to avoid the more popular destinations of Seaside and Cannon Beach to the north.

Duniway County assigned one deputy sheriff and one assistant to serve Grady, Standish Beach, and greater Naghatune Bay. For years, it had been a calm and boring posting, best suited to those either early or late in their careers. Local legends told of strange goings on for generations—like sightings of Sasquatch or the Bandage Man, and innumerable local hauntings. But more active magick struck by way of a lightning storm a few years earlier, and what had once been quaint and peculiar was now downright weird and sometimes dangerous.

It had been a genuine surprise to find myself in the same small town with Jim, years after our romance in Oregon City ended in disaster. Audrey kept insisting it was fate.

I got out of the car and pushed open the building's glass and steel front door. The interior was the same dull grayish white as the outside. A few potted plants added some living color, and Colin had hung posters of nearby beaches and a forested coastal ridge since my last visit. Audrey was lobbying for a more cheerful wall color—like warm sand or a dusty sage—but Colin kept reminding her of all the paperwork involved.

"That is simply unacceptable," a familiar voice protested. I shouldn't have been surprised to find Thomas Catesby standing by Jim's desk and haranguing him. Unbuttoned, Catesby's olive trench coat revealed an expensive-looking sweater and oxford shirt beneath. His vaguely European vowels and haughty demeanor were at odds with the rain-splattered fedora on his head. Even I knew you were supposed to take off your hat indoors when you were pretending to be fancy.

"*If* I am to undertake a thorough investigation, there is no question as to whether my access is appropriate." Catesby gave me a dignified dip of the chin to acknowledge my arrival but didn't alter his cadence. "I am frankly astonished there would be any doubt, but if you must, you are welcome to contact my university for instructions."

As Jim rose to his feet, I observed the tiny muscle twitch of his jaw that indicated mounting irritation. I couldn't count the number of times I'd been the cause of that tic.

"The sheriff's office does not take 'instructions' from you or your university, professor." Despite his agitation, Jim's voice was as steady as ever. He glanced my way and even managed an amiable smile when he turned back to Catesby. "And we do not comment to the public on an ongoing investigation."

"Be that as it may, *deputy* sheriff." Catesby's smirk telegraphed that he thought he was being clever. Jim looked like he wanted to laugh. "You will soon change your tune once you've spoken to the dean. Max!" Catesby glanced around with a perplexed look when his assistant didn't spontaneously appear at his side.

"Here!" The door opened behind me, letting in a cold draft, and Max pushed past to respond to Catesby's beckoning. "My apologies, professor. I hiked up and down the road but couldn't find a single teashop."

"You won't find one on Salt Road," I said. "The nearest teahouse is my shop. The Tea Reader." I tried not to wince when I added, "Or the Tea and Botanicals Dispensary."

Catesby scoffed. "I could have told you there'd be no decent tea establishment in such a godforsaken area as this *Salt Road*."

"We did tell you that." Colin sauntered over from the kitchenette and handed the professor a glass of water. "Well, not the 'godforsaken' part. We've got Lipton tea bags, or I can offer you coffee? Just made a fresh pot." He gestured to the coffee maker behind him.

Catesby scoffed again and looked as though Colin had inflicted a wound both moral and mortal. He turned his annoyance on Max. "Give these gentlemen my information and make sure they have the direct number for the dean at Cascade State, will you? I'll be waiting in the car."

Catesby strode out of the building with the weighty bluster of an aging diva, leaving Max to scramble to pull a contact sheet out of a damp satchel.

"The professor appreciates all that you're doing, and he really does want to help," Max offered to Jim along with the crisp sheet of paper.

"Does he now?" Jim let the paper drop onto his desk without looking at it.

Max's smile was heading in the direction of a grimace. I wondered how often the young assistant was left to explain what the professor "really meant" to say. "I know he can seem like a lot, especially at first. But he truly is brilliant. The best in his field."

"The best at authenticating tea?" I asked. "Isn't that a narrow job description?"

Max nodded with too much vigor. "One of the world's most respected tea historians. If you need his bona fides, you can call Dr. Edward Clair, the Dean of Antiquities at Cascade State."

"We'll be sure to check up on your professor," Jim said. "You folks staying locally?"

"The professor has rented a vacation home along the shore," Max replied. "On Dowitcher Drive."

I swallowed a groan. My cottage was on Dowitcher, which meant the professor was a nearby neighbor, and wasn't that a delightful development. Jim glanced my way and tried not to laugh.

"We'll be working at the Tea and Botanicals Dispensary," Max continued. "We're eager to get started and to have a look at the treasure that's been found. Despite the circumstances, of course."

Max's enthusiasm dimmed when Catesby opened the door to lean inside. "Max! I'm waiting."

With an apologetic shrug, Max hurried out of the building.

"I see you've met the local celebrity," I said to Jim and Colin as soon as the door closed.

"Yeah. Sorry about that, Suri." Jim crossed the floor to pour himself a cup of coffee.

I'm not morally opposed to coffee, like some residents of Grady. It's one of many funny divisions between Grady and our sibling town. You won't find a single coffee shop in Grady, whereas Standish Beach has a local coffee spot or a Starbucks on every corner. When I first came to Grady, I heard whispered lore about the fire that burned down the tavern where locals from both beachfront towns would gather, and somehow this enduring tea/coffee schism was the result. No one seemed clear on the details.

While some in Grady clung to their tea-drinking exclusivity like a religion or political affiliation, for me it was just a taste preference. No matter how much cream or sugar was stirred in, coffee always tasted bitter. I loved the smell of it, though.

"What are you sorry about?" I asked.

"About the TBD thing, and about the coroner being delayed with Ravi. Ennis was on vacation, whale watching down in Depoe Bay." Jim stirred a single sugar packet into his coffee as he walked back to his desk and sat. "It sounds like Ravi was acting kind of squirrelly even before he showed up at your teahouse, and the manner of his death doesn't sound like food or tea poisoning to me. For now, I consider it a death by natural causes. Though I can't rule out cyanide," he added with a wink.

"Not funny." I pulled up a chair, and it made a tiny squeak as I dragged it across the linoleum floor.

"Too soon?" Jim asked.

Colin went to his own desk on the other side of the room and pulled on a pair of noise-cancelling headphones.

"Yes, plus you're not the coroner, and you can't make that call." I shrugged out of my coat and settled the aqua-and-navy little kids' backpack I use as a purse in my lap. "Thank you for not shutting down my business in the meantime. Audrey gave me the news, getting her information from Colin. I just didn't think you'd resort to a game of telephone with me." I placed the box of scones and cookies on his desk.

A reflexive wince flashed over Jim's features before he could mask it with a sip of coffee. Then he winced again, because the coffee was too hot.

"It's safe." I nodded at the box. "Baked in my cottage last night."

Jim put down his coffee and rested his forearms on his desk, his signal that he was about to level with me. "It's not like that," he said.

"So what is it like?" I asked, with an unintended edge. I made myself take a breath. "No, I mean . . . I don't know what I mean."

We laughed together, and I felt better.

"About Catesby setting up over at the dispensary." Jim leaned back in his chair. "I'm not giving Karina preferential treatment. Catesby will give his report on the tea Ravi and Bud found, to see if maybe that's what killed Ravi. From that standpoint only, Catesby is working with law enforcement."

"So what was with all the pushback just now?" I gestured toward the door.

"The guy just irks me," Jim replied as he filed a couple of

papers into an organizer on his desk, including a flyer for a summer surfing competition in Standish Beach, a bulletin from the big cat sanctuary about an escaped leopard, an ad for the annual ghost hunting conference up in Seaside, and an announcement about the installation of a new sheriff in the county seat in Hattieville. "I have to make sure his authorization is in order first, though. And he keeps going on about needing security. For an old box? Securing the evidence from Bud was no picnic, either. And Bud's in rough shape, too."

I took a second to imagine what kind of laboratory examination the professor might need to perform on Bud and Ravi's cache of tea. Another second, and I understood that Catesby's university in Seattle was outside of Jim's jurisdiction.

"I get it," I said. "You don't have the space here for the professor to do his work. The TBD has a bigger kitchen than the Tea Reader, which is a potential crime scene."

Jim rubbed at the back of his neck, pushing aside his thick, dark blond hair that had grown a little too long. I rested my hand on his desk, not reaching to touch him but making the intimation.

"Jim, why didn't you just tell me yourself?" I asked. "You're investigating a suspicious death at my teahouse, so why not talk to me directly? I thought we were friends."

He stared at my hand on his desk, and I started to feel self-conscious. "Suri."

The front door opened and let in another gust of cold air.

"I know I'm early!" Karina exclaimed as she pulled back her hood and shook off the rain. Her eyes narrowed when she spotted me sitting with Jim.

Colin yanked off his headphones and jumped up from his desk to greet her.

She swung a cloth shopping bag bulging with food containers on her arm. "Where should we set up, boys?" Karina moved with effortless grace, like a princess vacationing incognito in our little coastal hamlet. Her light laugh made me want in on the joke.

Embarrassed by my winter frump, lack of makeup, and my hair in full February frizz, I slumped in the chair with my little backpack in my lap.

"You didn't have to bring us lunch again!" Colin helped her carry her bag to the kitchenette counter.

Jim gave me a lingering, cryptic look, and I found myself wishing I could read minds like some people in Grady assumed or feared I could. Was Jim really seeing Karina? Was this why he hadn't called me or come by to tell me about the investigation?

I leaned toward him and lowered my voice. "Jim. Talk to me."

Before he could respond, Karina laid a glass bento box on his desk. Four perfect quadrangles of warm edamame, chili-lime shrimp, rice noodles, and sesame seaweed salad looked like they'd been packed by an expert.

"I'm sorry, Suri, I didn't know there would be four of us." Karina placed a fork rolled up tight in a paper napkin next to Jim's lunch.

"Four?" I glanced over my shoulder and saw Colin tucking into his own bento box at his desk. There was music now, too, one of the classic rock stations from Astoria streaming via Colin's computer.

"You're welcome to mine, if you're hungry?" Karina smiled and held out an unopened glass box, but her eyes gave a clear entreaty to let her have my seat. I took the hint.

"Thanks, no, I have a million things to do." I grabbed my backpack purse and shoved my arms into my coat sleeves in the most inelegant maneuver possible. The cuff of my sweater caught halfway inside the coat sleeve, and merino fabric bunched up at my elbow as I pushed my arm through. I hated when that happened, but I'd fix it outside. My stomach grumbled loudly, because I'd been too distracted to have a proper lunch, much less breakfast.

Then came the fierce, stabbing pain of an ice pick headache in my left eye socket. I squeezed my eyes shut and held my breath for a few seconds until it passed. When I inhaled and opened my eyes, all three of them were staring at me. Colin held a forkful of shrimp and seaweed halfway between his bowl and his mouth, while Karina looked on with what appeared to be genuine concern and confusion.

But Jim was out of his chair and at my side, gripping my elbow. "Suri? You okay?"

"Fine," I said with a croak. "Just a little twinge." I twisted out of Jim's grasp and beat a hasty exit out the door.

Back outside in my car, I nearly pulled a muscle trying to get my sweater sleeve smoothed out inside my coat, while another ice pick headache stabbed at my left eye. I breathed and blinked slowly while the pain subsided. Through the front window, I watched Karina sit down in the chair I'd kept warm for her.

I DROVE straight home to my cottage. I did not stop at the Moroni Grocery, even though I was nearly out of sugar and fresh vegetables and was overdue for my weekly shop. I had a couple of cans of soup and a box or two of macaroni and cheese. I wouldn't starve. But I saved myself from having to face another human being when I was in danger of losing my composure.

Once I was safely at home, I stood in the small entryway, closed my eyes, and waited for the tears to come.

I got another ice pick headache instead.

I dropped my backpack purse on the hardwood floor, pulled off my wet boots in a clumsy scramble, and eased my way down the hall with the intention of lying down until either hunger or the next day's dawn woke me.

The bedroom door stood halfway open. Had I left it that way this morning? I couldn't remember. I wasn't in the habit of memorizing the angle of every half-open door each time I left the house. Jim had been urging me to install a basic security system, but that was one more thing I had to do, and it seemed like a hassle.

When was the last time he'd repeated this suggestion? Sometime around Christmas, or maybe January. The sharp, stabbing pain in my head lifted and left a dull throb in its place. Jim's last recommendation had come before the Tea and Botanicals Dispensary opened—before Karina Coyle came to town. The image of Karina sitting at Jim's desk and laughing with him over her neat little lunches filled my mind, and my stomach churned. Was this how Jim felt whenever he saw me with Eddie?

A strange clattering noise came from inside the bedroom. The sound rose to a loud banging, then softened to an arrhythmic series of thuds. If there was indeed an intruder, perhaps he was new to breaking and entering. Or had a squirrel crawled inside to escape the icy rain and gotten trapped? I wasn't sure which option was worse.

I crept back toward the front door and reached for the phone in my pocket to call Colin on his personal number, rather than reaching out to Jim or Eddie. That's when I heard the cursing coming from the bedroom. The voice was male and muffled, and was followed by more banging. I held the phone to my ear, waiting for Colin to pick up. I knew I should have retreated to my car for my own safety, but I was more puzzled than afraid. Like the proverbial cat, my curiosity was going to get me in trouble one day. Or deeper trouble, anyway.

"Hello? Suri?" Colin asked over the phone.

"Good," I whispered, even though I didn't think an intruder could hear me over all the banging. The sound of Colin's voice brought a surge of courage. "Just hang out on the phone with me, will you? I think someone might have broken into my house."

"A break-in?" Colin's voice rose with alarm. "Suri, are you okay? Are you at your cottage now?"

"Shhh," I hissed into the phone. "He'll hear you."

"He's there?" There were sounds of Colin's desk drawer sliding open, followed by jangling keys. "I'm on my way. Get out of the house and wait for me someplace safe! Can you go to a neighbor's?"

"No, no, no. It's fine," I said, when I didn't know any such thing. Stifled swearing came from the bedroom, accompanied by more frantic banging, and my curiosity overcame most of my fear. I kept Colin on the line as I warily pushed open the door and stepped into the room.

My bedroom looked untouched from the morning, meaning it was a rumpled mess. I'm not an untidy person. I make my bed every morning, but that doesn't mean tucking perfect hospital corners, or any other kind of corners. The pillows were at the head of the bed and the blankets were in approximately the right place. A stray sock lay on the floor beside the laundry hamper, and two stacks of books I kept meaning to finish—or start—teetered on the bedside table. Not even the dust on the potted snake plant on the low bookcase by the window had been disturbed.

A loud bang came from the tall armoire standing against the wall opposite my bed, followed by another string of curses.

"For crying out loud!" a familiar voice spat from somewhere inside. "Of all the boneheaded, cow-brained, ass-maggot dingle-burgers—"

"Trey? Is that you?" I stepped toward the armoire with caution even as Colin's voice called out from the phone in my hand, assuring me that he was mere minutes away and admonishing me to get out of the house. I pressed my ear against the armoire door and listened.

"Suri?! Is that you? Where in the bloody butt fungus am I?" Yes, definitely Trey. I didn't know how my ghost sidekick had ended up inside my bedroom armoire, or why he couldn't simply pass through the wood to free himself. He'd been absent so long, I was just glad he was putting in an appearance.

I turned the key in the lock and let the double doors swing open. At the back, surrounded by a couple of spring jackets, blouses I hadn't worn in years, and a stack of patched wool blankets, Trey Lindsey hovered half-in and half-out of the only formal gown I owned—like ghosts do, I guess.

"Suri?" He peered at me out of the darkness with a look of genuine confusion.

"Are you trying on my clothes?" I asked.

"As if," Trey huffed as he emerged from the depths of my wardrobe. "Your dress snagged me."

"You're incorporeal," I replied. "How is that possible?"

"Suri!" Colin demanded from the phone in my hand. "Are you there? Can you hear me? Are you okay?"

I lifted the phone to my ear. "False alarm! Just my resident ghost. Sorry to worry you."

"Did you say *ghost*?" Colin asked. With a cringe, I remembered that while he humored Audrey's witchy ways, he still wasn't sold on my paranormal activities, despite having more or less witnessed them for himself. It's remarkable what the brain can rationalize when necessary. "Are you feeling dizzy? Did you hit your head? Just sit tight. I'm maybe three minutes out."

"No, Colin, you don't have to come." But the call dropped and I couldn't get a strong enough signal to ring him back. Colin was making a trip out to my cottage for nothing, then he'd report back to Jim about a so-called ghost in my wardrobe, maybe with Karina present at the station to overhear. This day was getting worse by the minute.

Trey looked dazed. He blinked rapidly as if he'd taken a blow to the skull, but I didn't think a ghost could get a concussion. "How did I get in there?"

"I was going to ask you the same question," I replied.

He glanced at the armoire's open doors. "Could you . . ." His voice was scratchy and uncertain. "Could you close and lock the doors? It feels like something just wants to suck me back in there."

"And you're sure it's not just your natural affinity for picking apart my fashion choices?" I asked, but the bewildered look on his face told me Trey wasn't playing. I closed and locked the armoire doors and even removed the key instead of leaving it in place.

Trey appeared visibly relieved as sunlight streamed through a break in the clouds outside. I was still dripping wet, however, with a lingering, low-level migraine. A quick once-over from Trey let me know two things: that he'd sufficiently recovered from his ordeal in the armoire to cast supernatural shade, and that I looked every inch the sea wraith that I felt.

COLIN INSISTED on a full inspection of my domicile from front door to back and every square inch of floor, closet, and cupboard in between—while Trey groaned and made rude comments that Colin couldn't hear.

"Doesn't he have anything better to do?" Trey asked while Colin examined the laundry closet. "Isn't there a suspicious death to investigate? Or perhaps an appointment to keep with a tailor? Suri, I suggest you look away if you don't want to be mooned by Audrey's boyfriend," he said as Colin got down on all fours to inspect the dryer.

I laughed but tried to cover it with a cough. "I'm sure every-thing's fine, Colin."

"Can't be too careful." Colin's voice echoed with his head inside the dryer drum.

"I promise, it was nothing," I repeated for about the fifth time since his arrival. I'd agreed to let him take a look around after he'd made the frantic drive to my cottage, certain I was being held at knifepoint. I'd also tried to explain, again, that the disturbance had simply been a ghost in my armoire, but the young assistant deputy sheriff was tenacious as well as unfailingly polite. I could appreciate what Audrey saw in him.

"Just doing my job." Colin opened the washing machine door and stuck his head inside. "Plus, Audrey would never forgive me if I didn't do a thorough check."

"Okay, but I'm telling you it was a ghost. Trey? Audrey kind of knows him," I replied. "And he doesn't hang out in the washing machine."

"I do have *some* standards." Trey's smirk belied the disdain in his voice.

Colin hitched up his khakis as he stood and glanced up and down the short hall.

"There's nothing more to see," I said. "I apologize for the nuisance. I assure you, I'm quite safe."

Colin gave me an uneasy look. "You promise to call if there's any more trouble?"

I promised, and then sent Colin on his way with a couple of cookies leftover from the previous night's bake-a-thon.

Outside, a temporary pocket of sunshine gave way to dark, gray rain. I made a tall cup of herbal tea with the blend of lemon and rosehips Audrey had sent home with me. As for its promised effect, I felt neither prosperous nor cheerful, but the tea had a nice flavor. I sat at the small dining table with a bowl of chicken and wild rice soup while Trey paced up and down in the living area.

There are a few things most people don't understand about ghosts who hang around instead of crossing over, including:

1. Ghosts have no personal boundaries—more specifically, they do not respect yours. Perhaps modesty and decorum evaporate along with the ghost's connection to their lifeless body. Trey was beginning to grant me personal space upon request, but only after he'd been reminded four or five times.

2. Ghosts don't enjoy being sent on espionage or fact-finding missions, even though they are uniquely suited to the work. Unless they get bored, which happens easily and often. Then they might be eager to undertake something interesting and relevant to the world of the living.

3. Ghosts cannot fix you a cup of tea or heat a bowl of soup, no matter how miserable you're feeling.

"When I told you I needed some space, I didn't mean you had to vacate entirely." I dragged my spoon through the hearty soup and gave it a minute to cool. "I was getting worried."

"Worried I'd crossed over without saying goodbye?" Trey rolled his eyes and looked out the window at the churning ocean. "Not bloody likely."

It was curious that Trey hadn't moved on when the opportunity arose a few months earlier. I assumed he could change his mind at any time. Other spirits I'd worked with had been keen to wrap up their unfinished business and unsettled scores so they could hit the road for greener pastures, or whatever awaited them.

But this liminal, interim place is where Trey chose to remain, even after we solved the mystery of his own untimely death and brought him some small measure of justice. He'd gotten spooked —pardon the expression—by something he saw when that door to the beyond opened to him, but he wouldn't tell me what it was.

"I've been up at the Grazzini House, as you know. And I visited my family in New York." Trey watched the waves crash into the shore. It looked like a new storm was blowing in, with the beach grass on the dunes swaying with every gust of wind. "Just looking in. I hadn't been back since . . . Well, *since*."

"Ah." I spooned hot soup into my mouth. Chicken soup is supposed to cure all ills, but it couldn't turn back the clock on this disastrous week. "How was that for you? Is everyone doing all right?"

"Everyone's fine." Trey didn't look away from the window. He sounded dismissive and unconvinced.

I ate my soup and pretended I wasn't interested in his visit, though I was certain he knew I was faking. I'd encouraged him to say his goodbyes to the family and friends he'd known in life, on the chance they were holding him back from moving on.

From the stories he told, Trey had been a vigorous and entitled jackass who embraced life, though he'd not been especially considerate of the people around him. Only thirty-one when he died. He was still adjusting to his new existence as a ghost, and now he was sulking after a family visit. But he was back to hanging out in my living room, and that was something.

"So about why you were in my wardrobe . . . ?" I slurped my soup.

Trey turned to me with a shrug, though he wore the beginnings of a smile. His complexion was less spectral-ash, too, which I took as a good sign.

"Just making sure you're prepared to keep up appearances," he said. "I swear to God, Suri, we need to have a serious discussion about your choices. How much fleece does one woman need? You can do better than this sad mountain spinster thing you've got going on."

I smiled back at him, but the corners of his mouth dropped.

"I don't know how I ended up in there, or why I was stuck," he said. "I couldn't get out, and I didn't know where I was. I was starting to panic when you showed up."

"How long were you stuck?"

He gave me an incredulous look. "You know me and time, Suri."

Trey wasn't the most punctual ghost. He said he had no use for clocks anymore because nothing ever changed. Every minute, hour, and day was little different from the one before. That's what he usually said, anyway, before trying to draw me into a transcendental discussion on the intangible nature of time. The more likely truth was that an ingrained problem with tardiness had followed him into the afterlife.

"That's weird." I gulped down more tea, wishing it could bring me focus and cohesiveness of thought. I made a mental note to ask Audrey about developing a line of cognitive function teas. We could name them something cute like Certain-Tea and Clari-Tea. But someone else had probably already done that, and I would forget the idea by the time I went to bed.

The thought of my bed made me feel even more sluggish. It was only late afternoon, but the shadows were growing long outside and I could have easily turned in for the evening. But then I'd have to face tomorrow too soon. Was there any point in rising early if there would be so few customers at the Tea Reader? What if no one came at all? Apart from the teahouse and bookshop, I had little reason to get out of bed.

My face tightened. I had a reputation for being cranky and difficult, but now I was sounding morose even to myself.

"You're looking especially dull and glum," Trey said. "Barely any color to you, like you're a piece of furniture."

"What?" I looked down at my clothes and realized he was right. My jeans were faded and worn. My dark gray sweater looked lumpy. The only true splash of color came from a pair of hot pink socks from Loki's delivery box at the bookshop.

Trey started pacing again, agitated. When I asked what was bothering him, he shook off the question. "Something's not right here. Something just feels off. A 'disturbance in the Force,' or some crap like that."

I started to laugh, but my brain sparked a pathway from the Force to Audrey and Colin's sci-fi movie and game nights and the reason they'd had to cancel. I told Trey what happened the day before in the teahouse. We hadn't spoken of it at the Grazzini House, out of respect for Agatha's memorial.

"Ravi King? The obnoxious treasure hunter guy?" Trey asked.

"You think all the treasure hunters are obnoxious," I replied. "Actually, I'm pretty sure you think everyone is obnoxious."

He held up his hands as if to say, *Obviously*, before chastising me about landing in the midst of yet another suspicious death. "I'm beginning to wonder if you don't attract just ghosts, but also the people who are about to become ghosts."

"Please don't say that." I waited while he looked out at the ocean again. The tall incoming waves crested white and looked angry.

"No, I've not run into Ravi," Trey said. "But I've not really been around."

"Could he have moved on right after he died?" I asked. I didn't see ghosts everywhere I went. If all the newly dead hung around the world of the living for any length of time, I'd expect cities and even rural villages to be jam-packed with them.

"You're the expert," Trey said. "You tell me."

"You're a ghost," I replied. "*You* tell *me*."

"I'm an expert only in my own experience."

And here came the ghost philosopher again. I took another gulp of tea, which was only lukewarm now. We'd had variations of this conversation before. Neither of us had been handed a guidebook—how to be a ghost, or how to be a living medium.

"Whatever," I replied, but something still bothered me about Ravi not putting in a spectral appearance, even if he wasn't concerned about the suspicious nature of his death or any unfinished business he was leaving behind. Then I remembered the letters traced in the fogged up window. I told Trey about it. "It could have been someone playing a prank. In really poor taste."

"But you don't think so," Trey said.

I shook my head in confirmation. "I don't."

The concern on Trey's face transformed to annoyance. "So now you want me to go looking for Ravi, somewhere in the 'spirit realm,' to see what happened. Right?"

"Would you?" I lightened my face and voice, but he shot me a dirty look.

"Why do I keep helping you?" He glanced around the living room, looking like he wanted to kick something, but he wasn't corporeal and couldn't connect with any of the furniture.

"Because you're a decent person, always looking to do good in the world?" I suggested.

He gave me a look that was even more dour.

"Or maybe because whatever you saw when Drew Gaines crossed over scared you bad enough that you want to try to score as many brownie points as possible while you still can," I said. For a second, I thought I saw fear in his eyes, and I felt ashamed for being the person to put it there. Regardless of the friction between us, I didn't want to be a bad friend.

"I'll do it," Trey said, then vanished into thin air.

CHAPTER FIVE

L ate the next morning, I carried three reusable grocery bags full of the Tea Reader's remaining cookies and muffins down Main Street to the Tea and Botanicals Dispensary.

When no one—not even Murray Overhill—had come into the teahouse by 11 o'clock, Barbara made the call to close for the day, and I didn't argue. She'd use the extra time to go over the financials again, in case there were areas we could make more cuts or ways to increase our business. We were now looking at laying off staff, which made me feel sick to my stomach.

Barbara shook her head at my mention of Audrey's kombucha as a lure to bring back our customers, but she did grab the spare toner cartridge from Monday morning's mystery box. Sadly, nothing else from Loki's delivery gave me much hope that the Tea Reader's numbers would soon turn around.

Then Karina had called and asked to buy out the contents of our bakery case. She said she needed to entertain a few guests with foodstuffs that didn't contain cannabis, but I figured she was just trying to be nice. After all, her shop was putting mine out of business. As much as I disliked charity, her order would pay for next week's loose leaf shipment.

The Tea and Botanicals Dispensary was packed to the walls with my Grady neighbors and plenty of visitors from Standish Beach. Every table in the place was full, with small clusters of people standing between the tables while they drank their tea and ate their spacey cookies, or whatever cannabis confections are called. Even the couple whose romantic breakfast at the teahouse had been interrupted by the unfortunate incident of Ravi King's death were looking cozy at a table in the TBD's front window.

The place was loud, too, and full of lively conversations and clinking glassware, plus the sounds of a busy kitchen in the back —which made me wonder how Karina could justify buying all of my baked goods when she clearly had the means to produce her own.

Not everything at the TBD was infused with cannabis, but I didn't know the ratio of regular food and drink to pot products. The shop also had what I could only think of as a bouncer at the door, I guess to check IDs for anyone underage trying to sneak in. He was tall and lean, with short blue hair, and probably in his mid-thirties. His name tag identified him as the assistant manager.

"Are you Suri?" he asked before the door closed behind me. He didn't smile when he pointed to the tag pinned to his black-and-teal uniform polo shirt. "I'm Bard. Karina asked me to bring you to the back, if that's okay with you?"

"You're new in town, too?" I asked. "Like Karina?"

Bard rolled his eyes with an irritated sigh, as if I was the one-hundredth person to ask him that same question this morning and his unspoken snark was my door prize.

He tapped his foot while I perused the massive menu board that took up the entire back wall, above the sales counter and so many glass cases. Upbeat jazz music filtered down from tiny speakers mounted in the ceiling. "Or would you prefer a cup of one of our CBD-infused teas, or one of our new Valentine's candies?"

He gestured toward the counter where a TBD barista was giving an older lady a tour of their red and pink edibles, including heart-shaped gummies.

"Made right here in our own kitchen," Bard explained, "even though we're technically part of the Pot Stop chain. But we're selling out of Heart Warmers and pretty much everything else as fast as we can make them."

"I see." I shifted the heavy bags in my hands and noted that Bard didn't offer to take them from me. "But I think I'm good, thanks."

He leaned close. "If there's something you want that you don't see on the menu, just let me know." He gave me a quick wink, then his eyes went wide as he looked over my shoulder.

A draft of cold air heralded Bud Barlow's arrival behind me. With a glassy gaze, Bud blinked hard as he glanced around the busy dining room. The din of the crowd didn't cease, but the noise lowered a decibel or two.

"Bud." Bard sounded surprised, and his face went pale. I couldn't blame him. The recently deceased Ravi King had been Bud's best friend, and I got the sense Bard didn't know quite what to say.

Bud gave a slow nod. He looked smaller in his grief, and softer around the middle. He pulled off his knitted hat to reveal a hairline that had receded another half-inch since the awful events in the teahouse.

"Can I get you anything?" Bard's voice creaked in his throat. "I don't think we have an open table, but I'll see what I can do?"

Bud shook his head and shuffled through the crowd toward the sales counter. The TBD's boisterous conversation resumed its overwhelming volume.

"He looks terrible," I said as Bard and I watched him go. Bard blew out a ragged sigh and shivered. "Are you okay, Bard?" I asked.

"I'm fine," came his curt reply. "You're right. Bud looks bad. That whole thing with Ravi must have been terrible for him."

Bard motioned me to follow him through the maze of crowded tables. I thought I recognized his graceful gait, but the room was too loud for me to ask if he'd been out walking along the shore in the rain the night of the bake-a-thon at my cottage. That was fine, because I didn't feel like friendly chitchat anyway.

As we passed, I returned some of the curious and sympathetic smiles from my former Tea Reader customers, and pointedly ignored the others. Lifting my chin, I focused on keeping my cool, because there is no greater humiliation than failure in a small town where everyone knows your business.

A PAIR of swinging doors with circular windows separated the TBD kitchen from the customer area. Taylor Driskell pushed through from the kitchen and nearly dropped his tray of candies when he saw me.

"Taylor?" I asked. I shifted the heavy bags of baked goods in my hands.

"Suri, I can explain." His dark hair was pulled back in a ponytail, and he wore the same black-and-teal polo as Bard, emblazoned with the TBD logo. "I'm just here part-time, you know, while the teahouse is getting sorted?"

"Taylor, it's fine." I was glad at least one of the Tea Reader baristas had found gainful employment elsewhere. Maybe Karina had a job for Cyndi, too.

"No hard feelings?" Taylor asked, but Bard cleared his throat and Taylor hurried toward the counter instead.

"This way." Bard held one of the swinging doors open and I waddled through under the weight of Karina's order. The glint of polished chrome tables, appliances, and fixtures dazzled me. This was a true industrial kitchen, leaps and bounds beyond our simple setup in the Tea Reader.

Back when I was new to Grady, the commercial real estate agent had pushed me toward this property. He'd extolled the tremendous possibilities of the empty building, which I could configure any way I liked, and how all it would take was someone with a little vision and a lot of money to make the space their own. But I'd opted instead for the former restaurant at the other end of the street, where I converted the small dining room into the bookshop and replaced a few counter tops to remake the lounge and kitchen into the teahouse.

Three different businesses had come and gone in the TBD space since then—an overpriced house plant boutique, a New Age crystal shop that was popular with summer tourists but had been shunned by locals, and a short-lived surf shop that couldn't compete with the prices or selection of similar enterprises in Standish Beach—and it had been sitting empty for the past year. Maybe Karina was the person with vision and money the real estate agent had prophesied. She'd transformed the space into a thriving business that was bursting at the seams as soon as it opened.

"Are the muffins finally here?" Catesby asked in mock astonishment when he caught sight of me in the kitchen. "We'll, *thank God*. It's about time. I've been on the edge of starvation for the better part of an hour."

"What a jackass," I muttered, apparently loud enough for Bard's ears.

He chuckled. "Between you and me, the sooner he's out of our kitchen, the better. Too much hassle. I don't care about the treasure he's investigating, and I won't be sorry to see him go."

Max hurried over from Catesby's side to help me with the bags. Without the many winter layers of scarves, hat, and coat, it wasn't clear if Max was a he or a she, or neither. While we unpacked the bags onto a shiny, stainless steel table, I asked about Max's pronouns.

"They/them is fine, thanks," Max said with a quick smile before splitting one of the berry muffins onto a heavy china plate. They pulled a squeeze bottle of honey out of the canvas satchel they seemed to always be wearing.

"I'm pretty sure the muffins are sweet enough already." I stacked unopened boxes of cookies on the industrial kitchen table. Bard had disappeared back into the dining area, and Karina was nowhere in sight.

Max spread a small amount of honey on both halves of the muffin. "The professor is very particular, but I try to keep an eye on his health. He can be his own worst enemy sometimes."

I glanced toward Catesby and wondered if Max was worried about diabetes. Max recapped the bottle, tucked it inside their satchel, and hung their bag on a nearby chair before darting back to Catesby.

Dressed in a three-piece brown tweed suit with gold buttons, Catesby drummed his fingers with impatience on the far side of the kitchen. He was almost a caricature, presenting himself how the average American probably thought a self-important Oxford University professor might dress and behave. In contrast, Max looked every inch the harried graduate student, in an oversized sweater and corduroy pants and with black hair in a short, choppy cut.

With nothing better to do, I wandered over to have a look at Catesby's setup. There wasn't as much laboratory equipment as I'd expected, considering the professor's protestations about how much room and security he would need to conduct his work. There was something that looked like a tall breadbox with dials on it, and a wooden rack of petri dishes and glass test tubes next to plastic bottles of various liquids. A small wooden chest the size of a shoebox had pride of place. It appeared ancient but still solid, with runic-looking symbols carved into the dark wood around the base. Beside it, in a plastic container, sat the leather pouch that had rolled out of Ravi's hand as he lay dying. But the rest of it—a laptop, a stack of file folders, a couple of notebooks, and various pens collected in a heavy mug—was completely pedestrian.

Catesby eyed me with a suspicious grin as he took a generous bite of the split muffin. He made a show of considering the taste and texture, then nodded to indicate that my offering was adequate. He laughed as he sucked a bit of honey off of his thumb.

"Excellent, as to be expected," Catesby said with what appeared to be a genuine smile. He lowered his voice and leaned toward me, as though we were old chums. "To be honest, the food here is fine—the stuff that isn't laced with THC or CBD, that is. But it's just so *generic*. So much that's been frozen and *reheated*. I'm grateful for quality goods baked locally."

"Good to know," I replied.

He leaned back and gestured toward the equipment on the table. "I can't very well continue such important work on an empty or upset stomach." He patted his belly and glanced at his assistant. "That's your cue, young Max."

"Maybe you should take a break, professor?" Max suggested. "Head back to the rental house for a few hours?"

"Preposterous." Catesby narrowed his eyes. "We're only just getting started."

"Upset stomach, right." Max dug through their canvas satchel, and Catesby turned his good humor back on me.

"Young Max Turner possesses a brilliant mind, of course," Catesby said. "And I would simply be lost without *them*. But a mind reader *they* are not." I wasn't sure why the professor sounded so burdened by the use of Max's pronouns.

Max rolled their eyes at every emphasized syllable that dropped from Catesby's mouth. They produced a bottle of pink, over-the-counter stomach-relief liquid and handed it to the professor.

"I've been having stomach issues of late." Catesby took a gulp and looked pained as he swallowed. "Overwork, perhaps, but the food in this place certainly hasn't helped."

"'This place'? You don't mean all of Grady?" The instant the words were past my lips, I knew I shouldn't have poked the bear.

"*Well,*" Catesby exhaled and handed the pink relief back to Max. "That remains to be seen. One can hardly expect a quaint, seaside village to supply the more sophisticated and cultured offerings that a palate such as mine has come to relish, nay even require. For the time being, these baked delights of yours are an encouraging start."

He consumed the rest of the berry muffin in three quick bites —an impressive feat considering that Audrey's muffins were closer to jumbo size than mini. Again, he licked his fingers clean, then wiped his hands on a linen handkerchief pulled from his tweed blazer pocket.

"Now, you are the proprietress of the Tea Reader," Catesby said. "You should know your teas, yes?"

"Uh, sure?" Even the newest Tea Reader barista knew more about tea than I did. My expertise lay more on the bookshop side of the operation. But even with Catesby's more generous attitude, his condescension was stifling. I didn't want to give him the opportunity to feel superior or get the idea that he could teach me something.

"Perfect!" Catesby clapped his thick hands together, while I heard Max blow out a long sigh behind me. "And we have already concluded that the plant matter found in the 'treasure box' is indeed a blend of loose tea leaves."

"And not just a really old salad?" I asked.

Catesby roared with laughter. "I thought I detected a kindred spirit in you, Ms. Mudge."

My smile felt rough around the edges, and I kind of hoped

the professor would notice. I was interested in his and Max's work with the treasure, and I was grateful for the large bakery order, now that I understood it was for actual consumption and not just Karina's charity. But I lacked the patience for a full tour of Catesby's small mobile lab.

Catesby launched into a tour of his mobile lab all the same. The petri dishes were self-explanatory, and the plastic bottles contained various fluids that would react or turn colors and tell Catesby all about a sample's origins and specific gravity—maybe? My eyes were glazing over and my ears filling with cotton. The professor was especially proud of the breadbox with knobs, which was a portable gas chromatograph mass spectrometer that would, I guess, read the tea leaves and reveal the secrets of the universe.

"All of this for some old tea?" I asked.

Catesby laughed. "Some old tea indeed." He pressed his hand to his heart. "I tell you, Ms. Mudge, it is a refreshing delight to meet someone with such insight and wit in such a peculiar and out-of-the-way hamlet."

Ah, so we were back to the big city snobbery. No doubt Catesby believed he was as charming as they come. I still couldn't place his accent. It wasn't consistent, with unpredictable prolonged vowels and choppy th- sounds scattered among his softer syllables and dropped Rs. So, there was a good chance Catesby was not who he pretended to be, but who was?

Max skirted around us to take a seat at the table. They opened the laptop and got to work.

"And what have you learned so far?" My question was for Max, but Catesby jumped in to answer instead.

"We believe the tea in question to be quite old, yes," Catesby said, then cleared his throat.

"We really can't be sure." Max looked up from the laptop screen with an apologetic glance at Catesby. "This equipment can't establish a date for the wooden container." They gestured toward the treasure box nearby. "That will be the job of the archaeology department, when we return to Cascade State. But for the tea? It's tough without being able to examine the site itself. Treasure hunting is basically looting, and so much data gets lost."

Catesby cleared his throat and gave Max a pointed look.

"But, uh, we're considering thirteen hundred to sixteen hundred years as the age range," Max said. "That estimate will change as we dig deeper. It's odd that it's so well-preserved."

Catesby's smile pinched inward. "Yes, yes, because we've only begun our work. Soon we'll be able to determine what *kind* of tea it is, or was, as well."

"Preliminary indications place the primary ingredients in the lamiaceae family," Max said as they transcribed handwritten notes from a spiral notebook into a document on the laptop.

"The herbal family that includes sage, mint, thyme," Catesby explained to me. "That sort of thing."

"And not native to this area," Max added. "Common in more temperate regions of Europe, Asia, and Northern Africa. I'm concerned about the scrollwork on the box, though. Are we sure these treasure hunters aren't pseudo-archaeologists trying to prove the presence of Viking settlers or something problematic like that?"

"I hardly think so, Max," Catesby replied in a condescending tone. "Given that Mr. King himself was a person of color. And I remind you that our primary interest is the contents of the box, not the box itself."

"Sure," Max said with a sigh. Their shoulders seemed to tense as their fingers rested on the keyboard, then they put their head down and went back to typing.

"Quite right." Catesby shoved his hands into his pockets. "It's a curious thing, this 'treasure tea.'" Catesby pulled a face instead of making actual air quotes. "And clearly of massive historical significance. I would venture it's likely safe to drink, even after all this time, though not especially palatable."

"Safe to drink?" I asked. I'd wondered about whatever Cyndi

said she saw Ravi and Bud sprinkle into their teapots. Could old, bad-tasting tea have killed Ravi? "Not poisonous?"

"Poison?" Catesby chuckled. "Certainly not. Though it might give you some indigestion."

"There's magick here, right? In the Naghatune Bay area?" Max looked up from the laptop screen. "I was reading about it, but there's not much in the scientific literature, as you might guess. But I'm genuinely curious. Maybe that's why the tea and the box are so well preserved?" Their question seemed intended for me, but Catesby swooped in to respond.

"Magick indeed!" Catesby chuckled. "Next thing, young Max, you'll be proclaiming a belief in ghosts!"

Max looked chastened and went back to typing on the laptop. I held my tongue. I didn't want to engage in a debate about survival beyond death with a blowhard like Catesby.

"As you can see," Catesby continued, "we're already making excellent progress. I would be delighted to speak to you further about our findings at a later time. Perhaps over dinner?"

His phone rang before I could refuse. Catesby's face lit up when he saw the name of the caller on the screen.

"Ah! It's *Proof TV* returning my call," Catesby announced in triumph. "I told you they'd be interested in this truly fascinating case. Groundbreaking, even."

Max grumbled something unintelligible, earning a sharp look from the professor.

"Dr. Thomas Catesby here," he said as he answered the call. "But just a moment, if you will." Catesby walked me toward the kitchen door and ushered me out. "I will get your contact information from Ms. Coyle, then, and give you a ring? Thank you so much for stopping by."

"But, no," I said as the double doors swung closed in my face. Through the window, I watched as Catesby chatted on the phone and picked up another Tea Reader muffin. After dipping into Max's satchel for the squeeze bottle, Catesby slathered the muffin with at least three times as much honey as Max had allowed. He grinned at me through the glass as he lifted a quarter of the muffin and crammed it into his mouth.

WHEN I TURNED to head for the TBD exit, I collided with Karina. Even though I'd been delivering an order, I felt like I'd been caught trespassing.

"Oh, Suri! I'm so glad I ran into you. Literally." Karina chuckled and shifted the heavy grocery bags she was carrying. Every gesture was punctuated by that pleasant, airy scent of hers. She cocked her head toward her office door, next to the kitchen. "Do you have a minute? I was hoping to talk to you."

Because, of course she had her own office. I suppose the entire Tea Reader bookshop was my personal space, since barely anyone—other than Audrey—came through to visit with me. When there's a lull at the teahouse, Barbara will often sit with a laptop in the dining room to do the books and place supply orders. But Karina's office, with its minimalist furniture and tidy use of space, was a beige and white testament to her success.

"I'm afraid I grabbed the last bag of flour Mrs. Moroni had on the shelf, and she's all out of sugar, too." Karina set her purse and grocery bags on the floor next to her smart, well-ordered desk. Papers were stacked neatly inside tiered baskets in silver metal that matched her desktop computer, which for some reason reminded me that I'd never completed my master's degree in library and information science. "I'll have to see what I can grab from the kitchen here. I've got some baking of my own to do."

I took the chair she offered—a lightweight, Scandinavian-looking thing that was more comfortable than I expected. But I declined a cup of tea from the compact beverage maker sitting atop a low credenza. She inserted a pod with an orange label and within seconds, the small office filled with the aroma of spiced raspberries, which blended smoothly with her perfume.

"I hope you don't mind that I hired one of your baristas," Karina said.

"You mean Taylor?" I asked, then tried to laugh as if I were feeling breezy and carefree. "No, I'm glad. He's diligent and smart. It's good that he's found a place with you while the Tea Reader is closed." I swallowed a tight lump in my throat.

She smiled. "It's a relief to hear that. I didn't want you to think I was poaching your employees! But you're right about Taylor. He's friendly and gets along with everyone, too. Even Bard, and he can be a tough sell."

"Bard?" I asked. "Your assistant manager."

"He's very efficient," Karina replied. "But he's got his own way of doing things, and there can be some friction with the baristas. But Taylor's a good fit, and that can be hard to find and keep. Just a couple of weeks ago, at the end of January, we lost Stacey for reasons I don't quite understand." Karina sighed. "It's a shame. I really liked her."

"Not every barista is meant for every teahouse, I guess," I said. "Just like not every book will be right for every reader."

Karina's smile dimmed as she looked down. "I want to apologize for yesterday."

I didn't know what she was talking about, and I told her so.

"At the deputy sheriff's office, when I arrived for lunch," she said.

"When you brought them lunch," I replied.

She folded her hands on her desk. "I didn't know that you'd be there. And you have every right to be upset with me. So I wanted to talk this out with you."

The tea machine beeped to signal that it was done, and Karina wrapped her hands around the mug of hot tea. She made repeated attempts at meeting my gaze but kept looking away.

"Is that why you bought out our bakery case?" I asked. "Out of guilt, or to force a meeting with me?"

"No! Well, not entirely," she replied. I appreciated the honesty. "Professor Catesby really did ask for food to be ordered in. He's got quite an appetite."

"I know the Calico Café doesn't open until spring, but you could have had something delivered from Standish Beach. One of the fish-n-chips places maybe, for some local flavor."

Karina's face darkened with frustration. "You've seen how particular and impossible he is. Do you think he would have accepted fried fish? No, he insisted on sweet snacks from here in Grady. And I feel bad about your business closing."

"We're not closed." It was a knee-jerk, defensive response. I took a breath. "It's temporary. I hope."

She nodded in sympathy. "So do I. Anyway, I didn't want there to be any bad blood between us. We're both independent businesswomen." She cleared her throat.

"And we both have an eye for Jim Vandenhauter," I spoke again without thinking.

"Mmm." Karina looked away. "But I didn't know that you and he . . . I mean, if I'm getting in the way, I would happily step aside. Or maybe not happily? I just thought, since Jim and I have found ourselves together in the same town again . . ."

"Again?"

Karina leaned back in her leather office chair. "I thought he would have told you. We were together, for a time, I think about a year after . . ." She gestured toward me.

"After the incident," I said. Saying that innocuous word, and not even trying to describe the event itself, brought a roaring sound to my ears as my heart started to race. I turned my attention to the tea maker in the corner, and I watched how the light from the standing LED lamp glinted on the machine's white plastic surface. I inhaled the soothing aroma of Karina's tea and perfume. I stretched my toes inside my boots to remind myself where I was now, not then.

Karina's brows drew together, then relaxed. "I was going to say, 'after you were together.' But Jim told me about what happened in Oregon City. And then, of course, there's his scar."

If she'd seen his scar, she'd seen Jim without his shirt. But if they'd been seeing each other, now or years ago, that made complete sense. Maybe this was what Jim had been trying to bring up with me when I visited the station, before Karina arrived. Exes move on. Wasn't that what I was doing with Eddie? I chuckled and told myself to get a grip.

"What's funny?" she asked.

"It's nothing. And no, you're not in the way of anything. Jim and I will always have a complicated relationship, I guess."

A quick smile of relief lit up her face. "I'm glad to hear that. I knew that talking to you was the right thing to do. Jim didn't want me to approach you, but I knew that if we could just sit down with each other, everything would be better. I'm kind of headstrong that way."

Bard poked his head into the office. "Sorry to interrupt, but you wanted to know when that package arrived?"

"Yes, thanks!" Karina's cheeks flushed when she glanced at me. "Well, with Valentine's Day coming up, you know."

She stopped there and let my imagination run wild, which wasn't particularly considerate. Bard handed her a padded envelope with Victoria's Secret branding all over it, and my suspicions were confirmed.

Bard glanced at me, then back at Karina. "If you've got a minute, I thought I could run a few product ideas by you?"

"Not now." Karina waved a hand in the air, then waited for Bard to exit and close the door behind him. "Off the record, we're kind of a test kitchen for the Pot Stop. To try out new recipes and product offerings they can take national. That's why the shop name is different."

"In a tiny place like Grady?" I asked.

"Starting small, right?" She laughed. "Yeah, it's not obvious. But with Standish Beach and all its tourists and surfers nearby, it's not a bad fit. Honestly, I got my foot in the door with this project because the Pot Stop CEO is my godfather, and I'm determined to prove my worth."

"And your employees contribute their ideas, too?" I thought of Audrey and how boring the Tea Reader menu would be without her inventive baked goods and tea drinks.

"They can try." Karina gave me a look that I think was supposed to communicate commiseration. "But, no. I've got my hands quite full with trying out my own recipes. Grady is just a stepping stone for me."

I stood. "Well, I should be going. You've obviously got things you need to do."

Karina rolled her eyes, not understanding my haste. "You have no idea. The professor is such a handful. Demanding half my kitchen and ordering my staff around like they work for him? What a diva! Everything has to be to his precise specifications. Nothing is ever good enough."

I smiled. Audrey's two-day-old muffins were good enough for Catesby, so what did that say about the TBD's offerings? Or perhaps the professor's gustatory requirements were as invented as his accent.

"Max seems okay, though," Karina continued. "More down to earth. Practical and polite, but always apologizing for the professor. Telling me what he *meant* to say and thanking me for the space." She waved a hand in the air. "It's like Catesby likes to inconvenience other people just to prove how important he is." She took a sip of her tea. "I get being professionally ambitious. That's me, too, and yes, sometimes I can be kind of aggressive about it. And I don't need to tell you how ambition can sour a romantic relationship, right?"

"I guess." I edged closer to the door, but Karina was on a roll.

"But I just don't think a girl—no, a woman—should have to settle." Karina took an assertive gulp of tea, all thoughts of Catesby apparently exhausted. "Thank goodness there are men like Jim Vandenhauter in the world. He's not intimidated by that kind of drive. He's content to be who he is, and where he is."

Karina's phone rang. As she pulled it out of her bag, I saw it was Jim calling—not just from his name on the screen, but from a photo of Jim and Karina, too, their faces pressed together as they smiled for the camera. But he didn't merit a special ringtone.

"Speak of the devil!" Karina exclaimed. I showed myself out while she took Jim's call. It was none of my business, but I worried that whatever inner fire drove Karina might end up breaking Jim's heart.

I exited the TBD onto the slick sidewalk and pulled my collar close against the icy rain. Bud came out the door behind me.

"It's too much." Tears brimmed in his eyes as he pulled his hat on. "I thought I could, but I just can't be around so many people."

"You've been through something dreadful." I touched his elbow to offer comfort. "Maybe it's too soon."

"Did you see the treasure in the back kitchen?" Bud appeared agitated and insistent, even with tears spilling down his cheeks.

"I saw it," I replied. Grief can present in many different ways, and I wanted Bud to feel reassured. "I'm sure they'll take good care of it. The treasure is safe."

"Good," Bud said. "That's good. Good, good," he muttered to himself as he turned and headed down the sidewalk at a brisk pace.

I'D LIKE to say that I went home, put on some smooth jazz, took a long hot bath, and invited Eddie over for a home-cooked meal, because I wanted to see him and not because of anything Karina said about Jim.

I mean, I did go home. I tuned the radio to the jazz station, because I wanted to feel sophisticated. I tried to find a station that played music like what I heard at the Tea and Botanicals Dispensary, but the public radio station out of Seaside was playing only experimental jazz. I made it a full fifteen minutes listening to an East Coast group called The Devil's Workshop before I admitted to myself that I couldn't stand their music and was just pretending to be sophisticated. What I really wanted was Golden Oldies, so I picked up WOLD out of Hattieville and drew a lavender-scented bath. I called out in the empty cottage for Trey to keep his distance for the night, in case he was lurking in the shadows rather than checking up on the whereabouts of the recently departed Ravi King.

Trying to relax, I soaked in a hot bath of Epsom salt and lavender oil and listened to The Temptations, Elvis, and Strawberry Alarm Clock until the water cooled, but I didn't work up the nerve to text Eddie about dinner. It felt wrong to have a cozy date so soon after Ravi's death. I was too tense to be good company, anyway, though I had a feeling Eddie could make me forget my worries. Instead, I microwaved a can of spaghetti, and when Leslie Gore's "It's My Party" came around on the radio, I cried into my noodles.

Thank goodness Trey wasn't around to witness my pathetic state. After changing the sheets as an act of self-care, I put myself to bed early. It had been a hell of a day, in the middle of a hellish week, and I was grateful for sleep when it came.

Which is why I was especially grumpy when I was awakened in the middle of the night by an argument in my living room. I opened my eyes in the darkness to the sound of someone shouting, "Don't be ridiculous!" It sounded like Professor Thomas Catesby, but the phone charging on my bedside table read 3:17. Assuming I'd dreamt the disturbance, I closed my eyes and was drifting toward sleep again when I heard Trey's distinctive voice reply, "Man, you just can't be here."

I slid out of bed, did a sloppy job of pulling on my heavy bathrobe, and padded out of the bedroom in a pair of thick wool socks. The house was dark but far from quiet. I snapped on the lights and squinted at the two men in my living room. I was only half-awake and didn't have enough spare brain cells to be surprised by the sight of Thomas Catesby standing in front of the picture window.

Did the professor think his vague dinner invitation entitled him to enter my cottage without my permission?

"No," I said firmly, then yawned. I softened my eyes, determined to remain drowsy enough for an easy return to sleep. "Whatever you have to say to me can freaking wait until after dawn. You have no business being in my house in the middle of the night. Or at any other time." I ran my fingers through my tangled hair and knew I should be embarrassed by my rumpled state, when Catesby was dressed again head to foot in tweed with every square inch of fabric perfectly pressed.

"Right?" Trey gave a dramatic shrug. I shot him a look to let him know that I'd deal with the unwanted guest.

"I never agreed to have dinner with you, either," I told Catesby. "And, hell, I guess I knew you were presumptuous, but really? Breaking into my house in the middle of the night?" I waited for Catesby to say something, anything, in his defense or to embark on some long-winded explanation about how he was in the right and even the victim in this situation.

But Catesby just stood there, watching me. He looked paler than when I'd seen him in the TBD kitchen the previous afternoon.

"Are you feeling okay, professor?" I remembered Catesby's digestive upset. "How's your stomach? You're not going to puke all over my floor, are you?"

Catesby's jaw loosened in an expression of astonishment. "I

assure you, Ms. Mudge, I do not know how I came to be inside your domicile at this hour, or at any time of day. I must therefore assume I was transported here against my will, and I can and will exercise my right to alert the authorities. As for your question, well, I believe perhaps I might be rather ill after all."

Trey scoffed and crossed his arms. "You do know, man. I told you."

Catesby glanced from Trey to me, his eyes wide and afraid. "Or, yes, I fear I may be having a nightmare? I am indeed sorry for involving you in it. Now, if I may ask for your assistance in helping me to wake up—"

Trey laughed. "Pinch yourself all you want, dude. It's not going to help."

"Pinch myself?" Catesby retorted. "The very idea. Any sensation can be manufactured by the mind in a dream state, and pinching oneself is therefore entirely useless. Not to mention unseemly and undignified."

I started to ask the professor what help he thought I could offer if he believed he was simply dreaming, or maybe sleepwalking, but I froze before the first syllable was out of my mouth. I turned to Trey. "He can see you."

Trey nodded. "Exactly."

"He can hear you, too," I said. My brain was waking up, and it was irritating. I had little hope of getting back to sleep now. "You're having a conversation with him."

Trey's smile was smug but grim.

"That means . . ." I turned to face Catesby. "Professor, I'm sorry to be the one to tell you this, but I think you're dead."

CHAPTER SIX

G hostly shouts of "That's preposterous!" and "You are seriously deranged!" and the like were hurled back and forth as I placed a call to Jim before the sun was even up. Trey tried to reason with Catesby—going so far as to demonstrate how they both were incorporeal by asking Catesby to turn on a lamp, fluff a pillow, or open the front door—while I sat at the dining table, listened to Jim's phone ringing, and dreaded the possibility that Karina might be the one to pick up.

But it was Jim who answered, sounding very much alone, and I couldn't help the relief in my voice even as I reported that I was pretty sure—no, I knew for a fact—that visiting academic Thomas Catesby was dead. Jim knew me well enough not to ask how I'd come by this information.

Then I waited. Or, *we* waited, because Catesby was still haranguing Trey and me about the injustice of our distasteful prank and how this *entirely and irrevocably* altered his good opinion of me. Whatever. I ignored him as much as possible while I fixed myself a cup of tea. Unfortunately, the sight of me sipping my Earl Grey with honey made Catesby's eyes bulge out of their ghostly sockets.

"How dare you loiter there and enjoy your tea without offering your unwilling guest—nay, your hostage—the same hospitality?" Catesby spluttered.

"Loiter? This is my home." I placed the mug on the dining table and invited Catesby to pick it up for himself. He hesitated, then swiped his hand through the cup as though it weren't there. Trey laughed, which didn't help.

"Balderdash! Inconceivable!" Catesby shouted as he made a show of stomping away from me, without a single footfall making a sound.

"Just wait until he realizes he can't slam a door behind him," Trey chuckled. "He'll have to find another way to make a dramatic exit."

So it went for the next hour, while Jim called around to the house Catesby and Max had rented for their stay, then to Karina, and even to Dr. Edward Clair, Dean of Antiquities at Cascade State University —all to officially inquire about the professor's whereabouts.

In the meantime, I tried asking Catesby where he'd been when he expired, but as he refused to concede his own death, he was uncooperative and refused to consider the question.

When the theme from *Super Fuzz* started up on my phone, I answered immediately.

"Found him," Jim told me without preamble.

"Where?" I felt Catesby's eyes on me, but didn't give him the satisfaction of looking his way.

"On Haystack Lane, headed into town," Jim replied. "Max Turner, the assistant, reported that Catesby had experienced some indigestion and nausea late in the day, then said that he needed some air just before midnight, when he stepped outside to go for a walk. His body is in the middle of the road. I've set up some flares, but it's not like there's any traffic this time of night."

I glanced out the window. Sunrise was a couple of hours away. The rain had taken a break some time after I'd gone to sleep, but it was bitterly cold outside and the sidewalks and streets would have frozen over.

"Was it a car? A hit and run?" I looked at Catesby. "Or did you slip? Maybe hit your head or something?"

"What? Did I? Oh." Jim gave a nervous laugh on the other end of the phone. "He's there with you now."

Offended, Catesby turned his back to me and pretended to be fascinated by the darkness beyond the window glass.

"Can you handle those questions?" Jim asked. "I don't know how to question a ghost."

"You're lucky I have some experience in that area," I replied with a yawn.

"I need to finish securing the scene, and call the coroner." Jim sounded weary, and his day was only beginning. "Then I'll head your way."

"We'll be here," I said. "But give me a call first? I might need to get some sleep in the meantime."

"Suri." Whatever Jim wanted to say never made it past his lips. Through the phone, I heard Colin's arrival, and I listened as the deputy sheriff and his assistant started setting up a road block. I hung up and finished my tea while Catesby stood at the window and delivered an extemporaneous monologue about the critical significance of his work and how he was too important to die.

"And yet the end comes for all of us, eventually," I muttered into my empty mug.

"THIS IS INTOLERABLE!" Catesby scoffed for probably the forty-ninth time. He'd been pacing around my living room for several hours, and I'm not sure he'd once taken a breath. Not that he needed to breathe any longer, but whenever this fact—or any other proof of his death—was brought to his attention, his outrage ratcheted up that much further.

In an uncharacteristic display of selflessness, Trey offered to babysit the new ghost while I tried to get some more sleep before the sun rose. I drifted in and out of unconsciousness, but my sleep was restless, and my dreams of heart-shaped sugar cookies and muffins drenched in gooey honey syrup were punctuated by Catesby's real-time outbursts in the living room.

By the time Jim arrived at my cottage, alone, I was on my third cup of strong black tea. I was grateful he hadn't brought Colin with him after the whole "ghost in the closet" embarrassment. Jim sat at the dining table with me, and with his own cup of tea and a plate of buttery crackers out of a box—don't judge me—while he learned how to interrogate a petulant and uncooperative ghost about his own demise.

"There's been a mistake, and a rather basic one at that," Catesby insisted again, as he stood over Jim and yelled in his face. That Jim was oblivious to his bluster only antagonized Catesby. Done with his ghost-sitting duty, Trey had left the scene as soon as Jim arrived, which meant I was more or less on my own to contend with Catesby. "Foolish, small-town law enforcement can't be trusted to properly identify a body or recognize a living, breathing human being standing directly in front of them."

When Jim didn't respond, Catesby stormed in silence across the room and turned to glare at us from the corner. I relayed Catesby's words to Jim, who suggested that he'd be happy to show the ghost his own lifeless body, if that would help.

"Perhaps a photograph?" I suggested.

Jim pulled out his phone and held up the screen for Catesby to see. "Is, uh, is he looking? Can he see it?"

With an air of grudging compliance, Catesby ambled toward us and leaned down to examine Jim's phone. On the screen was a tweed-wearing, deceased professor, staring up at the sky. If not for the eyes being open, the corpse might have looked like he was sleeping. Catesby's smug smile vanished from his face.

"Well, obviously, this is a trick," Catesby protested. "Some malicious fakery. And quite mean spirited, I might add."

"To what end?" I asked. Jim, privy to only my end of the conversation, glanced around what looked to him like an empty room. I was glad he didn't need any convincing that the ghost was present. "Why would the deputy sheriff try to pull a fast one on you?"

"Naturally, that would fall under the categorization of hazing." Catesby lifted his chin in indignation. "It's well known that minuscule, insignificant hamlets such as yours are unwelcoming to outsiders."

"So you think local law enforcement would waste time and resources to play a prank on you?" I asked.

Catesby waved a hand in the air. "What else have they got to do?"

"How about investigating the other suspicious death that occurred just a couple of days ago?" I replied. "Remember Ravi King, and his find in the hills? The whole reason you came here in the first place?"

"*Well*." Whether that was a concession or not, Catesby turned his back to us and resumed gazing out the window. The early morning sun was low in the sky, casting long shadows of my little cottage over the beach grass and sand dunes.

I couldn't blame Catesby for the shock he was experiencing. He'd died unexpectedly only a few hours earlier, and it happened far from his home and in unfamiliar surroundings. How long had it taken Trey to come to terms with his death, under similar circumstances? In both cases, I needed the fledgling ghost's help to figure out what happened to them. In Trey's case, it had turned out to be murder. What were the chances it was the same for Catesby?

I turned to Jim. "I think he accepts that it's his body, at least.

Not that you can put in the official record that the ghost identi-fied his own corpse."

Catesby huffed and kept his gaze on the scene outside the window, where birds scattered across the sand to inspect and gobble up what the outgoing tide had left on the beach.

"Sorry, Jim," I said. "I shouldn't have invited you over. It's too soon to get any useful information out of him. I just wanted to try to help before he, well, you know."

"Before what?" Jim and Catesby asked in unison.

"Before he crosses over, in case that is about to happen," I said.

Catesby was at my side in a silent instant, making me jump. "Is that possible?" he asked with a mix of excitement and fear. "Will it happen soon? Where will I go? What do I need to do?"

"I don't know," I replied, then looked at Jim. "There's a lot I don't know. Maybe Ravi moved on right away, and that's why I couldn't find him to ask questions and help you."

Jim closed his little notebook and slipped it into his shirt pocket. "I appreciate your trying all the same." He started to get up, but fell right back into his chair again.

"Jim?" I was on my feet, checking his pulse and feeling his forehead for a fever, but his skin was cool to the touch.

"Just a little dizzy, I guess." Jim looked pale as he rose to his feet and took a few unsteady steps across the floor. He staggered toward the breakfast bar and braced himself against it. "Sorry, Suri. I don't feel all that great right now."

Then he vomited all over my Pendleton rug.

CHAPTER SEVEN

After I helped Jim get himself cleaned up in the bathroom, I directed him to my bed to sleep off whatever was ailing him. Given that Ravi had so recently expired on the teahouse floor, I'd wanted to call an ambulance for Jim, but he swore he was fine and just needed to rest for a while. I was glad I'd put fresh sheets on the bed the night before. His uniform was in the wash and even my oversize lounging sweats were too small for him, so he was currently ensconced in my bed in nothing more than his underwear. I tucked him in and closed the curtains to darken the room so he could rest.

A little before 8 a.m., I put in a call to Colin to let him know what had happened. Audrey was with him and making breakfast, and she promised to bring over a load of bland, easily digestible comfort food before lunchtime. After that, I was subjected to more bellyaching from the ghostly Professor Catesby while I cleaned up the mess Jim had made of my living room. I sponged away as much vomit from the rug as I could, then hung it on the railing outside to freeze, I guess, or maybe to dry in the sun. It would have to be sent out for a proper cleaning. I hoped the deputy sheriff's office would reimburse me.

To mask the lingering smell of sick, I lit a eucalyptus-scented candle and set it on the old chest I used as a coffee table.

When I cracked the door open to check on Jim a while later, I overheard him on the phone with Karina. He was thanking her for her concern and urging her not to come over—thank goodness for that—then telling her how much he'd enjoyed their dinner the previous evening. Jim was in my bed, cozy beneath the yellow-and-blue quilt my grandmother had made for my eighteenth birthday, while he talked to another woman about her rose-and-honey cupcakes, which I really hoped wasn't a euphemism.

I closed the door and marched to the kitchen for another cup of tea. I might also have texted Audrey with a list of foods to help me eat my feelings.

Catesby hovered in the middle of the living room looking morose as I took a seat at the dining table with my fourth or fifth cup of tea since my rude awakening in the wee hours of the morning. I wanted to go back to bed and pretend none of this day had happened. But my bed was occupied, and taking a nap on the couch was out as long as Catesby the Unfriendly Ghost was hanging about, demanding attention.

"Just say it." I stared into my mug and watched steam rise from the dark tea.

"What is it you would like me to say, madame?" came Catesby's smug reply.

I didn't look up. "Whatever it is that's got you in such a snit, that you're standing there waiting for me to ask about. And while you're at it, what's with all the flowery, formal speech and two-dollar words? Can't you just talk to me like a normal human being?"

Catesby sniffed. "This is simply the way in which I express myself. Perhaps it is too much to expect for my vocabulary and sentence construction to be comprehended by the less erudite masses."

I laughed, and Catesby looked surprised. "Oh, I understand you just fine. It's just that you sound like an ass."

A knock at the front door saved Catesby from having to reply, or maybe saved me from any further verbal swagger. I walked down the hall and was thanking Audrey for coming so quickly before I even opened the door. I stopped mid-sentence when I instead found Max Turner standing on my stoop. "Max? What are you doing here?"

"I'm sorry, Suri," they said. "Ms. Mudge, I mean."

"Suri is fine."

"It's just, I don't know anybody here, and I didn't know where else to go." Their eyes wandered over the cottage's cedar siding, then down the concrete steps leading up to my door, before finally meeting my gaze. "Uh, can I come in? It's kind of cold out here."

"Of course." I wasn't excited about having another uninvited guest inside my home, but I also wasn't about to let young Max freeze on my stoop. Max removed their boots in the hallway without being asked. I felt my mood lighten with the simple courtesy.

"Would you like some tea?" I asked, leading Max toward the living room. "I don't have anything fancy here. Just whatever I can buy in a box."

"Thank you. You save the good stuff for the teahouse. Makes sense." Max wandered into the living room, oblivious to Catesby's presence or that the ghost was studying their every move.

"Well, now." Catesby stepped in Max's direction. "I would have expected more tears from you, young person." Catesby's lip curled. He circled Max, looking them up and down. "Same clothes from last night, too. I could charitably chalk that up to grief, or more likely, simple laziness. What's your excuse, Max Turner? Wandering and lost without your mentor? Yet not the least forlorn to be rid of me?"

I held my tongue and set a fresh mug of water in the

microwave. Contrary to Catesby's appraisal, Max looked disoriented, not relieved. Their face was blotchy and their eyes red— what you'd expect from someone who had been weeping—and their short hair stood out every which way. But Catesby held a grudge against Max, and he hadn't let go of it in death.

"Smells like a spa in here. Eucalyptus?" Max asked. I nodded toward the candle on the coffee table. They took a deep breath in. "It's nice."

"I'm sorry, Max. I'm guessing you've been notified about the professor," I said, then gave Catesby's ghost a hard look.

Max slipped out of their jacket and bunched it up in their hands in a gesture that reminded me of an overwhelmed and desolate street urchin. Their large eyes started to tear up as they blinked at me and nodded. It made me want to wrap them in a warm blanket and feed them chicken soup.

"Deputy Sheriff Vandenhauter called earlier this morning. After he found the body." Max made a small, strangling noise. Catesby rolled his eyes.

The microwave beeped, and I directed Max to take a seat at the dining table while I set a generic tea bag to steep—decaf, because I didn't want to amplify Max's distress. The buttery crackers I'd served Jim were still on the table, and I grabbed a container of local honey and a small jar of sugar on my way around the breakfast bar.

"Honey or sugar?" I set the hot mug in front of Max, then slid into my chair and wrapped my hands around my own cup of tea.

Max stared at the sugar and honey, then shook themselves out of a daze. I'd looked at sweet things like that before, too, when I was trying to get into shape. The poor thing was possibly on a diet, and at the worst possible time. Food can be a great comfort in grief, even if the effect is temporary. But Max left the sweeteners alone. "No, I'm fine. Thank you."

I remembered Max's care in doling out berry muffins to the

professor the day before. Maybe I had misinterpreted their reaction to the sugar. "Max, was Thomas Catesby any chance diabetic? Could that be what killed him?"

"Surely, you must be joking!" Catesby exclaimed, and I had to stop myself from countering with the old joke that my name was Suri, not Shirley.

"Pre-diabetic." Max sat up tall and looked almost hopeful. Even with the death of a loved one, uncertainty can be a heavy weight. "Do you think that's what happened?"

"I don't know." I also didn't know how long it would be before the coroner could provide Max with the comfort of concrete answers. Letting the warmth from my tea mug seep into my fingers, I tried not to think about how little sleep I'd gotten and how rough the rest of the day was going to be. I focused instead on the fact that Max still hadn't told me why they'd appeared on my doorstep.

"It must be a terrible shock," I said. "And here you are, away from home, and now alone."

Max almost hid their face behind the ceramic mug as they took small, uncertain sips. "I called the dean. That was right after I talked to the deputy sheriff."

"And Catesby's family?" I asked. "Do you need help reaching out to anyone, so they can make arrangements?"

"No," came Catesby's firm reply. "There's no family to notify. The dean will see to an appropriate memorial befitting someone of my stature and importance."

Max swallowed. "I emailed the professor's father in Milwaukee. He, I mean Professor Catesby, didn't know I was in touch with his family from time to time. He didn't like people knowing where he came from, I guess. But his parents worried about him, you know? They're older and just wanted to know how he was doing. So, sometimes I send updates." Max gave a nervous laugh. "Professor Catesby would've killed me if he knew."

Now that Catesby did know, he looked positively livid. It was almost encouraging to see the color rise in his ghostly cheeks. "Who says I won't chastise you now, you deceitful little waif?"

It wasn't easy to ignore Catesby's histrionics and waving arms, but I tried.

"And it shouldn't have been a big deal, even." Max relaxed into the chair and seemed relieved to be talking to someone. "So what if the great Professor Thomas Catesby grew up in Wisconsin instead of at the Sorbonne or whatever? So what that his dad is a mechanic and his mother is a hair dresser? Those are good, honest jobs. But the professor didn't care when his sister and brother opened their own repair shop, expanding the family business. He acted like it was something to be ashamed of."

Max took a big gulp of tea while I watched Catesby for his reaction. His face was beet red, but he kept his jaw clamped shut. It was a pleasant change.

Another quick knock came from the end of the hall, followed by the sound of the door opening. "Don't get up!" Audrey called from the front hallway. I heard her slipping off her winter boots. "I come bearing gifts, and pretty much everything you need to eat your way through the apocalypse!"

She wasn't kidding. Audrey appeared on the threshold to the living area with multiple fabric bags hanging off both arms and several more in her hands. She raised her eyebrows when she saw me sitting with Max.

"I caught Mildred Moroni as she was restocking her shelves." Audrey unloaded the bags onto the breakfast bar and started putting away cans of soup, beans, and boxes of bouillon cubes into my cupboards. "I figured you hadn't done any shopping since I was here the other night, so I went ahead and got you, well, everything."

"Audrey." Frustrated tears caught in my throat, and I swallowed hard. "Audrey, I don't even know if I can pay you this week, and you're buying me groceries?"

"I know you're good for it." Audrey tossed a plastic container of home-baked cookies to Max. "Eat."

Max opened the box and started nibbling on the end of a heart-shaped sugar cookie decorated with white and silver sprinkles.

"You made more cookies?" I asked. "Audrey, the teahouse is effectively closed right now."

Audrey slid a few slices of bread into the toaster, more comfortable in my kitchen than I was. "Sure, but I had all the ingredients already. And I wanted to do something useful with it all, and with my time."

I winced. Audrey would have opened the teahouse with Barbara this morning, to serve her scones and special tea blends to our regular customers, if not for the competition down the street and Ravi King's unfortunate demise in the Tea Reader dining room. And I would have been sitting in my dimly lit bookshop, pretending to be open for business and maybe helping a customer or two while I read the latest cozy mystery from Dale Ivan or June Lucas. But none of that would happen today.

I needed to check in with Barbara. I should probably have been calling the part-time baristas, too. It was a short list in the winter months, just Cyndi and Taylor during the week and Barry and Andrew on the weekends. But what could I tell them, other than to encourage them to find other work? I couldn't promise the Tea Reader would re-open by a particular date, or at all.

I wanted to reach out to Trey, to ask if he'd found out what happened to Ravi King, and to Catesby, too. But I already had one quarrelsome spirit stalking about my living room, plus three living guests. Both Audrey and Jim knew about my special talent, and even relied on me for it from time to time, but Max Turner was an outsider. Word about my abilities was getting around, but I was still trying to keep this information close. Naghatune Bay attracted too many spiritual seekers as it was, and I didn't want anyone coming to town looking for me in particular.

"Is Jim awake?" Audrey placed a stack of napkins and a plate of buttered toast on the dining table while bowls of chicken soup heated in the microwave.

Max perked up. "The deputy sheriff is here?" They drained the rest of their tea and reached for a slice of toast.

"Sick, I'm afraid. He was here asking about your boss." I tried to swallow the last words before they were out of my mouth, but I couldn't take them back. Max didn't seem curious about why Jim would consult with me about Catesby's death, and my shoulders relaxed as the moment passed.

"Sick?" Max's face blanched. "What's wrong? Is he okay?"

Audrey shot me a questioning look. "Stomach upset, right?"

"Yeah." My attention turned to the ghost of Catesby, standing by the couch and shaking his head. He'd fallen silent, something I would have considered an impossibility only a few minutes prior.

"I felt sick to my stomach, too," Catesby said. "Indigestion. Nausea. I was dizzy. My heart was pounding painfully in my chest. I thought a late night walk in the crisp winter air would clear my head."

The ghost started to cry.

~

THE GODS, if they exist, were having their Greek-tragedy fun with me this week. Before I could find an inconspicuous way to calm Catesby out of Max's earshot, before I could reassure Max that Jim likely had a stomach bug and wasn't going to die, before I could take hot soup and toast to my ailing ex-boyfriend recuperating in my bedroom, the doorbell rang.

It was such a seldom-heard tone that I froze as soon as the chime sounded. Everyone always knocked, and I'd thought the doorbell wires had shorted out after a visit from Loki a couple of weeks earlier.

Audrey hastened down the hall to open the door, and she reappeared with Loki close behind her.

"Speak of the devil," I muttered.

Max and Audrey frowned at me, but Loki's face brightened. "Good morning to you as well, Ms. Mudge."

"Hey, so I'm sorry to be rude, but whatever it is, can it wait?" I asked. "I really have my hands full right now."

"Ah. I was hoping to speak to you about a cat," Loki replied.

"You mean Simba?" Audrey replied. "But she's fine. She bounced right back after what happened at the Grazzini House."

"A cat," I said. "In other words, yes, this can wait."

"Suri?" Jim appeared on the threshold to the living room in nothing but his underwear, letting the wall hold him up. Max gasped at the sight of him, and I nearly did, too. Jim's skin was gray and his eyes glassy. He kept grimacing and clutching his chest.

"Jim!" I forgot about Catesby's tears and pushed past Loki. I reached Jim just as he started to slide to the floor. "Audrey, call the doctor! Call Colin! Call 911!"

"Your friend there looks like I did," I heard Catesby in my ear. "Or how I felt, right before the end." For once, he didn't sound smug or condescending. I told him to shut up and give me some room.

"I'm sorry, Suri." Max thought I'd been talking to them. "But what can I do? How can I help?"

"Audrey will tell you what to do." I pulled one of Jim's arms over my shoulder, steadied him on his feet, and turned him around. He swore he didn't need to be sick again, but I steered him toward the bathroom anyway. I got him inside seconds before he started vomiting.

Maybe it was a stomach bug, albeit a bad one, but I couldn't get Catesby's comment out of my head. What if what was wrong with Jim was the same thing that Catesby had experienced? And if Catesby was now a ghost in my living room, what did that mean for Jim?

"Ambulance is on the way," Audrey called from outside the closed bathroom door. "How is he? What do you need?"

I sat on the cold floor, rubbed Jim's naked back as he retched into the toilet, and tried not to cry.

It wasn't Dr. Settle from Standish Beach who arrived first. It was Coastal Fire and Rescue. I gulped when I heard their sirens outside the cottage. Eddie was on duty today.

And Eddie was the first up the steps, the first through the front door, and the first pushing into the bathroom. "Suri?"

"I'm okay. It's not me." A not insignificant part of me melted when I saw the anguish in his face turn to relief. But his eyes narrowed as he looked from me to Jim, who was slumped in a tight ball on the floor in his boxer briefs. "Jim came over this morning on an official call, asking questions about a suspicious death."

"Another one?" I couldn't read Eddie's expression as he squeezed into the small bathroom and rested his massive first responder bag on the tile floor. I scooted out of the way to make room for Eddie to kneel beside Jim and check his vital signs.

"It's his job," I added, expecting Eddie to push back. "His uniform's in the wash, because he was sick all over it."

"Just tell me what happened so I can help him." Eddie's voice was calm and his movements deliberate and professional. He attached a pulse-oximeter to one of Jim's fingers and listened for Jim's pulse and breath sounds with a stethoscope. I felt foolish and petty for anticipating jealousy or snark when Eddie was trying to save a life. "Jim? Hey, buddy, can you hear me?"

Jim was semi-conscious. His eyes began to roll up under his lids, but he managed a vague moan in response to Eddie's questions.

Another fire fighter, I think her name was Tracey, appeared in the bathroom doorway. "How's he look?"

In the hall, I saw Audrey and Max peering over Tracey's shoulder. That left Loki and Catesby in the living room, but that was a concern for another time.

"Pulse is rapid and weak." Eddie draped the stethoscope around his neck. "Pulse-ox is on the low side, 84, but steady. Patient is cool to the touch and appears to have been vomiting. Signs of dehydration." He peeled back Jim's eyelids. "Pupils dilated, but reactive."

In the doorway, Tracey entered everything Eddie reported into a tablet encased in thick rubber. "Conscious?" she asked.

Eddie shook his head. "Non-responsive."

Tracey called toward the front door. "We need the stretcher."

Eddie turned to me. "Suri, tell me what happened."

"He was here following up on, on a body that was discovered on Haystack Lane in the early hours of the morning," I said, my breath high in my chest and my heartbeat pounding in my ears. "Because, you know why."

Eddie touched my knee. "Hey, it's okay. Take a breath."

I did as he suggested and felt instantly better. "Jim said he was feeling dizzy, and then he puked on my carpet."

"How long ago was that?" Eddie asked.

"I don't know. I think it was around 6 or 7?" I looked at Jim lying motionless on the floor. He was still breathing, even if those breaths looked shallow to my eyes. "I made him lie down after that, and I think he slept for a while. I know he was talking on the phone, so I thought he was okay."

"Did he have anything to eat or drink that you saw?" Eddie asked.

"Just some tea I made, Lipton or something from a bag," I said, remembering that he hadn't touched the crackers I'd put out for him. "But it was the same tea that I had, and I'm fine, right?"

"Okay. Okay, that's good." Eddie grasped my wrist and was gentle about pulling me to my feet so Tracey and another rescue worker could come into the bathroom with a rolling stretcher.

Eddie and I stepped into the bathtub, pulling his gear bag with us, to get out of the way as they lowered the stretcher to the floor.

"Anything else you can think of?" Eddie asked. "What happened after Jim went to lie down?"

I lifted my hands to shrug, and they were shaking. "I don't know! Audrey came over and was helping make some food, something bland so Jim could keep it down. But then he just appeared in the hallway and looked so weak and pale and awful."

They loaded Jim onto the stretcher, covered him in a blanket, and strapped him in. It was just like Oregon City, when Jim was bleeding on the floor in the library, shouting into his radio for backup. My lungs froze, and I stopped breathing.

"Suri." Eddie grasped my hands and turned my body to face him, but I was transfixed, watching them raise the stretcher and lock the rolling legs into place. "Suri, look at me."

I met Eddie's warm, familiar gaze, and I started breathing again.

"That's better." Eddie gave me a small smile.

"What's wrong with Jim?" I asked.

"I don't know," Eddie replied. "But we're going to get him up to the hospital in Seaside, where he'll get the care he needs. All right?"

"Is he, but will he be okay?" The sudden thought of Jim as a ghost haunting me—or worse, my having to help him move on —threatened to stop my breathing again.

"I don't know, Suri," Eddie said. "But you've done all you can do. You were right to call for help. Now the help's arrived, and we'll take care of him from here." He squeezed my fingers tight in his. "Okay?"

I nodded dumbly and watched them wheel Jim out of the bathroom and into the hall.

～

"POISON," I repeated the word with the phone pressed to my ear. "Are you sure? What kind?"

I stood in the kitchen, watching a few slices of bread brown in the toaster, while Max and Audrey sat in the living room, looking stunned. I had no idea when Loki had left—not unusual for him, but mildly unnerving for me. A few hours had passed since the rescue crew took Jim to the hospital. Other than ironing his newly laundered uniform—without any burn marks—I didn't know what to do with myself.

"I'm afraid I don't have that information," Eddie said on the other end of the call. When the phone first rang, I'd worried that Eddie was breaking protocol or violating HIPAA by giving me an update—until I learned that at some point, and without consulting me, Jim had designated me as his next of kin. "Someone from the hospital will be in touch when they know more, and to let you know about visiting hours, if Jim needs anything from home, that sort of thing."

Eddie let the silence hang on the line. I listened to him breathe and tried to figure out what to say.

"He was in his underwear because he'd vomited on his uniform and I had to put it in the wash," I blurted into the phone. Max and Audrey looked up in surprise, and I realized I probably should have stepped into the bedroom for this conversation. "It's not like he was here overnight."

Audrey threw me a glance that was somewhere between a smirk and a concerned frown. Max pulled a pair of earbuds out of their pocket. I turned my back to them.

"Suri, it's okay. I believe you." Eddie's voice was tinged with laughter, and the tightness in my chest began to loosen. Everything was easy with Eddie, and I wondered why that wasn't enough for me. Why I couldn't just relax and let go. "That must have been scary for you this morning. My question is, are *you* okay? I can come by after my shift, if you want. Whip up some homemade paella? It's the best comfort food."

I surveyed the kitchen counter and breakfast bar. Every surface was claimed by either dirty dishes or the bounty of fresh bread, cookies, crackers, and more that Audrey had brought with her. A half-dozen cans of chicken broth sat beneath overflowing cupboards.

"I think I'm good on the comfort food front," I replied. "But I appreciate the offer. I'll let you know."

"I'm here for you, either way," Eddie said before hanging up.

The toaster popped. I smiled and slathered Tillamook salted butter across slices of crispy bread and watched it melt.

"Your fireman's quite the hero today." Audrey had her legs tucked beneath her on the couch, with a blanket draped over her shoulders. The morning's brief window of sunshine had given way to a wintry mix of wet sleet and snow. It was a good day to nestle in by the fire, which Max had thoughtfully built in the hearth without being asked.

"I know, maybe not *your* fireman. Yet." Audrey gave me a meaningful look, with no hint of teasing in her voice. "But it sounds like he wants to be."

Max stared out the picture window at the gray, icy day while listening to something with a mellow beat through their earbuds. The big window onto an ocean view inspired quiet contemplation for all of my guests, eventually. That view, even when the weather was cold and miserable, was probably my favorite feature of the cottage.

None of us had anywhere we needed to be. With the shock Max had endured so early in the morning, I wasn't about to throw them out and make them trudge through the sleet back to their rental house to sit there alone.

I lowered my voice, though it wouldn't matter if Max heard me over their music. "I thought you said Jim and I were destined to be together."

"I don't think I ever said it like that." Audrey shrugged. "And I could be wrong. Also, you do get a say in the matter."

"Oh, thank you very much." I carried the plate of toast over to the old chest and set it down. The eucalyptus candle was close to burning itself out. "Anyone want more tea?"

Max patted their stomach. "I think I'm going to float away as it is."

"Can we call anybody for you, Max? Maybe a friend from school?" I settled into the upholstered chair next to the couch and reached for a slice of warm toast.

"Not now," Max replied. "I mean, not yet. I just, I need to figure this out. Process what happened. Losing my mentor like that. It's a lot." They went back to watching bits of falling ice scatter across the back porch.

"You haven't offered me anything." Catesby materialized out of thin air in the middle of the living room. I'd forgotten about him for a solid two hours, and I had not missed his presence.

"Oh, for crying out loud." An ice pick headache stabbed at the top of my head, and I shielded my eyes against the shaded lamp on the side table.

"Suri? Is someone here?" Audrey was learning from my reactions when I had a welcome or unwelcome spectral visitor.

Max took out their earbuds. "Someone's here?" They glanced toward the hallway.

On reflex, I squinted in the direction of the front hall and felt genuine relief that Loki hadn't wandered in again and that some fresh problem hadn't been deposited on my doorstep. I'd managed, at least, to put Loki off for a few hours, but there was no telling when or where he might ambush me next. I took long, steady breaths and waited for the pain in my head to pass.

In the meantime, Audrey's cheeks burned bright red. "Suri, I'm sorry. I didn't mean to." She didn't elaborate, but her meaning was clear. She hadn't meant to spill my secret to a stranger.

But Max greeted the new topic with eager ease. "You mean a ghost, right? Are you seeing a ghost?" They looked around with wide eyes. "Here, now?"

"Clever, aren't they?" Catesby stood beside me as he watched Max. "Do you think young Max knows I'm present?"

When I didn't respond, Max leaned forward to offer their reassurances. "It's okay. I heard some people talking in town, but I wasn't sure how to ask you about it." They fiddled with their earbuds, tangling the cord in their fingers. "And so, when Deputy Vandenhauter told me about Professor Catesby, and after I'd made those calls, I guess I just wanted to know if he's okay. You know, wherever he is now."

"Is that why you came to see me?" I asked. The ice pick released its grip. That was a long one.

Max sniffed hard and started to cry, clutching their hands together as they hunched forward. Audrey scooted closer to rest a hand on Max's back. I jumped up to grab a box of tissues from the bathroom.

"I hate to see Max like this." Catesby followed me and waited in the bathroom doorway while I reached into the closet. "He . . . She? *They*. They deserve better."

"That almost sounds like regret." I opened the fresh box of tissues but lingered in the bathroom, out of earshot of Max. "It almost sounds like you might have cared about someone other than yourself, more than you'd like to let on."

Catesby's grimace looked remarkably similar to the wince he'd made when his stomach was acting up at the TBD, before he died. After a lifetime of self-absorption, maybe he had a limited range of facial expressions. Or maybe I was, again, getting way too irritated with people and ghosts and situations that were beyond my control.

"Max Turner is a fine graduate student. A superior academic assistant, and a brilliant young mind." Catesby drew himself up tall and affected an air of simultaneous dignity and humility that appeared to be a hefty expense to his ego. "I may not have been as kind to them as I might have been."

"'May not have been,' huh? Are you done? Can I go back in

there now to comfort someone who actually gives a crap about what happened to you?" I was back to being flat out of patience. I was exhausted. My head hurt. And I still didn't know what was wrong with Jim. I took a breath. "I'm sorry. I shouldn't have snapped at you. I'm having a bad day, but I think it's safe to say my day hasn't been as bad as yours."

Catesby paused while my meaning sank in. "Ah, yes. With my being deceased, and such."

I made a move toward the door, but Catesby held up a hand and shifted to block my exit, as if I couldn't walk right through him.

"Please do what you can for Max, will you?" he asked. "They didn't deserve to be treated so poorly, and should you find an appropriate moment to communicate my sincere apology, it would be appreciated."

And so here it was. Maybe guilt or remorse was the gravity that kept Catesby hanging around the world of the living. If it were that simple, I could convey his regret to Max right now, and the ghost would disappear. But Max had mentioned Catesby's estranged family in Wisconsin. I got the sinking feeling I might be on the hook for delivering more messages of contrition. The whole medium messenger thing was not my idea of a good time. And it doesn't pay.

"Sure." I walked directly through Catesby's ghost and back into the living room.

Max was sitting up and wiping away tears, but their red eyes and hitched breath hinted at more grief to come. I deposited the box of tissues on the coffee table and sat back down.

"Are you feeling better?" I asked.

"I'm really sorry." Max coughed. "Maybe I shouldn't have come. Or I at least should have asked you right away, if, you know." Max started to get up from the couch but then sank back down as fresh tears streamed down their cheeks. "I know he was a lot. And I know a lot of people didn't like him."

"What's this?" Catesby asked, again appearing by my side and making me jump.

"I mean, people *really* didn't like him." Max laughed through their tears and reached for a tissue to blow their nose. "He was definitely an acquired taste or something. How does that expression go? When everyone wants to be seen with someone important, but they don't really want to be friends? Like a photo op with a celebrity or politician. Riding on someone's coattails?"

"This is preposterous," Catesby grumbled, his pomposity returning in force. "I genuinely have no idea what they're going on about."

I shushed Catesby. Max looked up, eyes bright with hope. "Is he here?" They asked. "Can you hear him? Is he okay?"

"I retract in full what I told you in confidence earlier," Catesby said to me. "Obviously, Max Turner is a two-faced, gossiping—"

"That's quite enough," I replied sharply. To Max and Audrey, it appeared I was chastising empty air, but my irritation was real. I turned to Max. "Professor Catesby wants to apologize for his ill treatment of you."

Max blinked in silence. More tears rolled down their face and dripped off their chin. Audrey tucked a dry tissue into their hand.

"He said you are an excellent student and assistant, and that you have a brilliant mind," I continued. "And that he feels bad about not being kinder to you."

"That is *not* what I said," Catesby complained with an exasperated huff.

"Close enough," I replied.

Max watched me closely. "That doesn't sound like the professor."

"Clever Max. Didn't I tell you?" There was a hint of pride in Catesby's voice. "You should know better than to paraphrase, Ms. Mudge."

"For Pete's sake!" I exclaimed, when I wanted to say much

worse. "I am paraphrasing for the sake of expediency. You are one haughty ghost." Now he had me using big words, too, damn him.

That elicited a smile from Max as they dried their face with the fresh tissue. "*That* sounds like the professor."

"He says you're quite clever," I replied.

The smile vanished from Max's face. "I just wish I could have done better. That I'd been smarter. That I'd . . ." Max choked on a sob.

"Indeed, I feel badly for Max, but I am uncomfortable with such displays of unconstructive emotion," Catesby said.

I wanted to point out his hypocrisy, given the many displays of unconstructive, indignant emotion he'd no doubt subjected others to in life—and now me in death. But starting an argument with a ghost wasn't going to help Max in their grieving.

"But he's okay?" Max looked at me with an expectant but fragile expression. "Is he having any trouble, with crossing over? Is there anything he needs me to do?"

There's a thought. Perhaps I could charge Max with passing along whatever additional messages Catesby might have, and wrapping up his unfinished business. Kind of like having an intern. I liked the idea, a lot. I looked at Catesby and waited.

"Apart from the obvious?" Catesby said.

"The obvious?" I asked.

"Finishing my work, of course," the ghost replied. "Publishing my papers. Securing my legacy. This must be Max's priority now."

"You are a stubborn piece of work." I turned to Max. "He's going on about his legacy and unpublished papers."

Max's face fell, but they nodded in acknowledgement. "Reputation and renown were always important to the professor."

Along with putting on unnecessary airs, I added silently. Max looked like they wanted to say more, perhaps something along the lines of my quiet judgment. But with the ghost of their former mentor present and listening, it was no surprise that Max would hold their tongue.

"And of course, the matter of determining what, precisely, happened to me," Catesby said. "I do not recall being struck by a vehicle, nor seeing any car on the road that night. And I'm quite certain I did not slip on the ice, not merely because that would be a thoroughly undignified means of meeting one's demise." He nodded toward Max. "It rests on Max's shoulders now to ensure my good and long-standing memory. A significant piece of that is solving my murder."

"Murder?" I asked. "Who said anything about a murder?"

"You're not serious?" Audrey asked with nervous laughter. Beside her on the couch, Max froze in place.

"Murder?" Max asked in a small voice as a new wave of anguish rolled over them. "The professor thinks he was murdered?"

"That's what he said, but he doesn't actually know," I said. "Sometimes death comes by way of a simple accident, and we wish it meant more." In Catesby's case, I hoped that was true.

Audrey's phone chirped with the instrumental love theme from *Mystery Science Theater 3000*—the ringtone she assigned to incoming messages from Colin. The quick tempo drums and guitar used to annoy me, but now seemed kind of sweet. But the smile vanished from Audrey's face as she read the text from Colin.

"Audrey?" I asked.

"He's sick," she replied, her hands shaking. "Colin's sick, too. Just like Jim."

CHAPTER EIGHT

After a stop at Catesby's rental house to allow them to change into fresh clothes, Max rode along with us to the hospital in Seaside. They were too upset to be left alone in the empty beach house, and not one of the three of us could think clearly enough to come up with a better solution.

Despite a migraine that was coming on strong, I got behind the wheel of the Subaru. Audrey was newly in shock over the news about Colin, whereas I'd had a few hours to sit with Jim's illness. But about halfway to Seaside, the pain got bad enough that I had to pull over to let Max drive the rest of the way, even though they didn't know the roads, which were slick with ice. Regardless of their own distress, Max was steady at the wheel and made slow and steady progress.

By the time we made it to Seaside, what should have been a forty-five minute drive had taken closer to two hours. I worried we'd missed the hospital's visiting hours window, because that was the kind of luck I was having. The reality, when we arrived, was even worse.

Both Jim and Colin were in critical care. Plus, they were under county police protection due to the suspicious nature of their illnesses. They'd both been poisoned, but the doctors were telling me they didn't know with what. My "next of kin" status with Jim got me at least that much information.

I called Mayor Phil in Grady to tell him what I knew, and he sounded even rougher on the phone than I felt. He was commiserating about what a terrible week it had been and telling me he hadn't slept well when the call dropped. My phone battery was drained.

Max, Audrey, and I camped out in the critical care waiting room. We were a sorry-looking bunch—exhausted, grieving, confused, and afraid. The only good news was that the ghost of Thomas Catesby seemed to have remained behind in Grady. But the sun was sinking low in the sky, and we needed a plan.

Audrey scrolled through Travelocity and Airbnb on her phone and made calls looking for a room we could share for the night, but the convergence of whale watching tours, winter storm seekers, and Seaside's annual ghost convention had every room in the area booked. With business tanking at the Tea Reader, I wasn't sure I could afford beachfront hotel prices, anyway. We were probably going to have to hit the road back to Grady, though that meant traveling on frozen roads at night. I found grim humor in the fact that I was, at least in part, being forced out of town by a ghost convention.

Max was looking for a place where we could grab some dinner. None of us had eaten much more than toast and cookies for the day, and I wasn't keen on giving the hospital cafeteria a go.

Because my phone mysteriously wouldn't hold a charge, that left me to not so casually amble past the nurses' station like clockwork for any updates on Jim or Colin.

"Suri Mudge?"

Which was how I met Chief Deputy Chris Banich.

"Ms. Mudge?" He asked again, then introduced himself when I blinked at him without a word. He was short and stocky with graying temples and a day-old beard, and he wore a jacket embla-zoned with the Duniway County logo over street clothes instead of a full uniform. Quite the contrast to Jim's clean, pressed edges. Banich explained that he'd been assigned by newly installed Sheriff Kay Butler in the county seat in Hattieville, and the hospital in Seaside was his first stop on his way to Grady to take over the case.

"The case?" I asked.

A slow, incredulous smile spread across his face. "Well, as I've heard it, you've had two suspicious deaths already this week in Grady, and it's only Thursday. Now both your deputy sheriff and his assistant are in critical care after being poisoned. I'd say that warrants looking into."

"Oh," I said. "That." I felt just as obtuse as I imagined I sounded.

Banich gave a polite dip of the chin, but there was little doubt that he was in charge. He was older, nearing middle age, with the extra padding around his middle to prove it. He pulled his badge from his jacket's inner pocket and offered his creden-tials for my inspection.

"They must have changed the uniforms in Hattieville," I said as he put his badge away.

My comment earned an obliging smile. "I'm more of an investigator," he said. "Plain clothes." He gestured toward the waiting area, where Audrey and Max huddled together over their phones, scheming about lodging and sustenance. "Do you have time for a few questions?"

"If you don't mind that I'm almost entirely braindead," I replied, and two weary-looking women at the far end of the waiting area looked up. I wanted to smack myself. On this very floor, there likely lay patients who, in fact, were braindead and whose families were struggling to come to terms with their horrible loss.

Banich guided me toward a couple of empty seats away from

the grieving women and far from Audrey and Max as well. "You were going to be one of my first calls as soon as I got to Grady," he said. "Might as well get a jump on things."

"I understand." I found myself holding an insulated cup of hot tea, thrust into my hands by Audrey. She gave me a look of wary curiosity as she crossed the dark green carpet back to Max.

Banich watched her go. "That's Audrey Medina, right? Assistant Deputy Sheriff Colin Jung's girlfriend." He pulled a notebook out of his jacket pocket. It was one of those fancy, refillable folios, made of leather and larger than the notebook Jim carried, and in better shape, too. Banich uncapped a heavy-looking, executive-style pen with gold accents. The offices in Hattieville had bigger budgets and better everything than the converted gas station in Naghatune Bay. "And who's that with her?" he asked as Audrey sat down next to Max.

"Max Turner," I replied. "Thomas Catesby's assistant."

Banich nodded but didn't write anything down. "And Mr. Turner came with you to Seaside from Grady, or did he come down from Cascade State to meet you here?" He squinted at Max from across the waiting area and let out an uncomfortable sigh. "Or, Ms. Turner, maybe? Difficult to judge at this distance."

Distance had nothing to do with it, but I didn't want to get off on the wrong foot with the Chief Deputy by accusing him of being narrow-minded, especially if he could help Jim and Colin. "I'm not sure what salutation they use," I replied, placing subtle emphasis on the pronoun and hoping Banich would take the cue.

He did, but not with grace. He sighed again and scribbled something in his notebook. "Right. Well. Did this Max Turner come to the hospital with you?"

"Yes. An awful lot has happened today, and it seemed cruel to leave them alone in a strange town after their mentor just died," I said. "They don't know anybody in the area, and Grady isn't always welcoming to strangers."

"So I've heard." If there was any emotion or judgment in

Banich's voice, I didn't detect it. "And Catesby and Turner came to town three days ago?"

"No, it was Tuesday. So, two days ago?" I knew Banich was testing me, trying to catch me in a deception. It was a shrewd method of interrogation, one Jim had used when he questioned Audrey about her ex-boyfriend's unfortunate demise on the beach outside my cottage the previous autumn. Banich was trying to gauge my trustworthiness, but I was tired and found his approach annoying. "The days and hours are kind of running together at this point."

Banich raised his eyebrows.

"I've not gotten much sleep," I said.

He looked again at Audrey and Max, with an intensity that made me uncomfortable. They were speaking quietly, probably comparing notes and online reviews as they searched for a local diner that hadn't been overrun by the tours and conventions in town.

"And did Turner there seem especially eager to accompany you to the hospital?" Banich asked.

"What do you mean?" I glanced at Max, then at Banich's notebook, filled with scratches and scrawls that an Egyptologist would have been hard-pressed to decipher. Banich's insinuation caught up to me. "To get away from Grady, you mean. To get out of town."

Banich cocked his head and waited, watching me, his expression blank.

I lowered my voice. "No. Max came to me this morning to ensure . . ." I nearly finished with "that the recently departed spirit of Thomas Catesby wasn't traumatized," but caught myself. Banich noticed my hesitation, and the tiny lift of one corner of his mouth irked me.

"To ensure what, Ms. Mudge?" he asked.

"Suri. Everyone calls me Suri, so you might as well do the same," I said, to buy some time. I had to think fast, and I was certain Banich saw through my delaying tactic. I blew out an aggravated sigh. "To ensure that I was okay." I tried not to frown at my own weak lie.

"That *you* were okay?"

"Yes. Well, you know Ravi King dropped dead at the Tea Reader just a few days ago. Of course, that was quite a shock." I was speaking a little too fast and too loud, plus I kept glancing away from Banich. I took a breath and forced myself to slow down and look him in the eye. "Ravi was a good customer. Bud, too, his partner. It wasn't a real surprise when business dropped to almost nothing after that."

"So you've been open for business, after King's suspicious death in your establishment. Local law enforcement didn't shut you down." It wasn't a question. Banich scrawled more indecipherable squiggles in his notebook while I felt my heart starting to race. I'd been trying to take the spotlight off of Max and instead focused it on myself—or worse, on Jim.

"Ravi wasn't poisoned." As much as I was trying to keep my breath calm and my voice steady, I worried I was coming across as hysterical instead.

Banich let the silence grow as he watched me, almost daring me to continue. All the little secrets Jim had told me about getting suspects and witnesses to talk, and I was defenseless when they were turned on me.

I rolled my shoulders back and lifted my chin. "Ravi wasn't poisoned," I said again, my voice stronger than I felt.

"You know this for a fact?"

"No. Of course not," I replied, and there was the same quirk at the corner of Banich's mouth. I tightened my hands into fists to keep myself from stammering in exasperation. "The coroner was on a whale watching vacation and hasn't released a report yet, I don't think. But we've had other customers since then, and there have been no other reports of ill effects."

Banich motioned with his pen to indicate our surroundings.

"Yet here we are in the hospital, with both the deputy sheriff and his assistant having been poisoned."

I sat on my hands and clenched my teeth, but it was no use. Anger got the better of me, and the piercing pain of the migraine came roaring back at my right temple. "You are an irritating and odious little man."

Banich let me stew in silence again before he leaned back and laughed. He capped his pen and placed it in a loop inside the notebook folio. "Relax, Ms. Mudge. You're not in any trouble." Another pause. "Are you?"

"What?!" I hissed, and he laughed again.

"All the same, I'd be wary of Max Turner," he said, as though he hadn't just upset me for seemingly no reason. "Or anyone you don't know well." He glanced again at Audrey. "Maybe not even then."

I stood up, prepared to express my loud indignation, but Banich didn't look the least bit intimidated or impressed. So I pretended I was Professor Thomas Catesby. I affected the haughtiest air of privilege I could muster. "I don't know what you're about, Mr. Banich, but to sow unnecessary mistrust and to prey on people who are worried about their loved ones while they sit in a hospital waiting room is quite uncalled for. Unseemly, even, and possibly unethical."

Banich kept his seat, looking bemused as he slid his notebook folio inside his jacket pocket. "Who said anything about unnecessary mistrust? I'm on my way to Grady shortly, and I expect nothing less than your full cooperation. Especially seeing as how you and your business, and everyone associated with it, might well be sitting on crucial evidence and information, whether you know it or not."

I cleared my throat. "We're not suspects, then?"

Banich didn't so much as twitch. "Everyone's a suspect, Ms. Mudge."

I'd heard that line before, but coming from Jim it always

sounded more like he wanted to retain objectivity while upholding the law to the best of his ability. From Banich's mouth, the same words took on a sinister edge, in which every person walking the Earth was a criminal waiting for an opportunity. "I don't like what you're implying, even indirectly, about me or my friends."

The twitch at the corner of Banich's left eye indicated he'd heard me but was choosing to ignore my remark. "In the meantime, I expect you'll contact me immediately should you think of anything that might aid in my investigations." He held out his card and waited with an air of boredom while I decided whether to take it.

"You sure have a lot of expectations, Mr. Banich." I stood over him, not taking his card.

He smirked up at me. "I do. And I'm a real son of a bitch when my expectations aren't met."

Jim would have been proud of me for swallowing the nasty comments I wanted to make in that moment. But the real reason I held my tongue was that I found Banich unnerving in a cold, hollow way that made my skin crawl. My mind went blank when I searched for a witty, snarky, or disarming retort.

I tugged the card out of his hand, careful not to touch his fingers, and did my best not to stomp back across the carpet to where Audrey and Max sat.

THROUGH THE WIZARDRY of Yelp and Google, Max and Audrey located a burger joint within walking distance of the hospital that had fallen under the radar of the storm watchers, whale spotters, and ghost hunters. It was a slog on foot through the sleet and over the slippery pavement, but it was safer than driving, and the arduous journey made my avocado pastrami burger taste that much better as we hunkered down in one of Butch Burger's red vinyl booths.

Our appetites seemed bottomless at first. Max ordered a second plate of fried asparagus and made quick work of a triple-decker vegetarian club sandwich. Even Audrey, who only picked at her small salad at first, polished off a steaming bowl of chili and a couple of baskets of fresh cornbread. But after such a long day, we were too tired, and maybe too demoralized, for anything more than basic small talk about the weather and the food.

Then it was back to the hospital. After deciding to stay put for the night rather than risking the icy roads, Audrey tried to get some rest in the waiting room chairs, while Max grabbed their satchel and went for a roaming walk through the long corridors. At least Banich was nowhere to be seen.

I paced up and down in front of the critical care nursing station for a couple hours more before a young doctor took pity on me and took me into Jim's room. I gasped when I saw him, hooked up to machines and with wires and tubes running all over.

The man I'd known as a paragon of strength and principle looked small and helpless. Vials of recently drawn blood sat in a rack on the table at the end of his bed, along with a thick medical chart. *This isn't Oregon City*, I repeated silently. *Jim hasn't been shot.* But he was sick, and he was lying unconscious in critical care. The only indication that Jim was still alive was the beeping machines.

My heart nearly stopped when I heard a rhythmic click and the rush of air. "He's on a ventilator?"

"Just to give him some support." The doctor had a gentle voice and kind eyes. "His vitals are good. You can talk to him, if you want. He might be able to hear you." The doctor pulled an empty chair over to Jim's bedside and gave me a small, reassuring smile. He was very good at this. I hoped his profession wouldn't burn him out too soon.

Then he left, and I was alone with Jim.

I didn't know what to say. I sat and listened to one machine chirping as it monitored his heart rate, and to another machine breathing for him. The equipment wasn't as noisy as I'd expected. I reached for Jim's hand. When his fingers didn't close around mine, I squeezed harder.

"We never did have that talk." I laughed and wiped away tears. "A couple of months ago, you said something about forgiving me, as long as I could forgive myself. And we never circled back to that. There was always something more pressing, for me or you, or both of us."

Jim didn't squeeze back.

"I might know what you meant, but maybe not? So I need you to get better, okay? So you can set me straight."

The ventilator whooshed and clicked. The heart monitor beeped steadily. Jim's eyes remained closed.

"And I'm glad you have Karina," I said, wanting my words to be true. "And that I have Eddie. I guess things between us will always be complicated, and not just because, because we used to be *us*. There's everything that happened because of us, and everything that's happened in Grady." I paused. "I don't even know what I'm saying anymore. Just that a lot of people care about you, Jim. We need you to get better. Grady needs you. Karina, too. I need you to be okay."

Jim still didn't squeeze back.

WE WERE BACK in the same booth at Butch Burger the next morning, after spending the night in the critical care waiting area. With the blankets and pillows offered by the hospital staff, we'd made ourselves as comfortable as possible—which wasn't comfortable at all. Between trying to snooze across several padded chairs and later on the carpeted floor, my neck and shoulders were painful and tight—enough to distract me from a persistent tension headache. Neither Audrey nor Max looked like they'd fared any better.

Over stacks of pancakes and plates of fried eggs on toast, we sipped hot generic black tea with massive amounts of sugar and lemon, and watched more rain spatter against the window glass.

"At least it's warmed up," Max said brightly. They'd demolished a tall stack of pancakes and were digging into a second helping. Of the three of us, Max was the only one who looked alert. "The roads back to Grady should be better this morning."

Sitting beside Max on the vinyl bench, Audrey exhaled a jagged sigh. She checked her phone for any call or text from Colin's mother that she might have missed in the five seconds since she last looked at the screen. With no family relationship to Colin, Audrey was out of the loop on his medical updates. She had a shaky history with mothers of boyfriends. The last one had tried to kill her. All Audrey knew at this point was that Colin had been poisoned, the same as Jim, but she knew nothing about his prognosis.

Jim's condition had not changed. Without knowing how or with what he'd been poisoned, there was no telling when or if he'd improve. I'd spent a few hours by his bedside, but he remained unconscious.

Since there was nothing we could do for them, we were headed back to Grady after breakfast. The idea of working with Gary Banich gave me an uneasy feeling in my stomach, but I was determined to do what I could to help him find out what had happened to Jim, if there was any chance of saving him.

I had, however, stolen a little vial of Jim's blood from his hospital room. It was an easy thing to do, and not premeditated, but I was feeling guilty about it. When the nurse came in at the end of her shift to do another blood draw, she left three glass tubes for someone else to collect. I simply slipped one into my backpack purse.

It was Audrey's fault, really. On the walk back to the hospital after dinner, she'd speculated that she could try magickal means to identify the poison, or determine if a curse was at work. But she needed some hair from either Jim or Colin. She'd been thinking out loud, not making a plan, but my mind started to spiral during the hours I lingered by Jim's bed. I hadn't had scissors or a knife to cut off a chunk of his thick hair, and blood seemed more useful, anyway.

But I didn't know much about magick. If I'd consulted Audrey ahead of time, she could have told me that hair was better.

"Working with blood is too powerful, potentially." Audrey took a sip of tea, made a face, and added more artificial lemon juice. "I'll do it. Of course I'll do it. But if something goes wrong, well, I might accidentally unleash something even worse."

"Something worse than Jim on a ventilator?" I asked.

"They're still alive." Audrey checked her phone again. She hadn't touched her toast and eggs. "I know time is of the essence, but I'd feel better if I could do more research first. And get some adequate rest before I try anything."

"So, a witch, a medium, and a scientist shuffle into a burger joint?" Max chuckled as they added more butter and syrup to their stack of pancakes. "Maybe the field GC/MS or something else in the mobile lab at the TBD could help identify the poison." Max shoved another forkful of pancake and syrup into their mouth.

I blinked at Max, watching them chew and swallow it down with a hefty gulp of tea. For a graduate student in science, they were tolerating our talk of magick with astonishing ease. "You can do that?" I felt silly for not thinking of it myself.

Max loaded up another forkful. "I can try. I don't have the same equipment as they have at the hospital, or back at Cascade State. And it's not my field. But we might as well use what we've got. I want to help, if I can. It's not like the professor's research is going anywhere."

On instinct, I glanced around the restaurant, looking for any sign of the lurking ghost of Catesby. Max's comment would have drawn his ire if he were about, but Butch Burger was about as quiet as a coastal diner could be mid-morning on a Friday in February, with multiple tours and conventions in town.

Not all ghosts roam the way Trey could. Some are stuck in place—tethered to their decaying bodies, attached to the home they inhabited or the place of their death, or sometimes bound to an individual they'd wronged or who'd wronged them. Others are more free-wheeling, flitting about to visit places and people for closure before they move on. While I was relieved not to find Catesby following me up and down the Oregon Coast, I hoped he wasn't bound to my cottage as a permanent haunting. I liked my little home, and it would be a shame to have to move.

"So, what are we waiting for?" Audrey drank down the last of her tea and slid her phone into her coat pocket. "Let's get back to Grady."

I gestured toward her plate. "You haven't eaten anything."

Audrey took a generous bite of toast, shoved most of a cold egg into her mouth, then grabbed my mug to choke the food down with a gulp of tea. She wiped her lips with a paper napkin. "Satisfied? Now can we go?"

Max had half a stack of pancakes left, but they didn't argue. My companions slid out of the booth, pulled on their coats, and stood by the table, waiting for me.

"We can help Jim," Audrey said, as If I needed motivation.

I opened my wallet to lay some cash on the table. "I know. I'm just really very tired." I pushed my arms into my coat sleeves and pulled on a warm fleece hat from the Chichi Boutique.

Max held out their hand, open palm up. "You rest. I'll drive." Misinterpreting my fatigue for hesitation, they added, "I want to help, Suri."

I reached into my pocket and handed over my car keys.

~

I HADN'T SLEPT in the backseat of my car before, and I was surprised how comfortable it was. Or perhaps I just needed rest that badly. Before Max had pulled out of the Butch Burger parking lot, I fell into a dead sleep, curled up under my winter coat, and dreamt about the Bandage Man haunting the coastal roadways.

I'd seen the spooky legend once with my own eyes, when he appeared on the beach to help dispatch a malicious and inexperienced sorceress who'd killed Trey and her own son while trying to target Audrey. In my dream, a tall, waif-like figure kept materializing on the road back to Grady, his dirty and bloody bandages fluttering in the breeze as he stuck out a brittle thumb to hitchhike.

By the time we were approaching my cottage in Naghatune Bay, I felt somewhere close to refreshed. I sat up, stretched my arms wide, and tried not to interrupt Audrey and Max's conversation about medicinal uses for common garden plants and flowers.

"The ratio is one to one to one—chopped mint, sugar, and water—to make the syrup," Max said as they steered my Subaru onto Dowitcher Drive. "You can use it in drinks or even make a candy with it. Not only can it help with indigestion, but it's also quite tasty."

"I haven't tried making candy before." Audrey laughed in delight. "And this is what you're studying?"

"Not exactly," Max replied. "But you pick things up. My roommate has done more with flowers, specifically toxic flowers. She wants to find a way to develop a new strain of lilies that aren't poisonous to cats. Every once in a while, she comes across some natural flavoring or edible flower I've never heard of. She even has an apiary as a hobby, up on the roof of the apartment building. My focus is botanical spectroscopy."

"You're going to have to translate that," Audrey said.

"Okay, so bees can see ultraviolet wavelengths—light that we can't see. So pollinators are attracted to the spectra of each flower —the light and colors and patterns of the petals," Max explained. "They don't see flowers the same way we do. Then there's the electric field around the flowers."

"I thought bees were attracted by the smell?" Audrey asked.

"It's a little more complicated than that," Max replied. "For instance, down at Oregon State, they're doing work on how bees are drawn most to blue, white, yellow, or ultra-violet flower blooms. What I'm hoping to do is find a way to breed a kind of super flower to support and save the honeybees. That's kind of a long-term goal. For right now, I'm working on the spectral characteristics of flowers that are native to the Pacific Northwest."

"But I thought Catesby was a tea expert?" Audrey asked.

"He is—was," Max replied. "He became my mentor when I arrived at Cascade State, when I was more up in the air about what my research would be. And I thought I'd really lucked out, because Thomas Catesby! He's published more than a dozen books and gives lectures all over the world." Max paused. "I mean, gave. I'm having a hard time using the past tense."

"A dozen books?" Audrey asked. "All about tea?"

"Most of them are more academic than mainstream," Max said. "I guess I was naïve. I didn't really anticipate how much influence the professor would have on my work. He didn't take kindly to my wanting to branch off into botanicals and pollinators."

"He wanted to keep you under his thumb," Audrey replied. "He got you to do most of his work for him, too, right? And then took the credit for it?"

"Yeah," Max said. "And when I got some grant money for a new spectrometer, a unit that hadn't even been released on the market yet, the professor said he needed the money to fund his research. Before I knew it, the money was almost gone. I had to buy something used off of eBay."

I watched the trees go by outside the window, along with the occasional rental property tucked into the landscaping like fairy houses in the woods. But their windows were all dark and wouldn't show signs of life until tourist season picked up in the spring. The trees gradually gave way to sand dunes as the road curved to follow the bay and the shoreline as we drew closer to my property.

"But being Professor Catesby's mentee and assistant opened so many doors for me," Max said. "The other researchers at Cascade State were happy to almost bend over backward whenever I needed anything, even if it was for my own work. And it's not like he used me as a packhorse. For this trip, he refused to let me even touch his bags when I offered to carry them."

"But he overshadowed you," Audrey muttered. "Trying to control your every move, never giving you enough room to even breathe."

"Uh . . ." Max replied. "I mean, I don't think—"

"I know what it's like to be attached to an overbearing man," Audrey said. "It's the pits."

I leaned forward. "You don't mean Colin, do you?"

Audrey and Max both jumped.

"You're awake," Max said. "I think we're almost back at your house."

"Not Colin," Audrey replied. "I was talking about Drew."

"Hard to believe that was only a few months ago," I said.

"Not long enough," Audrey replied. I was tempted to tell her about my dream, but there was no sense dredging up bad memories.

Max pulled the car in front of my cottage. I was not surprised to find Loki waiting on my front porch. He had gotten lost in the shuffle the day before—with the discovery of Catesby's body on the road, the descent of the professor's ghost onto my sanity, then both Jim and Colin falling ill, plus young Max's distress.

I didn't have time for Loki's shenanigans today, either. He made me uneasy. He was intriguing in the same way a child might be drawn to insert pennies into an electrical socket, and the last thing I needed in my life was more destructive weirdness. He was probably coming around to insist again that I was special and had the potential to do real good in the world, if I would only allow him to train me as he had others before, whatever that meant. He'd been giving me the same song and dance for months, not long after I discovered he was the one who'd been leaving the mystery boxes of books and other trinkets on my bookshop doorstep. I'd humored him, to a degree, because those mystery drops were good for business.

But now I wasn't sure I had any business at all.

I climbed out of the backseat and zipped up my coat. "I'm sorry, Loki, but can we save the whole Mr. Miyagi thing for another day? I've not had a decent night's sleep in . . ." I had to stop and think. Two days? Three? I couldn't remember, and that was a bad sign. "It's been a while, and I've kind of got my hands full here."

"With the suspicious deaths surrounding the recently discovered treasure," Loki replied as he descended the trio of steps from the porch to meet me on the sidewalk. "And I hear they found a box of old tea?"

"You mean the tea treasure?" Max asked. "You know about that?" They sighed. "But, yeah, I guess everybody does."

I glanced at Audrey as Max handed me my keys.

"I'll take Max back to the rental for a change of clothes, then to my place for the same," Audrey said, heading toward her own car. "Meet you at the TBD after?"

I turned my attention back to Loki. "Right now, all I want is a shower and some clean underwear."

Loki raised his eyebrows.

"And fresh clothes and different shoes," I continued. "Then I've got this other thing I need to deal with."

"When you're ready, you know where to find me." Loki started to walk away, then turned back. "While you were out, you didn't happen to see a cat anywhere, did you?"

This again. "You should try the animal shelter or the vet in Standish Beach," I said. "Or maybe ask Bobby Jackson about running a lost cat notice in the weekly paper."

He studied me for an uncomfortable eternity, then turned to stray off the sidewalk as he headed toward a wall of beach grass and tall shrubs.

I fiddled with my keys and climbed the front steps. I turned to call after Loki that I actually didn't know how or where to find him, but he was nowhere in sight. It was as if he'd melted into the sand. I still didn't know who or what Loki was.

"I really do not need another freaking ghost right now," I muttered as I pushed open the cottage door and headed inside.

CHAPTER NINE

When I arrived at the TBD a little over an hour later, I found yellow police tape crisscrossing the shop's front doors, along with the requisite cluster of curious townspeople gathered on the sidewalk in the rain. Half the crowd complained about being denied their morning CBD tea and THC scones, while the other half whispered rumors and conspiracy theories. Everyone was unhappy about the weather.

Ignoring the murmured tales about Karina working for the mob, being possessed by a poltergeist sea witch, or both, I pushed through the crowd to the shop entrance. I wasn't surprised to spot Gary Banich on the other side of the glass, holding a clipboard and ordering about a trio of strange men in official-looking windbreakers.

I lifted my hand to knock, but Banich beat me to the door, letting me inside. He shut the door firmly behind me, cutting off much of the chatter from the onlookers outside.

"Ms. Mudge?" he asked with expectation.

"I wasn't prepared for you to just let me in like that," I replied.

Banich frowned, and I got the dreadful feeling I'd done something egregiously wrong in the fifteen seconds that had elapsed since my arrival. "I did ask you to meet me here."

"Did you?" The kink in my neck from my overnight at the hospital, the lack of sleep, and the squeeze of my headache were wearing me down, all exacerbated by the cheap caffeine of generic tea buzzing around my brain. I didn't remember taking a call from Banich.

"Have you checked your phone this morning?" he asked.

"No," I replied. "I didn't take a charger with me to Seaside and the battery ran out."

"And this morning?"

"I forgot." It was the truth. Between dealing with Loki on my cottage doorstep and rushing into a hot shower as soon as I was through the door, plugging in my phone had slipped my mind. I felt the heavy rectangle of glass and plastic inside my coat pocket and wished I hadn't been so scatterbrained. What if the hospital called with news about Jim? What if Jim needed me? "I don't suppose you have a spare charger?"

With an air of exasperation, Banich used his clipboard to gesture toward the TBD kitchen doors, and he walked with me through the dining room. The place should have been full, especially since the Tea Reader wasn't open. But, other than Banich's team, the TBD was empty.

"What's going on?" I asked.

A woman popped her head up from a table at the very back of the dining room, startling me. I hadn't seen her there. She was slumped forward, head in her hands. Her hair was a golden halo of frizz and tangles, and dark lines of mascara and eye shadow streaked down her face.

I nearly didn't recognize her, but there were only so many people in this little town. "Karina?"

"Suri?" My name was a plea on her lips, and her eyes filled with desperate hope as she pushed her chair away from the table. "I'm so glad you're here!"

Banich lifted a hand and motioned her to keep her place. "I'll ask again that you stay where you are, Ms. Coyle. I apologize for the wait, but you can see we've got a lot going on here this morning." He glanced around the dining room. "And who's got eyes on Bard Walker? We can't just let these people wander around."

I started toward Karina, but Banich grabbed my arm and held me back. "As for you, Ms. Mudge, I want to speak to you in the kitchen."

"But she's in obvious distress." I motioned toward Karina, who sank back into her chair, looking deflated in her tailored but rumpled clothing.

"He doesn't want to give us the chance to get our stories straight." Karina wiped at her eyes and tried to laugh.

"Get our stories straight about what?" I asked, but Banich pulled me into the kitchen. Before the double doors closed behind me, I caught a glance of Karina leaning over the table again and starting to sob. I turned to Banich. "Just what the hell is going on here?"

"Suri!" Audrey called out from across the kitchen. She stood with Max near the table where Catesby's mobile lab had been set up. Another one of Banich's men, wearing the same uniform of a khaki shirt, brown trousers, and dark green windbreaker with "Duniway County Sheriff's Office" emblazoned on the back, was sifting through a stack of notebooks and slipping individual sheets of paper into plastic evidence bags. Max groaned as each piece of their research was tagged and bagged to be carted away.

I crossed my arms over my chest and stepped in front of Banich. "I'll ask again. What is happening here at the TBD?"

"Funny name, like maybe everybody forgot what it's called, maybe from consuming too many of its products." Banich's tight smile of irritated patience had to have been deliberate. It telegraphed that he was humoring me, but that his forbearance had limits. It was an expert performance, probably something he'd practiced hundreds of times on his big cases in Hattieville, and one he was now trying out on a small town audience.

"Short for the Tea and Botanicals Dispensary," I replied. "Obviously."

"A lot has happened in Grady during your short absence, Ms. Mudge," he said. "And I'm not convinced these events are unconnected and unrelated."

"You mean the deaths of both Ravi King and Thomas Catesby?" I asked. "Isn't it enough that my business is shut down, but you have to do the same to Karina, too?" There's never a convenient time for an ice pick headache to stab you right between the eyes, and naturally this was the moment the pain elected to blind me for a few seconds. I squeezed my eyes shut and pinched the bridge of my nose. I reminded myself to breathe while I waited for the pain to pass.

"Ms. Mudge?" Banich cupped my elbow to hold me steady. At least his concern sounded genuine. "Ms. Mudge, are you all right?"

"Could I have a cup of tea, please?" My voice wasn't much above a whisper as I blinked my eyes open. Damn, that was a bad one. "Nothing with cannabis, of course, but maybe something herbal? Decaf? Audrey will know."

Banich gave me another tight smile, but this one looked less artificial. "You don't want to be consuming anything out of this place."

"Well, nothing with pot in it," I said, shrugging out of his grip. "Even though it's legal. Or is there a problem with their license? Is that why you've got the TBD shut up tight, and half of Grady outside grumbling on the pavement?"

Banich started to answer, but Audrey cut him off as she made her way over to me. "Mrs. Moroni is sick, Suri! And Murray Overhill, Emmaline Kapul, Joe Stanley, and Mayor Phil, too."

"Sick?" I asked. "All of them?"

"Just like Colin and Jim." Audrey looked frightened, and that alone was enough to rattle me.

"But Joe Stanley didn't have anything from the Tea Reader, did he? He never comes into the teahouse." I looked to Audrey for confirmation.

"The only coffee drinker in town." Audrey crossed her arms and looked at Banich. "Whatever's making everyone sick, it didn't come from the Tea Reader."

"Nothing has been definitively ruled out," Banich replied.

"You think it's the Tea and Botanicals Dispensary." My stomach dropped. Whatever relief I'd felt with the certainty that the Tea Reader hadn't poisoned anyone vanished. I thought about Karina's tear-streaked face as she sat in her own shop's dining area, waiting to be questioned by Banich or one of his deputy drones. She'd said Banich didn't want us talking to each other to "get our stories straight."

And had I just thought of law enforcement personnel from outside Naghatune Bay as "drones"? Perhaps I had become a true local, suspicious of anyone who wasn't a resident. I filed that away for later.

"Or you suspect it's both of us," I said. "So, what? You think that Karina and I have been working together to poison our customers? The very people who keep our businesses afloat?"

"Now you're putting words in my mouth," Banich replied. "And whatever 'shock' you were feigning a minute ago seems to have worn off rather quickly."

The metaphorical poison daggers Audrey was shooting from her eyes at Banich were almost comical. I might have laughed if not for the cold reality that Banich considered me a murder suspect, whether he'd say it to my face or not.

"I get headaches," I said. "Sometimes I get an ice pick of pain that hits like, well, like an ice pick, right into my skull." When I saw the familiar skepticism on Banich's face, I had to remind myself not to get into an argument with him about invisible illness and masking pain. There were more pressing matters. "Which doesn't change the fact that you think Karina and I are poisoners."

"Maybe not deliberately." Banich rubbed his forehead, the first indication of stress or frustration I'd seen slip through. "Look, there's a lot we don't know. And I'm sharing this information with you as a courtesy to Deputy Sheriff Vandenhauter, out of respect for the assistance you've given him in the past."

"The assistance I've given him in the past." I watched Banich for any sign that he knew about my paranormal talent, or if he was being sarcastic and cruel. The man was unpleasant but also impenetrable. "I can't say you've given us much information at all."

"This is an active investigation, Ms. Mudge," Banich said as we watched one of his deputy drones carry Max's laptop computer out of the kitchen.

"So you keep saying," Audrey said.

"They're taking everything!" Max appeared at Audrey's side, looking anguished. They kept rubbing at their face, and I wasn't sure if the gesture was self-calming or an effort to stay awake.

"You can have your computer back after we've copied the hard drive," Banich said as he consulted his clipboard.

"How long is that going to take?" Max demanded. "People are sick! The deputy sheriff and his assistant are in the hospital."

"I am well aware of the situation, Mr. Turner," Banich said with weary resignation, then looked up. "Ms. Turner?"

"Mx," Max replied. "But just Max is fine." They dug their hands into their short, black hair, with little tufts standing up between their fingers. "I'm trying to tell you that I can help. I can try to identify the poison that's making everyone sick. Don't you want that?"

Another deputy drone passed by with a plastic crate of Max's spiral notebooks and stacks of petri dishes. Max grabbed the rim of the crate and tried to wrestle it out of the assistant deputy's hands.

"*Mx.* Turner, if you would be so kind as to allow my team to do their work," Banich said.

"What can it hurt?" I asked. "Do you honestly believe Karina used Ravi King's death at the Tea Reader to orchestrate Thomas Catesby's need to use the TBD kitchen, in order that she could then use his equipment to synthesize some fancy poison to feed to her customers, plus take out Catesby himself while she was at it?"

My question hung in the air while Banich stared at me and waited for me to listen to myself. None of what I'd said made sense, which I'd thought was the point, but maybe there was a kernel of truth in there. I winced.

"I realize you have to consider all possibilities," I said. "But why not let Max help?"

"I can set up at the rental house, since it's just me there now," Max offered, the thin hope plain in their face while they clung to the crate of notebooks and supplies. "You can even have one of your goons there, too, to make sure I don't tamper with anything or try to skip town or whatever."

"Goons?" Banich and I asked in unison.

"Please let me help," Max pleaded.

Banich nodded to his underling, who handed the crate over to Max.

"You will be working under strict supervision," Banich said. "And this accommodation is being made only because Ms. Mudge here is vouching for you."

I wasn't sure I'd done any such thing, but it sounded all right. Banich could station one of his people at the rental house to monitor Max, but Audrey and I would be there, too.

"Keep in mind that any false move, any deviation, doesn't come down on just you," Banich told Max. "Yours isn't the only head on the chopping block."

"I don't think I like that phrasing," I muttered, but I accepted the small win for Max.

Determined relief washed over Max's face as they supported the crate on one hip and started back toward their workspace. "I just need to grab a few other things."

"Found him!" One of Banich's deputy drones leaned through the kitchen doors. "Bard Walker. Said he was in the bathroom."

"Unsupervised? For how long?" Banich asked with a heavy sigh. "This shouldn't be that complicated, people. We're supposed to be better than this."

"Yes, sir," the underling replied with a sheepish dip of the chin. "I'll stand by the door myself and won't let either of them out of my sight."

When Banich turned back to me, I looked him dead in the eye. "You've got questions? Ask them."

Banich seemed surprised. "Wouldn't you prefer to have a lawyer present?"

"What I would prefer is a long nap at home in my own bed, followed by a good read and a hearty bowl of soup," I said. "And Jim and Colin recovered and out of the hospital, while we're at it. And this whole mess far behind us. But I don't think you can offer me any of that right now, can you? So let's get on with your questions instead."

Audrey hid her laughter behind her hands. Banich started to walk me toward Karina's office when there was a new exclamation from Max on the other side of the kitchen.

"Where's the gas chromatograph mass spectrometer?" Max sounded on the verge of panic. "And, and the cache of tea? The tea from the treasure is supposed to be right here? And the testing solutions?"

"Whatever's not here has been bagged and entered into evidence already," Banich replied. "You'll have to proceed without those items, for the time being."

Max nodded, but their breath hitched in their chest.

Banich turned to me and dropped his voice. "Are you sure you want to spend your political capital on that one? How well do you really know Max Turner?"

There was so much in those questions I wanted to take issue with. That a term like "political capital" was laughable in a small community like Grady or even greater Naghatune Bay. That Banich's anti-LGBTQIA bias was dripping from nearly every word. That the Chief Deputy kept oscillating between treating me as a suspect and intimating that he and I were working together. The sheriff in Hattieville was new, and so was Chris Banich. I wondered about his training and record in law enforcement, but that would have to wait. For the moment, I couldn't shake the feeling that Banich was setting a trap.

"You've carted off most of Max's research," I said instead. "Something they've probably devoted years to. Max is away from home. They've lost their mentor, and now they've been robbed of their autonomy and control. Can you cut the kid a break?"

With a parting look of disgust aimed at Banich, Audrey walked over to help Max gather their things. Despite my little speech, Banich's wariness was creeping in. I had a shivery feeling I'd need to keep an eye on Max, for their own good if nothing else.

CHAPTER TEN

"Finally!" the ghost of Thomas Catesby exclaimed after I walked through the door of the rental house. He put on a grand display of pouting and broad gesticulations to demonstrate his displeasure. "I've been waiting for *hours*, first within the confines of your humble abode, and then here in this sterile and thoroughly unstimulating environment. Do you have any idea how *boring* the afterlife is?"

For the moment, I held my tongue. I stood in the living room of the rental where Max and Catesby had been staying before the professor's demise. After the turmoil of the preceding days, I had no patience for spectral foolishness. I felt dead on my feet, but I couldn't say that to a ghost.

I also didn't know why Catesby had sequestered himself here. Maybe, like Max, the recently departed professor felt like he didn't know any of the ghosts in town and hadn't yet tried to leave Grady.

Over by the dining table, Max kept close tabs on the "goon" Banich had dispatched to photograph every page of Max's journals. It was a straightforward process, with little to no conversation involved, but the deputy drone's presence was stifling. I felt almost afraid to breathe.

Hours later—or maybe it was only twenty minutes—Banich's man handed the journals back to Max, told us the house was "being watched," and headed out the door. We let out a collective sigh.

"I'm glad that's over." Audrey took command of the kitchen to prepare tea and toast, and to make a grocery list for everything she'd need to make the rental more homey for the coming days.

At least Barbara had agreed to take over feeding and watering Audrey's little Simba for the next twenty-four hours, so we wouldn't have that roving fuzzball of chaos to contend with.

"You're welcome to use whatever you can find in the fridge or cupboards," Max told Audrey. "I'm not particular, though the professor kept his items separate on one shelf. At least he didn't write 'SH' all over everything, like my roommate."

"'SH?'" Audrey asked.

"Sarah Hopkins," Max replied. "Her initials." They turned back to the dining table. "I'm not sure what good any of this will do me without the mass spec and my computer." Max arranged their notebooks and the few pieces of equipment they'd secured from the TBD kitchen crime scene. "Who knows when or if they'll turn all of that back over to me."

"Banich wants to solve this case as much as we do," I said. "I think he'd prefer to be back in Hattieville."

I looked around the main living area of the oceanfront rental. The first floor had a familiar open design, with undivided dining and living areas and a generous kitchen separated from the common space by an L-shaped, marble-top breakfast bar with built-in kitchen island.

Catesby's complaints weren't far from the mark. The off-white walls hosted watercolor prints of generic seascapes, and the ocean-facing windows were framed by pale aqua seashell curtains that matched the throw pillows. The furniture was heavy, bulky stuff made in the 1980s style of looking like everything had been constructed out of wooden shipping crates. It was a smart choice for a rental. Every piece could withstand the worst abuse of heavy-drinking frat houses while retaining a durable, functional appeal. But the place lacked character and charm.

As for Catesby's description of my cottage, I doubted that "humble" was intended as a compliment.

"And naturally, young Max has been outright *ignoring me*," Catesby lamented. "After everything I did for *them*, after I picked them out of the obscurity of the graduate student masses and elevated them to the position of assistant to the world's leading expert on the historic cultivation of the finest divine elixir to be discovered by man."

"I'm sorry, *what*?!" I'd had enough. Max and Audrey looked up as I turned to Catesby. At least with this audience, I didn't need to explain that I hadn't lost my mind and wasn't speaking to thin air.

"He's here, isn't he?" Max's voice was barely above a whisper. "I thought I felt something, but then figured it was just wish fulfillment or grief or guilt or something."

"Guilt?" Audrey asked as she set out plates of toast and sandwich fixings on the breakfast bar.

Max sank into one of the dining chairs. "I've been getting close to finishing my own work, though it's been slow. Once my dissertation is done and successfully defended, it will be time for me to move on and start my own career. I didn't want to just leave the professor like that, because he's depended on me so much."

"Ho!" Catesby scoffed. "That I depended on, on . . ."

"Them," I suggested. Max looked up at me.

"*Them*," Catesby spat. The ghosts seemed oblivious to the fact that Audrey and Max could neither see nor hear him and that he was performing his histrionics for an audience of one. "To suggest that young Max's impending *abandonment* of *me* would have been such a career-rending betrayal is preposterous."

"I don't think that's what they said." I glanced at Audrey and Max, who watched me with rapt attention. "Oh, fine. The petulant professor is balking at Max's characterization of their coming departure, or whatever. He used words like 'abandonment' and 'career-rending betrayal.' And 'preposterous.'"

"Ms. Mudge," Catesby hissed through clenched teeth. "That is precisely what I said Max Turner's departure would *not* be."

Max dug their fingers into their short hair. "That's what he kept saying to me, demanding to know how I could be so ungrateful, to want to leave after everything he'd done for me."

Catesby floated across the floor and pointed at Max. "*That*, at least, is accurate. I gave Max here, as a mere graduate student, opportunities most post-grads and even tenured professors only dream about."

"All those 'opportunities' he kept saying he gave me?" Max dropped their hands in their lap and looked up at the ceiling. "If you're really here, I need you to hear me say this, because you wouldn't listen before. Opportunities to do your work for you, more like. Opportunities to watch you use my grant money for your own purposes, like supplementing your budgets and getting your office chair reupholstered in full-grain leather. Opportunities to keep your career afloat while my work kept getting sidelined and punted down the road."

Catesby's mouth hung open. For once in his life—or death— he appeared to be speechless.

"He was even trying to get on *Proof TV*," Max continued, "because of budget cuts at Cascade State. He thought the publicity would bring more money. I told him pseudoscience shows like that would hurt his reputation—and my work, too, by association. But he thought he was too high and mighty to fall, I guess."

I lugged a solid footstool across the floor and sat down. "Now he's dead and you can return to your own pursuits."

Horror-stricken, Max looked at me. "What?! No, I didn't want him *dead*. Holy crap, Suri, I never . . . Despite everything, I still cared about the professor. I looked forward to being his colleague, some day."

I glanced at Catesby for a reaction, but the ghost muttered something unintelligible and turned to gaze out the window at another cold, gray, damp afternoon on the beach.

Max scooted their chair closer to me. "After they told me the professor was dead, I came to you because I was distraught. And I wanted to make sure he was okay, even after . . . You know."

"I'm sorry, Max." I brushed back my unruly hair and wished I had an elastic. "But you have to know how this looks to Banich. Our friends are in the hospital, half the town is down sick, and we've got two people dead—"

"Ravi died before Max even got here," Audrey interjected.

"You're right. It's silly to suspect you, Max," I said. "Yet here we are."

"But it makes sense," Max replied. "I can understand why the police might think that. Probably why they didn't want me to have access to the equipment or my notes." Max wiped at their tired eyes. "If I didn't think it would cause more problems for you, I'd just go back to Seattle. But that would get you in trouble with Banich, right? And make me look even worse."

"*Our* notes," Catesby grumbled. "*My* work, *my* findings and papers to be published about the tea treasure."

The tea treasure. I'd nearly forgotten about it in the jumble of everything else—and there was so very much else. Banich had the right idea with his clipboard, though I doubted he had a persistent headache interfering with his memory and cognitive function. I needed to get everything out of my head and onto paper before I could hope to make sense of it.

"Max, do you have an empty notebook I might borrow?" I asked. "Or blank sheets of paper? I want to try writing everything down. I keep losing the details."

Max hopped up, dug into the police crate, and pulled out a thin spiral notebook. Then they emptied their canvas satchel onto the dining table and sorted through the mess of crumpled receipts, fingerless gloves, two empty water bottles, at least a dozen keys on a Cascade State chain, assorted plastic rulers, Catesby's pink stomach relief, and a vinyl wallet with a photo of the Space Needle on it. They grabbed a stack of brightly colored sticky notes from underneath a bag of cough drops and handed it to me, along with the notebook.

"And before I forget again . . ." Audrey reached into her bag and pulled out a phone charger. "I thought you might want this."

"Because my phone is dead." I groaned. I had again been too distracted to take care of my own needs.

I carried the notebook, sticky notes, and charger to the giant block of a coffee table. Catesby persisted in complaining quietly to himself by the window while I plugged in my phone. The battery was fully depleted. It would take a few minutes before I could access any voice messages or texts. I pulled a spare pen from my backpack purse, opened the notebook, and stared at the blank page. Where to begin? Maybe with a timeline.

"Hey, umm . . ." I called out. "What day is it?"

At the breakfast bar, Audrey laughed as she unloaded her bag around the corner from the food she'd set out. She laid out her witchy supplies of candles, polished stones, herbs and tinctures, and a few powders and blends I was pretty sure weren't ordinary kitchen spices. Did she keep a mobile cauldron in her car? Have wand, will travel? "It's Friday afternoon, Suri."

"Friday." The weight of the week pressed me into the couch. "But it's still February, right? I can't have been awake that long."

"Definitely still February. Only a few more days 'til Valentine's." Audrey gave me a wink as she held the flame of a small lighter to a bundle of dried herbs. She waved the smoke into her face and inhaled. At the first whiff of smoke, Max looked up in alarm.

"Something's burning?" Max was out of their chair and checking the wall outlets.

"Lavender and cedar." Audrey walked calmly through the open living area, fanning the smoke with her hands towards the corners and ceiling. "To refresh the senses, focus the mind, and drive out any negativity."

"Negativity, eh?" I glanced toward Catesby, who stared blankly out the window, unaffected by Audrey's space cleansing.

Max examined the stones, candles, and thick leather-bound journal on the breakfast bar, alongside the glass vial of Jim's blood I'd stolen from the hospital. "Is this a necessary part of your work?"

Audrey gave Max a pointed look. "Will any of this interfere with yours?"

Max hesitated. "I don't think so."

"Is it going to bother you?" Audrey asked.

"No, I don't think so." Max gave a nervous smile. "I'm just more accustomed to a different environment. Not that I really have the tools I need to work with."

"Max needs my guidance." Catesby moaned. "But I am neither seen nor heard. They're on their own."

Audrey uncapped the vial of blood, let a few drops fall into a heavy resin bowl, and handed the rest over to Max.

"I'm afraid to ask what you plan to do with that," Max nodded toward Audrey's set-up.

"Good luck to both of us." Audrey opened a plastic pouch of what looked like Italian seasoning and added a few pinches to the bowl.

"You're not baking anything with that, are you?" I couldn't help the wariness in my voice. "Nothing anybody has to eat?"

Audrey heaved a sigh. She had to be just as weary as I was, though she didn't look it. "Relax. No one has to eat any of this. If I do this properly, there won't be a trace left."

Max held the vial up to the light from the minimalist, bare bulb chandelier hanging over the dining table. "This should be enough. It feels weird not having the professor here."

"I am here," Catesby replied.

"I feel like maybe I'm second-guessing myself in his absence," Max said.

"Hardly necessary," Catesby told me. "My protégé is, of course, well trained.

"You've got this," Audrey said, then offered to make Max a cup of bolstering tea.

"No, it's okay," Max replied with a laugh. "Maybe I'm just not used to not being told what to do."

My phone chimed as it came back to life. I grumbled when I saw the missed calls and texts from Chris Banich, but they were all timestamped from earlier this morning, before I arrived at the dispensary, so at least it wasn't anything new. Then I saw the voicemail from the hospital. While Max and Audrey went about their individual pursuits, I steeled my nerves and opened the message transcript. I didn't breathe until I got to the end.

"Jim and Colin are stable," I announced to the room. Audrey choked back a sob. "But they've not yet identified the poison."

"I'd better hurry then." Audrey rested her hands on either side of the small ring of rocks and twigs she'd constructed on the marble bar. Three white candles burned around the circle, with the black bowl resting in the center. Her lips moved silently as she ignited a fresh match and touched its flame to the contents of the bowl. It went up like flash paper with a pink ball of fire that disintegrated in the air, leaving behind a sweet perfume of rose and vanilla.

"What the hell was that?!" Max exclaimed.

"That was my half of the experiment." Audrey peered into the empty bowl and took a few careful sniffs. She grabbed a pen and started writing in her journal.

Max looked at me with a worried expression. "I didn't realize we were combining our work."

"We all have to do what we can," I replied.

"Witchcraft?!" Catesby loomed over me with vicious outrage. "This is how you intend to solve the mystery of my demise? This is how you propose to secure my legacy and seal my reputation?"

"It isn't entirely about you," I replied. "We're also trying to help our friends. You know, the people who are still alive?"

"He's still here." Max watched me. "Casting aspersions with raised eyebrows? Tell him the scandal of illness will lend a shadow of intrigue to his last study—the case of the tainted treasure, the mystery he died trying to solve. Even *Proof TV* would want that story. And it will inspire debates and counter-arguments and wild conspiracy theories among his jealous peers and admirers for years to come. He'll love that."

"An interesting hypothesis." Catesby's gaze lifted as he considered the possibilities. "The curse of the ancient tea. The unsolved mystery of my untimely demise. Yes, I believe I can work with that." He lifted his chin and straitened his spine. "Ms. Mudge, I wish you and your colleagues to cease your work at once."

"Excuse me?" I asked.

"Your witch there." He pointed at Audrey, then made a sweeping gesture toward the coffee table, where my borrowed notebook remained mostly blank. "And whatever it is you're doing. And law enforcement as well, naturally."

"I have zero control over law enforcement," I said, and Audrey and Max looked over at me in mild alarm. "You want to stop their work, you'll have to do it yourself."

～

"I THINK I've worked it out," Audrey announced the next morning from the breakfast bar. She leaned back in her tall, padded chair and stretched her arms over her head to let out a long yawn. Max stuck two mugs of water in the microwave for tea, then loaded the coffee maker.

We'd called it an early night and headed to bed without dinner. Audrey was already snoozing in the guest bedroom by the time I made it up the stairs, which left me with Catesby's room. But I'd been too tired to care that I was using the bedroom of a recently deceased pompous ass, and fell asleep on top of the bed with my clothes on. I changed into my pajama bottoms only after I was up again this morning. I didn't know where Max had retreated for the night.

"Oh, yeah?" I stood before a formerly blank wall, now covered in multi-colored sticky notes. I was trying to keep track of the many clues, strange circumstances, and open questions— and there were a lot of all three. We had two deaths, two people in the hospital with many more sickened in town, a mysterious treasure box of old tea, a handful of new people in Grady, and plenty of residents and newcomers alike behaving strangely.

I'd made another call to the Seaside hospital as soon as I awoke to check on Jim. No change. He was still in critical care and remained unconscious. We had to assume the same about Colin.

"Yep. Bees." Audrey slid off her chair and started gathering breakfast supplies from the refrigerator. "Toast and eggs okay with everybody?"

"Bees?" Max asked. "Like, killer bees? In February?"

"You think everyone got stung?" I asked.

Too tired to laugh, Audrey yawned again, setting off a chain reaction with me and Max. We were all dragging, though at least we'd gotten some decent sleep.

"No, not like bee stings, I don't think. Not directly." Audrey cracked a half dozen eggs into a large iron skillet. "But bees are involved somehow in what happened. Maybe bee venom."

"In February?" I repeated Max's question. "Aren't they hibernating, or something?"

"I can explain my findings to you, if you want the details," Audrey replied. "Based on the color of the flame, the speed of the reaction, and also the blend of scents in the air."

"That sounds more scientific than I expected," Max said. Their open-mindedness was surprising, but then they hadn't seemed bothered that I could communicate with ghosts. "I didn't know magick could be like that."

Audrey shrugged. At the sound of the bell, I went to answer the front door, though I couldn't imagine who would come ringing before 9 a.m. on a Saturday.

"Good morning!" Karina sang with too much cheer as I opened the door. Her camel-colored wool coat matched her boiled wool slacks, and her rose-colored silk scarf picked up her blush-pink lipstick. She appeared to have recovered from the previous day's distress at the dispensary with Chief Deputy Banich. I congratulated myself on waiting fifteen full seconds before comparing Karina's photo-ready appearance to my flannel pajama bottoms and shapeless, oversized sweater.

"I'm sorry to just drop in on you like this, but I come bearing gifts!" Karina gestured toward the cardboard box and scientific instrument at her feet.

"My gas chromatograph mass spectrometer!" Max slid past me to lift the compact machine and give it an almost loving caress. "I thought I'd never see it again. How did you get it away from the police?"

Audrey appeared in the doorway. "Gas chromo-what?"

"Gas chromatograph mass spectrometer. GC/MS for short," Max replied as they carried the machine into the house.

Karina picked up the cardboard box and followed Max

inside. "To be honest, my assistant manager grabbed a bunch of things in a fit of paranoia as Chief Deputy Banich and his people filed in to take control of our commercial kitchen. An old habit from pre-legalization, I suppose. Now, I don't condone Bard's actions, but he made a good point that the professor's machine didn't kill Ravi, and it's not something someone would use to set off a string of poisonings. I understand that you're trying to find a cure, and I thought you'd need this."

As Max went about setting up the GC/MS on the dining table, Karina opened the cardboard box and lifted out a collection of plastic squirt bottles of various liquids.

Max let out a *whoop*. "These are the solvents I need. I can't believe you made off with all this!"

Karina next pulled out a shrink-wrapped laptop box. "It's not your computer, but something I had shipped in overnight," she told Max. "I'm guessing you can retrieve your files from the cloud?"

Max laughed and called Karina a miracle worker. I couldn't disagree.

"Do you want a cup of tea or something?" Audrey pointed at the coffee maker. "We've even got coffee, if you'd prefer."

Karina declined and made her excuses for needing to leave. As I walked her toward the front door, I filled her in on Jim's condition, though there wasn't any change.

"Thanks for all of this." I was stunned by Karina's unexpected generosity, especially since she should have turned everything over to Banich. Maybe she was a loyal boss, and this was her way of keeping Bard out of trouble.

Outside on the front porch, Karina turned to me with tears in her eyes. "Someone wanted to make it look like you were poisoning people, Suri, and then they did the same thing to me. We need to stick together. Anything you need, I'll help if I can." She reached for my hand and squeezed my fingers.

"You sure you don't want to stay?" I asked. Her business had put a heavy squeeze on the Tea Reader, but I saw Karina was trying to do the right thing now. And it sure looked like she could use a friend.

Again, she refused. "I'm on my way to Seaside. If they won't let me see Jim, I'll just camp out at the hospital. Maybe he'll feel that I'm nearby. I have to do something, Suri. You know?"

I did know. I recommended Butch Burger and warned her about the uncomfortable chairs in the critical care waiting area, then went back to my notebook and the parade of sticky notes I'd posted on the wall. Staring back at me were the names of the sick and deceased, the locations of the Tea Reader and the TBD, and every tiny fact I could think might be relevant—including Audrey's kombucha experiments, the possibility of weird drug interactions, and the black-and-teal TBD employee shirts. I'd organized everything in chronological order, then repositioned the notes in various concentric circles around possible motives and potential bad actors. But I was missing any number of pieces which simply hadn't occurred to me yet.

"This just doesn't make sense," I complained to the scattered rainbow of notes on the wall. I couldn't do any good at the hospital, and I didn't want to hide in my cottage or the empty bookshop. What made me think I could spot patterns or find a solution any faster than the professionals?

The GC/MS whirred as it warmed up on the other side of the room. Max looked positively joyful to have their instrument back, and at the prospect of putting their skills to effective use.

Audrey brought me a cup of hot tea. "Max said they need to prepare the blood sample with a solvent, and that it will take a while to run the tests." She studied my wall and my lack of progress. "Maybe a good time to take a break?" Audrey looked me up and down. "At least we could get you a change of clothes."

Banich might have assumed that Audrey and I would supervise Max, but he hadn't said so explicitly. We didn't work for him, and yesterday's wariness of Max had disappeared almost as soon as I was out of Banich's presence. Whoever he'd stationed to watch the house would have to suffice.

"Go." Max hovered over their new laptop, which was connected to the GC/MS unit. "This will take a while."

"And then you'll know what poisoned Colin?" The hope in Audrey's voice made my heart ache.

"Maybe," Max replied. "I'll start by following your lead on the insects. It could be a venom of some kind, like you said."

"Or botanical?" Audrey suggested. "Like a pollen or nectar?"

"You don't suppose it was bad cannabis?" I asked. "Or a poison added to the cannabis?" I glanced at the sticky notes. Some of them had been stuck and re-stuck so many times they were peeling off the wall. "Could Karina have done something? Is that what the bees are trying to tell you, Audrey?"

Max balked. "I can't imagine Karina would hurt anyone. It could have been an accidentally tainted supply. I'll see what I can find out."

"Max always tries to see the good in everyone," Catesby said in my ear. I started and held a hand against my suddenly racing heart. I'd hoped he'd been taking some time off to contemplate his next steps in the afterlife instead of obsessing over his reputation. Except here he was again. "It's both touching and maddening to see a young person be so big-hearted. I fear they'll be taken advantage of."

"You mean, by people like you?" I muttered. Catesby backed off.

"Come on. Let's let them work in peace." Audrey tugged at my elbow. "It'll be good to get out."

"Your curious friend makes an excellent suggestion." Catesby gazed again at the beach on the other side of the window glass. "I suppose I should contribute what assistance I'm able to offer, given that my legacy is at stake."

The ghost disappeared before I could ask what he meant to

do in his present circumstances. Max typed on the laptop keyboard and clicked a few on-screen buttons, and a new thrum joined the steady whir of the GC/MS. Audrey pulled on her coat and held mine out to me.

CHAPTER ELEVEN

Once inside my cottage, Audrey marched straight to my bedroom and demanded that I change out of my flannel pajama bottoms—which was fair, because I'd forgotten I was still wearing them.

She also ordered me out of the oversized sweater that was more comfortable than comely, with the promise that we'd find something in my wardrobe that was just as cozy while "not presenting as a fashion disaster."

As I pulled on my bathrobe to keep warm, I wondered if she and Trey had solved their communications problem and found a way to gossip about me and my clothes behind my back.

"I should take you shopping," she said as she rummaged through my drawer of jeans and sweatpants. "In case you ever want to cultivate a signature style."

"Do you mean I've been frumpier than usual?" I asked.

"Your words, not mine," she replied.

"She has a point." Trey materialized inside the doorway and gave my pink and navy polka-dot bathrobe a disapproving glare.

"I get it already. You think I'm disgusting," I said. I'd never heard a snarky comment from Trey about Audrey's personal style, which I didn't think was exactly fashion forward. But she had a consistent theme of all things science fiction. This morning she was sporting a quarter-zip fleece with a pair of lightsaber-dueling kittens on the front.

"What? No!" Audrey exclaimed. "Suri, I would never think that. I just thought maybe you'd feel better if your clothes more accurately reflected the amazing person you are inside."

I tried to tell her that I was trading barbs with a ghost and not disparaging her, but Audrey sat on the edge of my bed and dissolved in tears.

"It's like when I was feeling really low about everything that happened with Drew," she said, trying to catch her breath. "Because he was so awful to me. Accusing me of cheating on him if I tried to make myself look nice for him. You know?" Audrey pulled a TARDIS-print cloth handkerchief out of her jeans pocket and blew her nose. "And he was merciless about my liking *Farscape, Dr. Who, Star Trek*, and even *Star Wars*. Like, a lot of guys would be thrilled to have a girlfriend who loves sci-fi!"

"Like Colin," I suggested. I shot Trey a hard look and whispered, "See what you've done?"

"This is not on me," he retorted, unheard by Audrey.

"Exactly!" Audrey wiped at her wet face and took a deep breath. "But it was more than that. Breaking away from Drew also meant embracing myself. So I got my colors done. Dark Autumn." She laughed. "And I started literally wearing my heart on my sleeve. Or, close enough." She gestured toward the Jedi kitties on her pull-over, blew her nose again, and shoved the handkerchief back into her pocket.

I tried again to explain about the presence of the paranormal fashion police, aka Trey, but Audrey rededicated herself to her mission to dress me properly. She was on her feet and opening my wardrobe in search of something that might fulfill her vision of my signature style.

"You made Audrey cry," I hissed under my breath at Trey. "I can't believe you made her cry."

"I had nothing to do with it," Trey replied at full volume, since only I could hear him. "Looks like you mistreat all your friends."

"That is not even close to true!" I shouted back.

Audrey spun around in surprise. "Suri?" Understanding dawned on her face. "Is it Catesby again? Is he being a pill?"

"No, not Catesby," I replied. "Just a continuation of my argument with Trey." It was tempting to tell Audrey what he'd said about me mistreating my friends, because I knew she'd spring to my defense. But that would prolong and worsen the situation.

Audrey looked defeated. "Whatever's going on, I hope you two can work it out."

I glanced at Trey. He rolled his eyes and turned away, but he didn't vanish into thin air. That was something.

"What's this?" Audrey pulled a blue glass bottle from deep inside the wardrobe and rotated it in her hands.

I'd never seen such a thing, and I certainly hadn't stowed it inside my wardrobe. I looked to Trey, and he shrugged.

"Is this . . . ? Yes, this is a witch bottle." Audrey walked to the window and held the object up to the light to peer inside. "See how it's sealed with red wax and black string? This is a curse, Suri."

I lifted my hands and tried to push the sight away. "This is precisely the kind of thing I do not have time for right now." I turned away and shoved my fists into the deep pockets of my cozy robe. Who would place such a vile thing in my wardrobe? Who could have gotten into my house? I shuddered. I wanted to run to the bathroom, lock the door, and jump into a blistering hot shower. Choosing an attractive outfit had fallen way down the priority list.

"There's a tight coil of barbed wire in here," Audrey said. "And some jagged pebbles. Obsidian, I think. It's hard to tell through the dark glass. When someone plants a witch bottle, it can cause a string of bad luck, or sometimes serious injury. Or worse."

"Are you okay, Suri?" Trey hovered by my side. The last time we dealt with a curse, he'd ended up dead and I nearly joined him. "Do you think that thing is what trapped me inside your wardrobe before?"

I snapped a quick photo of the witch bottle in Audrey's hands, then posed Trey's question.

"Maybe." Audrey rattled the bottle. "Whoever did this, I don't think they wanted to cause significant harm. Looks like there's some sand and moss in here. To soften the blow, so to speak. But there's also a round, metallic-looking object. Maybe a magnet? That would make you feel sluggish or stuck, and could mess with your electronics. It might snare a ghost, too." She put the bottle down. "It's all a guess, but I don't dare open that thing to find out for sure. It looks like someone wanted to stymie you, Suri. Get you bogged down."

"I have been feeling kind of gloomy," I said.

"You've been downright dejected and morose," Trey added, earning him another sharp look from me. But he wasn't wrong.

"Could this thing be the reason the bookshop tablet has been on the fritz, and why my phone is being weird about holding a charge?" I groaned. My phone's battery, which should have been mostly full, read only thirty-seven percent. I groaned. "And your toaster oven nearly blew up in my kitchen. Is this bottle why I'm about to lose my business?"

"It didn't help," Audrey replied.

Thoughts of the Tea Reader drew my memory back to Monday morning in the bookshop, when I unpacked Loki's latest delivery box. I recalled the two copies of that witchy book, *Bewitching the Heart*, and how Karina had claimed one for herself. Had Karina planted the witch bottle? But why?

"This could be why you've been arguing with Trey, too."

Audrey carried the bottle into the hallway. "I'm gonna dig a hole and break this bottle underground, to shatter the curse."

She was down the hall and out the door before I could thank her.

"You think she's right?" Trey asked. "That some blue glass with sand and wire inside is the reason we can't stand each other?" There was an affectionate twist at the edge of his smirk.

"I didn't mean to suggest that you're a supernatural pervert," I said. "I'm sorry that I offended you. But you know we need some boundaries, not just about my space. I also shouldn't be ordering you around like you're my ghost servant."

"I prefer 'spectral sidekick.'" Trey stared at the clothes Audrey had pulled out of various drawers and piled on the floor. "I think this teal sweater would go nicely with these black jeans. Bootcut, right?"

And, just like that, we were talking to each other again.

WITH THE WITCH bottle buried and broken, Audrey left to claim her kitten from Barbara. Simba was adorable but unruly, and there was a limit to Barbara's pet-sitting generosity.

Trey made himself scarce as I got dressed. We hadn't fully resolved our differences. That would take time and deeper conversations. But for now, he was giving me some private space and even volunteered to do some ghostly reconnaissance work. I wasn't sure what I could do to repay him.

I was brushing my hair when I heard a quiet "*ahem*" in the hallway. Trey had returned. He informed me that Catesby was nowhere to be found at the rental house, despite the professor's bluster about needing to guide Max's work. I remembered the professor's earlier insistence that I somehow stop Banich's investigation in order to preserve the mystery around his death. I wondered if Catesby was off somewhere trying to take matters into his own ghostly hands.

Catesby might prove resourceful in his spectral state. It was possible he would observe or overhear something important about Banich's investigation, and maybe we could help fill in the missing pieces for the chief deputy. If nothing else, Catesby's side quest to secure his life's last glorious triumph, or whatever he was calling it now, would keep him occupied for a while.

Even so, I asked—politely—if Trey would mind keeping an eye out for Catesby, to steer him clear of any trouble he might get himself into, and report back if any promising clues were uncovered.

That's as far as Trey and I got before Banich started pounding on my cottage door. I didn't like visitors showing up unannounced, and he didn't like being refused entry. So we argued outside in the cold about suspects and motives.

"Once again," I insisted, beginning to feel like a skipping vinyl record, "it makes no sense that Karina would poison her customers or local law enforcement. She's trying to build a business here. And you know that she's dating Jim."

Banich gave me a smug smile. "And he's your ex, isn't he, Ms. Mudge?"

I crossed my arms against the cold. I hadn't pulled on a coat before I stepped outside. My frustrated sigh froze on the air. "Yes. And?"

"And with you and your barista, Audrey Medina, baking for the Tea Reader and reportedly selling those same goods to Ms. Coyle at the dispensary, doesn't it stand to reason that a jealous ex-girlfriend might seek to destroy a rival business and punish a former lover, in one fell swoop?"

"Hold up. What?!" I exclaimed. "You do not honestly believe that."

"It would answer a lot of questions." Banich chuckled, then

let out a sigh of his own. "But it's an incomplete theory. The pieces don't quite fit."

"But you're going to make them fit? Is that what you're trying to tell me?"

Banich winced. "That's not how I work, Ms. Mudge." I'd struck a nerve, but he didn't back down. "There are a lot of ways to make a death look like cardiac arrest."

"Is that how Ravi died?" I asked. "Or Professor Catesby?"

"You tell me," he replied.

I threw my hands in the air. "I don't know! What about Jim and Colin in the hospital, and the other people getting sick in town? Why are you here on my doorstep casting aspersions when you could be questioning actual suspects and following real leads?"

"Who says I'm not doing that right now?" Banich asked. "No one is above suspicion."

Ugh. I stood by my earlier assessment. Chris Banich absolutely was an irritating and odious man. Things were so much easier with Jim, as maddening as working with him could be. Not that investigating a suspicious death was ever easy. But the chief deputy was being impossible as he wasted both my time and his, even if he thought he was doing his job. Catching the hint of a smile on his face, I wondered if he was enjoying himself—or worse, thought we were flirting.

"By the way, how well did you know this Thomas Catesby character?" Banich asked. "We've done some digging into his career, and while I'm no authority on academia, I'm not sure how anyone makes a living as a self-declared 'tea expert.'"

"Well, Ravi King contacted him for a reason, even if it was just because of a Google search." I kept my mouth shut about the university budget cuts Max had mentioned, and the professor's recent media aspirations. While I didn't care for the late Thomas Catesby, I saw no reason to impugn his reputation posthumously.

I also didn't see how Catesby's academic work figured into the rash of poisonings that had occurred after his death.

When I suggested to the chief deputy that the poisonings might not be malicious, he met my logic with dismissive disdain. Banich countered that "the poisoner"—me, Karina, or whoever —might have been trying to throw suspicion elsewhere after they killed Ravi King. He brought up the old Excedrin tampering case from Seattle in the 1980s as precedent.

When I pointed out that poisoning an entire town to cover up a single murder seemed extreme, Banich gave me another superior smile, told me I hadn't been cleared as a suspect, and suggested that I shouldn't leave town.

I replayed every beat of the infuriating exchange as I walked up the steps of Lantz's Boarding House with a basket of heart-shaped shortbread. I'd kept the discovery of the witch bottle to myself, though my stomach churned whenever I thought about it. Someone had gotten into my house, and they meant to do me harm. For all I knew, witch bottles might have killed Ravi and Catesby both, and made everybody else sick. But could I trust Banich? Would he take a magickal threat seriously, or write me off as a crackpot?

Determined to think about it later, I pushed open the bright red door and stepped inside the boarding house. I had come to check on Cyndi, who'd been hit by the double-whammy of mourning her boyfriend, Ravi King, and then falling victim to the strange series of poisonings. My visit served multiple purposes. I wanted to see how my employee was doing, and I didn't want to disturb Max's work at the rental house. And with the witch bottle Audrey found in my bedroom, I was uneasy being alone in my own house.

"Ah, Suri! What a welcome surprise." Paula Lantz beamed at me as I entered. Paula was known for her warm welcome and her confused metaphors, but I caught the flickering wattage in her smile. "And aren't you a ray of fresh air! Good to know you're not among the afflicted. Three of my boarders are down with the scourge."

"The scourge?" I knew what she was talking about, but I hadn't realized that the rash of mystery poisonings had been given a monicker.

"Struck like an avalanche, too." Paula snuck a cookie out of the basket I carried and nibbled at the edge of the shortbread. "You'll be wanting to see Cyndi? She's in the northeast corner room on the second floor."

I left Paula with a second cookie, then climbed the carpeted stairs. Cyndi's door was ajar when I approached, and I heard voices inside. I knocked on the doorjamb.

"Suri!" Cyndi brightened at the sight of me. She sat propped up in bed, with various beverages and a stack of books and magazines on her bedside table. Despite her smile, her face was wan and drawn, and I tried to ignore the kidney-shaped emesis basin on the floor. Her visitor, Bud Barlow, looked about as desolate as anyone I'd ever seen, but he exhibited no signs of illness as he sat in a chair by her bed.

Cyndi glanced at the basket. "Audrey?"

We both chuckled while Bud let out an audible sigh. With no room on the bedside table, I rested the cookie basket on the end of the bed.

"How are you feeling?" With nowhere to sit, I stood beside her. "Is there anything I can do for you?"

"I'm not as bad as some others." Cyndi coughed. Bud handed her a glass of water, and she took small sips. "Bud has been such an angel looking after me since I got sick, and also since . . ." Her voice broke, and she started to cry. Bud exchanged her water glass for a fresh tissue.

"She's pretty broken up about Ravi." Bud looked like he was going to tear up, too, with anger or irritation simmering underneath. His partner was dead, possibly murdered. He had a right to be heartsick and enraged.

"I'm sorry about Ravi," I said to them both.

"Yeah." Bud gritted his teeth and looked at the floor. "It's the god-awful pits, that's for sure."

"It was just such a shock." Cyndi dried her eyes and asked for water again, which Bud provided. His active concern was touching. Maybe caring for Cyndi was a constructive outlet for his own grief.

"Has anyone else from the Tea Reader gotten sick? Do they know what caused all this?" Cyndi asked.

"No, to both questions," I said.

"Who would do this?" Bud blurted. He swore under his breath, then apologized for his outburst. "What happened to the treasure?"

"Doesn't the chief deputy have it?" I asked.

Cyndi shook her head. "He really grilled me about it. Bud, too. As if we'd know where it was."

"Karina said they got a few things out of the TBD before law enforcement could take everything away," I said. "I'm sure it will turn up."

"At least that Hattieville deputy doesn't have it," Bud grumbled.

"Bud's worried about what will happen to the treasure, since he and Ravi worked so hard to find it." Cyndi patted Bud's hand. "Maybe the treasure box can be a lasting symbol of what Ravi valued in his life. Adventure and discovery, and friendship." She coughed again, then rested back against the pillows and closed her eyes.

Bud stood. "You should eat. I'll heat up some broth." He looked to me. "You'll sit with her?"

I nodded, and he went out the door and down the stairs to the communal kitchen on the first floor. I closed the door and sat beside Cyndi. We made awkward employer-employee chitchat for a few minutes, until I remembered one of the gaps in my sticky notes on the wall.

"The day Ravi died, Audrey said you saw him and Bud sprinkle something into their tea?" When I saw the stricken look on her face, I softened my approach. "I'm sorry to ask, and I hope it's not intrusive. I imagine Chief Deputy Banich has asked you about it."

"About a thousand times. He always makes it sound like I did something wrong for just seeing that. Or like I'm responsible for getting poisoned, too."

It was no surprise Banich would have a callous bedside manner. I offered Cyndi one of Audrey's cookies, but she said she wasn't sure she could stomach regular food yet.

"Look, I'll tell you something I didn't tell that deputy from Hattieville," she said, and I leaned close on instinct. "What I saw? It was just a little something extra. A pinch of powder. You know."

"I don't know. You mean vitamin powder?"

She tilted her head. "You know. A little sprinkle from down the street."

"Something they got from the Tea and Botanicals Dispensary?" I asked.

"*Off the menu.*" Cyndi winked at me, as though I was supposed to know what she meant. Bud's heavy footsteps clomped up the stairs, and her expression turned more solemn. "Look, Bud is taking Ravi's death really hard. Harder than me, even. They were friends, you know? Spent all that time together in the woods and everything. Please don't ask him too many questions about that morning. It was so awful."

"Of course. I don't mean to upset anyone." I stood as Bud pushed the door open with his foot and carried in a tray with a bowl of steaming bouillon and a small plate of saltine crackers. "I'll let you eat and get your rest. But please call me or Barbara if you need anything?"

Cyndi promised, and I left while Bud settled the tray on her lap and fluffed the pillows behind her. The whole way back to my car, I wondered what the hell Karina had been selling "off the menu" at her shop.

~

CALLS TO KARINA went straight to voicemail. She probably had her phone on silent while she sat in the hospital, hoping for a chance to see Jim. Or maybe she was ignoring my calls.

I also put in a call to the county health department in Hattieville, but of course I got dumped into the voice messaging system because it was late on a Saturday afternoon. I recorded my concern and hoped it would remain anonymous. I couldn't remember if the coming Monday was a federal holiday or not. Who knew how long it would take someone to investigate the TBD's off-menu items?

My head throbbed, and I felt a little dizzy as I unlocked the bookshop's front door and stepped inside. The space was mercifully dark and quiet. I opened the pass-through doors and crossed over to the teahouse side. The emptiness of the dining room was disorienting.

I pulled out a chair at the table in the middle of the room, sat, and took a breath. "Ravi?" I waited in silence. "Ravi King, are you here?"

I let a full minute tick by. A few Standish Beach types in fleece hoodies and ill-fitting cargo pants laughed as they strolled past on the sidewalk. They were likely heading to the TBD, not knowing it was closed.

"Ravi? I need your help. My friends are in the hospital. You and the professor are both dead, and Thomas Catesby is . . . Well, *unhelpful.* I need to know what you put in your tea. Did you do this to yourself? Did Karina kill you?" No answer. Maybe Catesby would blunder his way into solving his own mysterious death, along with finding the antidote to whatever had sickened so many people in Grady. And maybe I'd grow wings and fly around the Moon.

"Ravi! Are you here?" I couldn't keep the frustration out of my voice. "Can you tell me what happened to you?"

"I am, in fact, on the premises and am hoping you can help me?"

I cursed as soon as I heard his voice. Turning in my chair, I found Loki hovering on the pass-through threshold. Had I forgotten to lock the bookshop door behind me? I balled my hands into fists on my thighs. "No, I was trying to . . . Look, we're closed."

"But I come bearing gifts." He gestured behind him toward the bookshop.

Despite my better judgment, I got up and followed him into the dark bookshop. I snapped on a single floor lamp to avoid aggravating my headache and to dissuade anyone else from trying to come in. On the sales counter sat another one of Loki's mystery boxes.

"Thank you," I said. "But like I said, the business is closed. For the foreseeable future."

"Yes, that is most unfortunate. But not, I believe, a permanent circumstance. Also, not the purpose of my visit." He cocked his head toward the cardboard box, and I decided to humor him.

This special delivery wasn't overflowing with random trinkets and used books across wildly unrelated topics. Instead, I pulled out a pair of lightly worn hiking boots in my size.

"For treasure hunting," Loki said.

"Nope. No. Not happening." I dropped the boots back in the box, but I didn't outright reject the gift. They were good boots. Since my old ones were losing their weather-proofing, I could use these for a hike or just walking in the rain.

Loki didn't seem perturbed, but he never did, did he? "Then perhaps you will indulge my curiosity on the whereabouts of the tea box treasure?" he asked.

First Catesby, then Bud, and now Loki. With everything else going on in town, why was the treasure box such a major concern?

"I don't know," I replied. "But it's apparently not in the hands of the visiting chief deputy, if that's what you were worried about."

The flicker of relief in his expression told me that was precisely the nature of his concern, at least in part. He leaned against a standing bookcase, his strong features exaggerated in the dim light. "I can assure you there's little chance the tea inside was poisoned, though I doubt it would have been palatable after all this time. It's merely a blend of thyme, wild basil, rose petals, and lemon balm. With the addition of intentional magick, of course."

"Of course," I said. "How the hell would you know the exact ingredients of the tea that Ravi and Bud found in that old box? Or was that just a guess?"

"Far from a guess." Loki smiled. I'd asked the question he'd wanted. "It was prepared by Frigga herself as a healing agent for my grief after my son Fenrir was imprisoned in his wolf form. Justifiably so, but still a source of significant anguish."

I stared at him. Because how was I supposed to respond to that? Frigga? Wasn't she an old Viking goddess? And this guy believed she'd made him a special tea blend, the way Audrey did for Tea Reader customers. I decided to skip over the whole "son is a wolf" thing. A quick glance confirmed I had a clear path to the bookshop door and could make a hasty, unobstructed exit, in case Loki's current delusion turned violent.

"My primary interest isn't the tea, though it is a pity to lose it," he said. "I doubt it could have harmed, much less killed anyone. You and your friends are working all that out yourselves?"

I nodded and waited for him to continue. Maybe if I let him spill the details, without interruption, he'd leave as quietly and peacefully as he came in.

"I desire the box itself," Loki said. "The chest is old, as you say, far older than you might suspect. Preserved with ancient magick. It was fashioned by Brokkr of the Svartálfar, as a peace offering to resolve a grievous misunderstanding that had extended to unfortunate consequences."

"Brokkr of the what now?" I asked.

"Svartálfar," he replied. "The black elves who live in Svartálfaheim. The chest was promised to contain the proper magick to call back the souls of my dispersed children, once they met their ends. This is, appropriately, how the chest came to also hold Frigga's grieving tea. In the wrong hands, I fear what might transpire."

"Right, sure." As I paused for another ice pick headache to pass—this time at the back of my skull—I entertained the idea that this Loki character genuinely believed he was an Old Norse deity. That would explain his name, which he could have chosen for himself. Then—because this was Naghatune Bay, where the impossible comes on holiday, and because my luck was exactly this kind of weird—I wondered at the remote chance that he was telling the truth. I shoved the thought away. On top of the migraine, I worried that such daft speculation would at last break my brain.

"Your headache?" he asked.

I nodded, but I didn't want to dwell on the pain. I grabbed onto something he'd said. "The box was supposed to house the souls of your deceased children?"

The corners of his mouth tugged downward. "That was promised, but all three are lost to me. Fenrir, in the last battle of Ragnarok. Hel, to her prison of a throne in the shadowy underworld. And Narfi, lost to the abyss."

An unpleasant suspicion arose, and I needed to tread carefully. "So you're telling me your box could trap a ghost? Do you know about anything else that could do that?" Loki had been inside my cottage the morning Jim fell ill, and I'd found him hanging around my doorstep after returning from the hospital in Seaside. Maybe he'd let himself in other times when I wasn't home. "Like a witch bottle placed inside someone's wardrobe?"

"Not really my line." He cocked his head. "I don't suppose you've seen a cat anywhere about?"

"No luck finding yours?" I asked.

"Not my cat," Loki replied. "Assuming any of us could belong to each other. My friend, perhaps? This is a very particular feline. Not native to the area. Determined and intelligent, with particular skills. You might have heard something about her?"

"Yeah, no. Sorry." Now that I thought about it, I couldn't remember the last time I'd seen him with his pet raccoon or his rotund orange-and-black tabby. I felt bad that he might have lost his emotional support cat, though that would explain a lot.

"I had thought she was leading me." Loki shrugged. "As to your witch bottle, there are several magick practitioners in the area who should be able to assist you with such a need."

"It's not something I need. It's something I found." I dug out my phone and pulled up the photo of the blue glass bottle Audrey had discovered in my wardrobe. "Someone put this in my house."

When I glanced up to show the photo to Loki, I found myself standing alone in the bookshop. I still didn't know who or what Loki was, regardless of what he thought of himself, and his vanishing act gave me the creeps. I cursed again.

CHAPTER TWELVE

"A little something extra," I muttered as I stood in front of the wall of sticky notes at the rental house. I hadn't gone to the boarding house looking for clues—at least, I hadn't thought so—and I wasn't sure what to do with this one.

I cupped my hands around another mug of tea. I didn't ask anymore what Audrey was putting in it. This cup tasted of mint and produced a pleasant, buzzy feeling in my chest, though she swore there wasn't anything but tea and non-cannabis herbs in the blend.

Simba the kitten ran around my feet a half dozen times like a furious, furry whirlwind before dashing across the room to leap at a string Max dangled from their fingers.

While I was gone, Max had moved the equipment to the basement mudroom, where a sturdy worktable was bolted into the concrete floor. They said the new setup could better protect the GC/MS from vibrations elsewhere in the house, and this meant the rest of us wouldn't have to listen to the machine do its work.

If the real reason for the change was that Max wanted some

time and space alone, though, I wouldn't have blamed them. Max was fielding calls from the university while trying to assist with the planning of their late mentor's memorial, along with inquiries from other professors looking to fill Catesby's advisory role for them. It was a lot to handle all at once.

But I'd been distressed, though unsurprised, to learn that Max had been sleeping in the basement, even before Catesby's death.

After a full day of running tests, Max hadn't been able to identify any poison in Jim's blood. At least, they hadn't found anything that made sense, and we were working on the assumption that whatever had made him sick would show up in his blood. Now was the time to decide what unlikely avenues to explore next, or what different solvent to try with the blood in the GC/MS, and there was only so much of the sample left to work with.

We all needed a long break, which was why Audrey and Max were playing with Simba while debating what movies we should queue up for the evening.

"Have you ever seen *Galaxy Quest*?" Audrey asked. Max shrugged, and Audrey clapped her hands in delight. "It's a classic! You'll love it."

"If you want classics, how about *The Andromeda Strain*?" Max laughed as they yanked the string out of Simba's reach, and the kitten gave an angry yowl. "Or maybe that's a little too close to reality right now."

"Double feature, then?" Audrey suggested. "And I can make a lasagne or something for dinner."

But I couldn't put the problem aside, not yet. There was something tugging from the periphery, something I was sure was so plain and obvious, if I could only will myself to see it.

"A little something extra, from down the street," I repeated Cyndi's words as I faced the wall. Today's migraine was receding by degrees. I squinted at the colored squares of paper stuck to the wall until my vision started swimming.

Max had read up on cannabis while the GC/MS was running, and like a good academic, they presented their sources when relaying their findings. It turned out that cannabis is wind-pollinated, so if Audrey's magickally divined "bees" clue was legitimate, the source of the poison was something other than cannabis contamination by pollinating insects. So what the hell had Cyndi been talking about?

Karina still wasn't answering my repeated calls or texts, and I tried not to read too much into that.

"Cyndi said Ravi and Bud sprinkled something into their tea. But Bud isn't sick, and Cyndi is. And Ravi's dead." I started rearranging the sticky notes again. "Jim and Colin are in the hospital." I had a hard time imagining either of them consuming pot edibles from the TBD or anywhere else. Not knowingly.

"You okay, Suri?" Max asked as they tossed a catnip mouse for Simba to chase.

"Just thinking out loud." I took another big gulp of Audrey's tea, emptying the mug. "Mayor Phil Lindquist is sick. Earl Greenbauer is sick. So is Cyndi. Gary Spalding. Mildred Moroni. Emmaline Kapul. Joe Stanley. And Murray Overhill." My casualty list was incomplete. I'd heard through the grapevine that there were at least a dozen more cases reported in Standish Beach. The local gossip mill was useful, for once. "This doesn't add up."

Hours earlier, I'd told both Audrey and Max about the "little something extra" in Ravi and Bud's tea, as described by Cyndi—and it didn't sound like the vitamin powder Audrey had told me about. This sent them both into a flurry of internet searches and active brainstorming, trying to line up everyone's symptoms with every conceivable powdery substance from the dispensary that might have made it into Ravi King's tea. Trying to incorporate Audrey's magickal findings, we spent a full hour going down a rabbit hole on the medicinal properties and potential allergic side effects of freeze-dried royal jelly. Without more information to go on, it was just a guess what might have been in that sprinkle, if it was related to the poisonings at all. Why hadn't Cyndi told Banich about it? For all I knew, Cyndi had killed Ravi so she could be with Bud, instead of just breaking up with her boyfriend. And then poisoned Catesby and half the town to cover her tracks.

I sighed and massaged my temples. Persistent pain and fatigue made my brain sluggish and dull, and I was grasping at straws. With only enough of Jim's blood left for a single run through Max's GC/MS and no clear idea what to test for, we were at a standstill. As much as I disliked him, I hoped Banich was making better progress.

"Come on, Suri, take a break." Audrey replaced the empty mug in my hands with a fresh one full of something frothy that smelled of cinnamon and sweet apples. Her boyfriend was in the hospital with a mystery illness, and she was expending her nervous energy taking care of me. "We've done pretty much all we can at this point."

"So we wait?" I asked.

"So we wait," she agreed. "And see what happens next."

Audrey wasn't clairvoyant, as far as I knew, but the doorbell sounded mere seconds later. I raised my eyebrows and followed her to the door.

Karina stood on the doorstep again, this time with a rolling suitcase, four cloth grocery bags, and none of the polish or confidence of her earlier appearance. I stopped myself from firing off a barrage of angry and suspicious questions when I saw how frightened she looked.

"I'm sorry to just show up like this, yet again. But can I stay here tonight?" Karina asked with a quaver in her voice. "I came back from the hospital in Seaside, and . . . Someone broke into my house. I don't know where else to go."

≈

AUDREY GOT Karina settled on the couch with a warm blanket, a mug of soothing tea, and a plate of vanilla shortbread —right next to my wall of sticky notes. I watched Karina for her reaction to my fumbled attempts to identify Ravi's and Catesby's most likely killer. The colored squares seemed to distract her from her fear and anxiety. I wondered what would happen if I posted a new note with "witch bottle" on it, right in the middle.

"Suri? You're on the trail of the Naghatune Bay Poisoner?" Karina cupped her hands around the warm mug of tea and took a long, calming drink.

"That's a good name," Max said.

"What do you make of all of this?" I asked Karina.

Tears welled in her eyes. "I feel like I'm in a twisted, alternate universe. Like everything around me is falling apart."

"Everything's going to be all right. I'm sure of it." Audrey sat next to Karina and wrapped a comforting arm around her. I worried that Audrey's need to caretake might override our suspicions about Karina, but then Audrey gave me a quick wink. "I know it looks bad now. Really bad. But we'll get through it."

"I spent the last hour with one of the deputies from Hattieville." Karina stared down into her tea mug. "My house was broken into, and Banich sends a young rookie to investigate? It's like he's not taking any of this seriously."

"Or that his resources are stretched to their limit," I said. Why was I defending Banich? He was obnoxious and awful and a bad listener, and he didn't deserve my sympathy.

"The good news? I don't think anything was missing," Karina said. "They made a hell of a mess, though. The few socks and sweaters that hadn't been rifled through, I packed up right away. I couldn't stand to be in that place any longer." She shuddered. "And just the idea of someone touching my things, my clothes. If they were trying to scare me, it worked. Even in a quiet little town like Grady, it doesn't feel safe."

Damn it. I understood how she felt. Hadn't I fled my cottage after discovering the witch bottle in my wardrobe? Maybe the same person broke into Karina's place. Or maybe she'd ransacked her own house to divert suspicion.

Karina finished her tea and set the empty mug on the coffee table. "I went to see Bard right after, and he's sick, too!" She wiped at her eyes. If she was the Naghatune Bay Poisoner, she was also one hell of an actress. She gestured toward my sticky notes. "He had a wall of clues like yours, Suri, trying to sort out what's happened."

"Bard's your assistant manager, right?" Max asked. Karina gave a quick nod, and Max added, "I keep getting Bard and Bud mixed up."

"And?" I asked. "What does Bard think?"

Karina shrugged. "No promising leads, I guess. But he wanted me to bring this to Max." She reached into one of the cloth bags at her feet and pulled out the treasure box and the plastic container of tea. "He wanted you to run your tests and see what you can find."

"Is that what I think it is?" Audrey pointed at the box, and Max let out a *whoop*.

I hadn't gotten a close look at the small chest when Catesby began his study in the TBD kitchen. About the size of a fishing tackle box, it was constructed of dark wood that looked very old. The inscription across the top had long since worn away, but intricate scrollwork carved into all four sides had survived, as had the runes running along the bottom perimeter.

"I didn't think I was going to see this again." Max pulled a pair of rubber gloves out of their pocket.

"Didn't you already test the tea, back at the TBD?" Audrey asked. "Before everything went haywire?"

"We were just getting started," Max replied, slipping on the gloves. "I didn't get a chance to run a full analysis. If I can get an idea of what's in this tea, maybe I'll know what test to run on the last of the blood sample."

"Blood sample?" Karina asked.

My stomach clenched. Should I tell the potential poisoner that we were onto her? Should we tip our hand by letting her know we had one last chance at identifying the poison so we could save the town? And what was her angle, bringing the potential evidence right to our door? I tightened my fists and unleashed a slew of silent curses. Banich had gotten under my skin. Suspecting Karina as the mastermind who targeted the whole town—threatening to put herself out of business in the process—still didn't add up.

"It's a sample from one of the people who got sick," Audrey said, not identifying Jim as the source.

I relayed to Max what Loki had told me about the tea being a blend of thyme, wild basil, rose petals, and lemon balm. I left out the part about "intentional magick" and his tale involving mythical elves.

"I'll get on it," Max replied before carrying the tea and treasure chest down into the basement.

Simba leapt onto the couch and raced across Karina's lap, making her jump. Audrey scolded the kitten and tried to grab hold of her, but Simba scampered across the coffee table, sending Karina's mug and cookie plate onto the floor. Laughing her way out of her tears, Karina reached forward to pet Simba while the kitten paused to clean her tail.

"Thank you. All of you." Karina wiped her damp eyes. "I hoped coming here was the right thing to do, and it was."

Audrey collected the mug and plate from the floor with a promise of refills. I followed her to the kitchen while Karina played with the kitten on the couch.

"Do you think she did it?" Audrey let the empty plate clatter on the counter by the sink to cover our whispered conversation.

"She might have poisoned Colin, and Jim, and everyone else." She turned on the faucet and ran the water at full blast, ostensibly to make more tea.

"I don't know what to think," I said. "If Karina is involved, at least she's here, where we can make sure she doesn't hurt anyone else." I thought about Max in the basement. Karina said she wanted to help, but what if she'd used her sob story to get close enough to thwart Max's work instead?

"We won't leave her alone with anyone, or with anyone's food or drink." Audrey's smile was rueful and wary. "That last part's easy, with me preparing everything."

"We should order out." I glanced across the living room at Karina on the couch. She held an uncooperative Simba to her chest as she sobbed again. The more the kitten squirmed to break free, the harder Karina cried.

With my suspicions overpowered by sympathy, I crossed the floor to stand over Karina. "I need you to be straight with me about something."

Karina let go of the kitten, and Simba bolted off the couch to scamper after a sticky note that had come unglued from the wall. "Anything."

"What's the TBD been selling off the menu?" I asked.

Karina blinked. "Off the menu?"

"Don't be coy." I resisted wagging a finger in her face, but barely. "Cyndi told me Ravi and Bud had gotten some special powder or something from your shop, *unofficially*. Maybe that's what killed Ravi, and Catesby. Maybe that's what's made everybody sick."

Karina stammered a few unintelligible syllables and blew her nose into a tissue that she pulled out of her purse. "I honestly don't know what you mean. Sure, cannabis is legal now, but the hurdles we keep having to clear, the exacting standards we have to adhere to . . . You think I'd jeopardize my shop and my career to engage in some small-town illicit sales?"

It was my turn to stammer. "Well, yeah. Maybe?"

Karina rose to her feet. "Suri. I would *never.*"

"Okay. So, then, what was Cyndi talking about?" I asked. "What did she see Ravi and Bud sprinkle in their tea, just before Ravi died?"

"I have no idea. Why should I?" Karina was calm and controlled, but with color rising in her face, just like Jim when he was good and angry. "Did you consider that perhaps Cyndi lied to you?"

I nearly laughed. "And then she poisoned herself to throw Banich off her trail?" I hesitated. Like Banich said, no one was above suspicion. "Actually, that would be a clever move." I glanced at Audrey. "Would Cyndi want to kill Ravi?"

"No. No, no, no." Audrey hurried toward us from the kitchen area. "I didn't see what they added to their tea on Monday, the way Cyndi apparently did. But Ravi and Bud definitely put something in their tea. People do that sometimes, like I said the other night. I just pretend not to see it."

I made a mental note to talk to Barbara about potential health code violations the Tea Reader might be liable for, if the teahouse opened again.

"We can ask Bard!" Karina pulled her phone out of her purse. "He knows everything that goes on at the TBD. Better than I do."

"If there's something you want that you don't see on the menu . . ." I remembered Bard's words from my first visit to the Tea and Botanicals Dispensary. Was he talking about Cyndi's powder? "But didn't you say Bard is sick, too?" I asked. "And wouldn't he just back you up, regardless? You're his boss."

Karina sat on the couch and slid her phone back into her purse. "It wasn't me, Suri. You have to know that. Why would I want to hurt Jim? I thought, maybe, he could be the one." She pulled a throw pillow to her chest and started crying again.

~

EDDIE UNSTACKED a trio of pizza boxes on the breakfast bar counter while I stored a hefty takeout container of tiramisu in the refrigerator. On the phone, I'd tried to explain that this wasn't, and couldn't be, an actual date night with Audrey, Max, and Karina in the rental house with me, but Eddie jumped at the chance to bring dinner for everyone. From Salty Pie in Standish Beach, we had a Sea Witch pizza—named after Audrey and topped with kale, ricotta cheese, pickled peppers, and veggie sausage—plus a pepperoni pizza and one veggie delight. Eddie also brought dessert, along with several bottles of wine, a few cans of cane sugar soda, and two massive green salads that Audrey was trying to divide among five plates.

Simba, napping on a dining room chair, let out a squeaking purr as she stretched all four legs and reformed herself into a compact, fuzzy ball.

Standing beside Eddie, I pulled out my phone. "Let me pay you back. What's your Venmo? Or do you prefer PayPal?"

Eddie's hands closed over mine. "My treat, Suri."

I protested because there were five people in the house, not just the two of us, but Eddie refused to let me reimburse him. Privately, I was relieved. With the Tea Reader closed for the foreseeable future, I was afraid to check my bank balance. I mentally cursed Chief Deputy Banich again. The two deaths and all the poisonings weren't his fault, but he had to know he was holding the financial fortunes of multiple Grady businesses in his hands.

Eddie slid a slice of veggie pizza onto a plate festooned with salad and carried it to Karina on the couch. She was doing better, but she remained ensconced in her comfortable nest of blankets and pillows. When everything turns to chaos, the instinct to cocoon or flat-out hibernate is strong. I followed behind Eddie with my own plate and glass of wine.

Eddie set down Karina's plate and turned to study my wall of sticky notes. It looked like the work of a person on the verge of a breakdown.

"I'm trying to keep track of everything that's happened," I explained. "Everyone who's gotten sick, who came to town when, who's been acting cagey." I did not glance at Karina. I'd discretely removed the sticky note with her name on it shortly after she arrived.

"It's a good idea." Eddie's eyes traced the tenuous connections I'd found. "I saw something similar on a call this afternoon. Someone else trying to make sense of it all."

"Bard?" Karina asked. "Bard Walker? Were you there with him? Is he okay?"

Eddie's jaw tensed, and I marveled for a moment that even his face was muscular.

"I'm not allowed to say," Eddie replied. "Patient privacy and all."

"I understand." Karina took a sip from her glass, let the wine linger in her mouth, then swallowed with a nod of approval. "Not long after I arrived here at the house, Bard sent a text that he'd gotten worse and called for help. Apparently, Banich showed up the same time as the emergency crew. Took a bunch of photos of his wall and made him answer a slew of questions while the EMTs were trying to treat him." She looked at Eddie. "Last update I got said he's recovering at home. Does that sound about right?"

"No comment?" Eddie shrugged.

"It just keeps getting worse and worse." Karina took a large gulp of wine. Her temporary calm broke. "Bard's my right hand at the TBD. He knows and runs everything. And now he's sick and under suspicion? I never should have left him at home alone."

"He's okay." Eddie sat beside her on the couch and took her hand to calm her. I felt warm just watching this man who was built like a tree be so caring and gentle. "I can't really tell you more than that," he said. "I'm not his doctor, and you're not next of kin, are you?"

Karina sniffed and shook her head.

"He's at home, like he told you. He's okay." Eddie looked up at me, and I felt an electric *zing* radiate from my solar plexus. Instead of standing there and beaming at him like a fool, I left my pizza and salad on the coffee table and went to the kitchen to fix a plate for Eddie.

"Isn't he the best?" Audrey nudged me as I grabbed three slices, one from each pizza box, and stacked them on a plate of salad.

"He's pretty great." I poured a glass of wine and tried to make my cheeks relax. Karina's assistant manager was sick now, too, along with many others. Ravi and Catesby were dead and my friends were in the hospital. This was no time to be grinning. I couldn't stop the blushing, though.

Max appeared at the top of the basement stairs and headed for the pizza on instinct. They grabbed a couple of slices and turned back toward the stairs. When Audrey suggested they take a proper break to eat, Max's faraway eyes came into focus. "Occupational hazard," they muttered as they bit into a slice of veggie pizza.

"Or bad habits." Audrey pushed a fork and a plate of salad toward them.

"It's because the people here care about each other," Eddie was telling Karina as I approached the couch. "It's reassuring to see, after so much time in big cities, where it's easy to fall through the cracks." He gestured toward my notes on the wall. "People like Suri are trying to figure this out so they can help."

Eddie smiled when I handed him his plate. I was glad I'd thought to call him. He bit off half the slice of pepperoni pizza and chewed as he stared at the wall of colored paper. "Did anyone else from your shops get sick?" He looked at me and then at Karina.

"No one but Cyndi," I replied.

"It's not just Bard." Karina blew out a heavy sigh. "It's everyone on staff except me. I know how that looks. And it's no secret what Chief Deputy Banich thinks about it, too. But I swear I didn't do any of this."

As soon as Max perched on the end of the couch to enjoy the food and company, their phone chirped. "Test is done." They were up like a shot and descending the basement stairs.

Following behind, Audrey stood on the top step and called down. "Anything?"

"What are we hoping for?" Eddie wiped pizza sauce off his fingers with a paper napkin.

"That it's just old tea, I think," I replied. "Max is testing the contents of the treasure box that Ravi and Bud dug up in the hills of Rock Coast State Park."

Eddie frowned. "Is it legal to go digging in a state park?"

"I don't think so," I said. "Not that it's stopped any treasure hunters."

"Just tea!" Max called up from the basement. They jogged up the stairs and leaned on the doorjamb. "Just tea. Like you said, Suri. Basil, rose, thyme, lemon balm, and traces of fennel."

"I don't suppose your machine can measure magick?" Audrey asked, then glanced at me. "I mean, because it's Loki, right?"

"Not that I know of." Max slumped on a stool at the breakfast bar and grabbed a slice of Sea Witch pizza. "So we're not any closer."

"What can I do?" Karina asked. "How can I make this better? If it's magick, I admit I'm only a hobbyist, mostly for fun. But I can try. Should I go digging around in the woods, too, to see if Bud and Ravi brought something harmful back with them that wasn't the treasure?"

"I wouldn't advise it." Eddie leaned back and stretched out his long legs. He'd been coming off another double shift when I called, and he was probably feeling tired and frazzled himself. "We had to rescue another treasure hunter from that area a few days ago. Lady got stuck in a rocky crevice with a broken leg. Then Luke and Carrie from the squad thought it would be fun to go have a look themselves. That didn't last long, with reports of mountain lions spotted in the area. And one of the leopards got loose from the big cat sanctuary, too, though I heard they recaptured it."

"Does that happen often?" I asked, remembering the bulletin about the escaped leopard on Jim's desk. That had been only four days ago, but it felt like ages.

"Maybe?" Eddie replied. "I hope not, though."

Simba meowed from the other side of the room to announce that she was done with her nap. She leapt down from her dining chair perch and performed a few cat-yoga poses before sitting for a long bath.

Cats. Loki hadn't been asking me about a mountain lion or a leopard, had he?

"So, stay out of the woods." Karina sank back into the couch cushions. "Note taken."

"Of course, they also stumbled across a small overlook over the ocean that they said was breathtaking." He looked at me. "Might be worth a visit."

"With mountain lions?" I replied.

"Oh, yeah. Teylan Point," Audrey said. "It's not a short hike, but it's supposed to be a good spot for whale watching, or romantic interludes."

"You've been there?" I asked.

Audrey shook her head. "I've read about it. We've been wanting to go, waiting for the weather to improve. Maybe when Colin's out of the hospital." Her voice cracked on the last syllable, and she turned away.

"My boyfriend's in the hospital, too." Karina pushed her plate aside, having hardly touched her food. "Please let me help. Is there anything I can do to prove I'm not involved? Something that will actually do some good?" She looked at Max at the break-fast bar. "Max, can I assist you somehow?"

Max dropped their unfinished crust onto their salad. "Let me run that test again."

A SECOND AND third test on samples of the tea yielded the same results. Even if Max's analysis had found anything suspicious, the old tea had been sealed in a plastic container. It was doubtful the tea cache could have contaminated the TBD edibles.

"This tea couldn't have hurt anyone beyond maybe a stom-achache." Max had shut down their equipment for the night. They were finally picking at their salad from dinner. "Not that Chief Deputy Banich will take the word of one of his suspects on the matter. And we don't have a sample of the mystery powder to test."

Eddie had left only moments before, after giving me a quick peck on the cheek in full view of everyone. Karina was buzzing about the living room in a sudden fit of cheer.

"Suri, I'm just so glad you have someone!" Karina practically sang as she fluffed the throw pillows on the couch. Simba the kitten raced circles around her ankles. Karina nearly tripped over the kitten, then reached down to give Simba chin scritches. "Jim and I were really worried about you."

"Hmm," was the only reply I could muster. She'd arrived in Grady barely six weeks earlier, and I had started sort-of seeing Eddie before she came to town. It wasn't like she and Jim had been sitting together on their front porch swing watching me struggle to find connection and meaning in my life.

Also, despite Karina's tears and protestations, I wasn't fully convinced that she wasn't involved, somehow, in the poisonings in town and Ravi's death. And in what had happened to Professor Catesby.

I mentally smacked myself. I'd nearly forgotten about the visiting academic, even as his protégé sat in the same room with me. The sticky note bearing Catesby's name had given up its glue and fallen to the floor. The absence of his noisy arrogance was a relief, but it had been hours since he'd departed to learn more about the treasure. It had been hours since I'd last seen Trey, too. And didn't we now have the treasure box here with us? So where were the ghosts?

"We forgot the tiramisu!" Audrey stood in front of the open refrigerator. "With all the talk of mountain lions and treasure hunts, we forgot about dessert." She glanced my way. "Should we call Eddie to come back? It feels wrong to enjoy this without him."

"I think we're okay without him for now." I stepped close and lowered my voice. "I haven't seen Trey since this morning. Or Catesby."

"You think something's wrong?" Audrey whispered back. "This feels bad."

"I'm happy to have some girl time," Karina announced brightly, then caught herself. "Even under the unhappy circumstances." She glanced at Max, who'd given up on their salad and was busy alternating between jotting in a notebook and typing on the laptop they'd carried upstairs. Karina shrugged and turned to Audrey. "Maybe we can have some fun in the kitchen? I've heard that you like to experiment. I have a couple of recipes I've always wanted to try, and I even brought supplies."

Karina nudged the cloth grocery bags she'd brought in with her, lined up on the floor against the breakfast bar.

"I think I need to lie down," I said. The headache wasn't bad, but it was persistent, pressing into my skull and making me feel heavier with each passing minute. Had the pain gone away while Eddie was present? More likely, Eddie was an affable distraction.

Audrey gave me a sympathetic look. "It's been a long day for all of us."

"I thought we could start with some candies? Have you ever made candy before, Audrey? It's simply heaven." Oblivious to the fading energy in the room, Karina unpacked her grocery bags onto the breakfast bar while Audrey loaded dinner plates into the dishwasher. Karina's supplies included boxes of cornstarch and jars of food coloring, alongside sacks of multiple types of sugar. The rental house kitchen was beginning to look like my cottage when Audrey came to visit, except this time Karina was the one in charge.

"I'll probably head to bed, too." Max closed their laptop. "I don't think there's anything more I can do tonight, and I'd just be in the way."

"Nonsense!" Karina gave a brief grunt as she lifted a one-gallon clear plastic jug, not quite half-full of oozy, amber-colored liquid, onto the counter. "We can teach you. It'll be fun! Promise."

Using a bar stool as a ladder, Simba climbed onto the breakfast bar. The kitten knocked a box of cornstarch to the floor as she slid across the marble before leaping into the air to land on Max's shoulder.

"Claws!" Max laughed, peeling Simba off their sweater and settling the kitten on the floor before they got up to place the corn starch back on the counter. Then Max groaned and backed away. They pointed at the container of amber liquid. "Where did you get that?"

Taking no notice of Max's wide eyes, Karina laughed and rested her hand on the jug's lid. "Right? Quite the find. When we ran out of sugar at the shop and even the grocery shelves were bare, I found this in the TBD kitchen. Pure honey! And extra sweet, too. It's been a lifesaver at the shop, and in my home kitchen."

Max rotated the jug around to reveal a thick strip of yellow tape with three letters scrawled in black ink: a large X followed by a smaller S and H. "You've been baking with this? And feeding it to people?"

"Of course!" Karina organized her supplies on the marble counter. "Now, I didn't consume any myself, of course. Have to maintain my girlish figure, you know." Her laugh sounded like she expected the rest of us to join in.

"'XSH?'" I asked, pointing at the yellow tape label.

"Extra Sweet Honey!" Karina exclaimed.

"No, no, no." Max sank into their seat and dug their hands into their hair. "This is not happening. This can't be happening. Half of it's already gone."

"What's wrong?" Not sure if they wanted to be touched, I rested a hand on Max's shoulder and felt their body shaking under my palm.

"Bees!" Max laughed nervously and looked up at Audrey. "You were right. You were right from the start."

"I'm not following," Karina said. "Is this some environmental thing about the dwindling population of pollinators? Because I swear the TBD is conscientious in sourcing many of our ingredients when we can. It's something I'm very strict about."

"But you found that in the TBD kitchen?" Max pointed a trembling finger at the honey again, as though gesturing toward one of the horsemen of the apocalypse.

"Well, yes," Karina replied, acting cagey. "It's February, and I got impatient waiting for the farmers markets to open so I could buy locally. I thought the honey had just appeared on the shelf, you know, like the magick here everyone talks about? But the professor said I should use as much as I wanted. To consider it a hostess present."

"It's the honey, isn't it?" I asked. "Not the mystery powder. You think that honey is the source of the poison." But how could Max know that? And where had the massive jug originated?

"I don't understand," Karina said. "What's wrong? It's just Professor Catesby's honey. It's not like he's using it."

"Whatever you do, don't touch it. Don't even open it! Get it out of the kitchen." Max grabbed their laptop and notebook and headed toward the basement stairs. "I really hope I'm wrong, but I know what last test to run on Jim's blood."

CHAPTER THIRTEEN

I awoke to the sound of light snoring and found Simba the kitten asleep on the pillow next to my head. It was Sunday morning—probably late morning, given the brightness of the sky outside the glass-block window. I'd finally gotten some solid sleep, curled up beneath a heavy quilt on top of Catesby's bed. I'd dreamt of multi-colored sticky notes pouring out of teacups and teapots in the Tea Reader, with rivers of paper flowing across the floor and up the walls, until the smudgy letters "KILLER" in the window were obscured and everyone and everything in the teahouse was engulfed.

I lay on my back and looked up at the ceiling. I would have expected a visit from the professor himself, though I'd left his things untouched. At the very least, Catesby should have raised strenuous objection to someone violating his private space.

But the ghost of the condescending academic remained absent. As did Trey. The object of their quest, the treasure box, sat on a worktable in the rental house basement, and there'd been no sign of the ghosts who'd sought it.

Max had promised to wake me if their tests turned up anything. In this case, I wasn't sure if no news was good news.

I splashed cool water on my face in the master bathroom. The space was light and airy in shades of seafoam and cream, and so much more spacious than the bathroom in my cottage. The towels were thick and thirsty, too. But I missed home. I pulled on the change of clothes I'd grabbed at the cottage and headed downstairs with the kitten trailing behind me.

The kitchen was a controlled disaster after Karina and Audrey's candy-making experiments. They'd used every ingredient but the mystery jar of honey. A half-dozen bowls sat lined up on the counter, full of hardened beans of sugar in varying shades of pink and red.

Simba padded across the floor toward Audrey, who was conked out on the couch, which meant Karina had taken the spare bedroom. While I considered a breakfast of leftover tiramisu, Max sat at the dining room table, staring at their laptop screen and looking haggard and defeated. Their dark hair stood up in short tangles, and the cuffs of their wide-legged jeans were damp.

"Max, did you get any sleep?" I asked. "Did you even go to bed?"

"I went out on the beach. I couldn't sit around, just waiting," Max replied, their voice soft as they stared ahead into space. "I ran the test. Can you call the doctors in Seaside? They'll listen to you. Tell them you know what the poison is. They should be able to treat it. Tell Eddie, too, so he can get the word out to the other people in Grady and Standish Beach."

"You found the source?" I nearly laughed. After so long, and with so many people ill, it sounded like we might have an answer. No one else had to get sick, or worse. I pulled out my phone to call the hospital. "Max, you're a genius! What is it? How did you know?"

"Oleander poisoning. Not common, but treatable," Max said. "And you'll also want to call Chief Deputy Banich. He'll want to come arrest me."

"Max?" I asked as I waited for Seaside Hospital to answer. "What are you talking about?" I thought about Catesby's ill-treatment of Max, and how Max still jumped to their mentor's defense. "Are you covering for the professor or something?" I glanced at the jug of honey, which Catesby had apparently given Karina permission to use. With a clearer head this morning, I saw Max was protecting the professor even now. "He's dead. You don't have to do this."

"Just do it," they said. "I'll explain everything the best I can. But the most important thing is to get the right treatment to the people who are sick."

"What?" Audrey sat up from a dead sleep on the couch. Her curly hair stuck out every which way, and she clutched Simba to her chest. "Did I dream you found a cure, or is it real?"

"Not a dream," Max replied. They looked hollow, like a condemned prisoner accepting the gallows. "I didn't isolate an antidote, but I found the poison. And the culprit."

I tried to follow the conversation between Max and Audrey while I relayed the pertinent information to the doctor overseeing Jim's and Colin's care. "Oleander poisoning. Max Turner of Cascade State University confirmed it just this morning." On the other end of the phone, the doctor let out an exclamation of surprise and relief. I glanced at Max. "I don't think they can talk to you right now," I said into the phone. The doctor promised to email the details for a home remedy to me, to Banich, and to the Coastal Fire and Rescue squad for the benefit of the people who'd fallen ill in Grady and Seaside—something to ease their symptoms while prescriptions were being filled.

By the time I got off the phone, Max was sitting on the floor with their knees pulled into their chest.

"But I don't understand! That doesn't make any sense!" Audrey stood over Max. Simba kept crying and climbing up her pant leg, begging for breakfast. "How could you have poisoned Colin? *Why* would you? You wouldn't have had any reason, and no opportunity. You're confused. Maybe you just need some sleep."

"None of this was supposed to happen," Max muttered. "This shouldn't have happened."

Karina shuffled down the stairs. Even with a serious case of bedhead and wearing yesterday's mascara, she looked like something out of a fashion magazine. Had she put on lip gloss before getting out of bed? "What's all the shouting about?"

"What were you thinking?" Max looked up at Karina with red-rimmed eyes. "You shouldn't have used that honey. You said you're so conscientious about your ingredients, but you didn't even know where that container came from. I don't know how it even got here. It's supposed to be back in the lab in Seattle."

"I told you, the professor himself said I could use it when we ran out of sugar in the TBD kitchen." Karina marched toward the coffeepot in the kitchen. "And he said I shouldn't tell you about it. From your reaction, I can see why." She cursed when she found yesterday's cold coffee in the pot and rummaged through the cupboards, looking for fresh grounds. "He had to sneak it out of his suitcase and onto the shelves when he sent you to the Moroni Grocery for more pepto. He said you're so miserly and controlling you wouldn't even allow a man of his stature and accomplishments to enjoy a little treat now and again."

That certainly sounded like something the late professor would say. I recalled Max's earlier comment about Catesby taking charge of his own bags instead of having Max act as his porter, on top of everything else. "Are you saying everyone got poisoned by a lab experiment?" I asked. "Was this part of Catesby's research? Are you saying Catesby did all this, deliberately?"

Was that pompous airbag truly so desperate for attention that he'd create a poisoning epidemic in Naghatune Bay, so he could swoop in to play the savior—and get to make a heroic appearance on *Proof TV*? Had he miscalculated and ended up a victim of his own scheme, or was his death part of his plan to cement the enduring legacy he seemed so concerned about?

"Call Chief Deputy Banich." Max nodded toward the phone in my hand. "Please, just do it. He needs to hear what I have to say."

I placed the call.

～

BY THE TIME Banich and one of his underlings arrived at the rental house, Audrey and Karina were at work again in the kitchen. Based on Max's information about oleander poisoning, Audrey formulated an herbal-plus-magick healing remedy to accompany the antidote that was already on the way from Seaside, to be administered locally by Eddie and his co-workers at Coastal Fire and Rescue.

"It's to help people relax and allow the healing to begin in their bodies and minds," Audrey explained to an incredulous Banich as he gazed down at a batch of pink-colored jelly beans that had been set out on the breakfast bar counter to harden. "An illness like this is a trauma. It affects every part of a person."

"Pink for Valentine's Day tomorrow," Karina answered Banich's unasked question while she spooned gooey syrup into silicone molds. "Along with Audrey's herbs, there's a little CBD tincture to encourage rest and relaxation. I wanted to include just a tiny bit of THC, too, but *someone* wouldn't hear of it."

"We're not having this argument again." Audrey added water, gelatin, and agave nectar to a large saucepan to begin a new batch of syrup on the stovetop.

"I suppose I should know better than to ask if you have a commercial license for this kitchen," Banich said.

"Please don't," Audrey replied as Karina excused herself to run upstairs. "This is a one-time thing."

"I think I've got enough on my plate as it is." Banich stepped away from the kitchen and claimed an empty chair facing Max at the dining table. The treasure box and the gallon jug of tainted honey sat at the far end.

I'd tried to get Max to eat something or change out of yesterday's clothes before Banich arrived, but they insisted they didn't deserve even basic comforts. Max did accept a glass of water, to hold on to if not to drink. Simba sat beneath Max's chair, batting at their shoelaces.

The ghost of Thomas Catesby was still nowhere to be found —probably a good thing for him, because I was ready to read him the riot act about the tainted honey, and about how poor Max was on the verge of throwing their life away to save their mentor's reputation.

Banich set his phone on the table and turned on the audio recorder. "Okay, Max Turner. Tell me where the poisoned honey came from."

"The Cascade State lab," Max replied. "That's where I last saw it. My roommate is pursuing research in toxic flowers, trying to make lilies that won't poison cats."

"Why would your roommate make toxic honey?" I asked, hovering over Banich's shoulder. "And then just leave it sitting around unsecured?"

Banich gave me an exasperated look. "Ms. Mudge, I'm allowing you to be present during this interview as a professional courtesy to Deputy Sheriff Vandenhauter. If you cannot restrain yourself from interfering, I will invite you to leave. In fact, none of you should be in the room right now."

"Oh, please, Chris." I crossed my arms and blew a strand of hair out of my face. "We're way past those formalities by now." I pulled up a chair.

Banich's young assistant deputy—Andy Davis, according to his name tag—raised his eyebrows at his boss. Banich sighed and turned back to Max. "What she said. How about it?"

"Well, there's a difference between a toxin and a poison," Max replied. "Some might call it an academic distinction, as the terms are used interchangeably in some fields. For instance, it could be more accurate to describe the honey as poisonous."

Banich's mouth flattened into a straight line. "I didn't come here for a vocabulary lesson."

"But I'm answering your questions," Max said. "My roommate didn't set out to make the honey, not on purpose. It came from her apiary, after her bees got into a one-off experiment she ran trying to make oleander non-toxic. But the reverse happened."

"The honey was extra poisonous," I said.

"Do you mind?" Banich asked in a huff.

"She labeled it with her initials." Max gestured toward the jug's yellow tape label. "SH, for Sarah Hopkins. Plus the big X to indicate that it wasn't to be used. I said I'd dispose of it for her."

"So, not XSH for 'extra sweet honey.'" I looked around for Karina, but she was still upstairs.

"My roommate doesn't know anything about what I've done," Max pleaded. "She's not even in the country right now. Please don't drag her into this."

"You know we're going to have to talk to her anyway," Banich replied. "So you didn't dispose of the honey, like she asked."

Tears filled Max's eyes. "I didn't. It was a brainless move of desperation. No one was supposed to get hurt! Not seriously. I doled it out in small amounts. Just enough to make him tired, or a little sick, so he'd slow down and take a break, so I could focus on my own work."

"Just enough to make who feel sick?" Banich asked. Simba dashed from under Max's chair to attack the hem of Banich's trousers. The chief deputy groaned and pushed the kitten away. Simba attacked again.

"Davis?" Banich handed the kitten over to his assistant, who looked uncertain about handling the squirming ball of fur.

"Catesby," I said. "The professor had a sweet tooth, and you carried that little squeeze bottle of honey for his tea and muffins."

Max's breath hitched as they nodded. "He thought it was a special honey my roommate had concocted, because that's what I told him. But it was laced with oleander."

"You deliberately poisoned Professor Thomas Catesby," Banich said. Max didn't refute the accusation.

"But why, Max?" I asked. "Are you sure you're not covering for the professor? He's gone. You don't have to take the fall for him."

"He didn't do this, Suri. I did. And you know why!" Max cried. "He had me doing everything for him. Grading student papers. Proofreading his papers, even writing them, to get published under his name. No mention of Max Turner. Doing his reading and research. He ran me ragged. There was no time for my work. I'm running out of grant funding and time and scholarship money to complete my dissertation. The professor *knew* that. He kept me under his thumb. Said I was too good to let go, or some more eloquent version of the same."

After an insistent yowl from Simba, Assistant Deputy Davis set the kitten on the floor. She dashed away to play hide and seek with herself behind a curtain.

"He took your grant money for your gas chromatograph mass spectrometer," I said, silently congratulating myself for putting all the right syllables in the correct order while my brain was reeling from Max's cogent confession. "And he spent it on his own wants and needs."

"Yes," came Max's soft reply. "He always wanted to put me in my place. Even here in the rental house, with plenty of room for both of us, he made me sleep down in the basement mudroom with the washer and dryer, and the inflatable surf mats, beach toys, lawn furniture, and yard equipment."

"Need I remind you there is a perfectly comfortable cot in

that space?" The ghost of Professor Thomas Catesby appeared beside me, facing Max. "With plumbing?"

At the other end of the table, Andy Davis held the treasure box in his hands, the lid open. Unbeknownst to Davis, Ravi King and Trey stood on either side of him. A fourth specter—a formless green cloud of mist—lingered nearby.

I gasped aloud, which Max and Banich took for outrage over Max's sleeping arrangements.

"I would describe it as more of a recreation room than a 'mudroom.'" Catesby continued. "It is wired for electricity, and you said the space heater kept the room feeling quite snug."

"But it was the best place to set up the GC/MS anyway," Max added.

Ten seconds before, there hadn't been a ghost in sight. Now there were three of them. Four, counting the weird swamp gas. Trey seemed to read my confusion as I looked from the ghosts to the box in the assistant deputy's hands.

"That box is some kind of ghost trap," Trey told me, unheard by every other living soul.

A chest to hold the souls of Loki's lost children. I looked at Trey and raised my eyebrows.

"The professor got sucked in when he was looking over Max's shoulder, and I fell in after him," Trey replied. "Ravi was already stuck inside. Along with whatever that green thing is," he gestured behind himself and shivered.

I angled my body to address both Max and Catesby, though no one else could see the ghosts. "Catesby shouldn't have treated you that way, is my point. You were in an impossible situation, Max. It sounds like Catesby more or less had absolute power over you. But to poison him? I'm just so disappointed, Max." I couldn't help my parental tone.

Max hunched their shoulders forward, shaking as they crossed their arms tight. "I couldn't see any other way. Maybe it was temporary insanity?" They looked up with weak hope, but

Banich's expression was as stern as ever. "You don't understand what it's like to be running on fumes—physically, financially, and mentally. And knowing that any complaint could hurt my scholarship or even get me blacklisted, because who crosses the Great Professor Catesby?"

"Now, that is a highly exaggerated assertion," Catesby protested to an audience who couldn't hear him. "I am not a tyrant."

"He sounds tyrannical," Banich said. My gaze went immediately to the chief deputy's face, but I saw no sign that he could either see or hear Catesby.

"I would like to second that characterization," Trey quipped. "I'm an expert on the matter, having been trapped in an old box with Professor Crankypants."

"Suri?" The ghost of Ravi King stood beside Assistant Deputy Davis, looking bewildered. "This isn't the teahouse, is it? Or did you redecorate?"

The spectral green blob formed into a vaguely human-looking face and gave me a grin that was both unnatural and unnerving. Before I could respond, it shifted into a silent, sideway cyclone and disappeared through the window glass.

Trey was visibly shaken.

"Ah." I tried to figure out what, if anything, I could say in the presence of Banich and his assistant. Audrey and Max knew about my mediumship, and Karina might have heard rumors around town. But I was already on thin ice with Banich, and I didn't think he'd take kindly to what he'd likely chalk up as "mumbo jumbo."

Banich followed my gaze to the other end of the table, where Davis closed the box's lid. "That brings me to another matter, which is just how you came to be in possession of that box?"

The temptation was strong to mimic Loki and make a sardonic comment, questioning the philosophical nature of physical possessions, but I held my tongue. Banich glared at his assistant, then at me, next at Max. Everyone in the room got a turn, and Banich wasn't stingy in spreading his vexation around.

"That is an important piece of evidence." Banich jabbed a finger in the direction of the treasure box. "A piece of evidence, I might add, that we've been looking for high and low. And you had it the whole time."

"Absolutely not," I replied, though my words were lost beneath Banich's urgent order to his assistant to stop messing with the artifact.

Banich blew a frustrated sigh through his teeth. "I should write you all up for interfering with an official investigation."

Audrey slapped a wooden spoon on the breakfast bar linoleum. "You like doing that, don't you? Writing people up. It's like your gut reaction, instead of taking a minute to find out the truth."

Banich looked about as stunned as I felt. Maybe it was the strain finally catching up with her, or the heat of the stove, but Audrey had more color in her cheeks than I'd seen all week.

"Like writing up Jim and Colin for consuming cannabis edibles, which they didn't." Audrey waved the spoon in exasperation. "And even if they did, it's *legal*."

"Not if they're on duty," Banich countered. "Or off-duty, if there are drug tests."

"You and I both know they did no such thing." Karina reached the bottom of the stairs. In a fresh set of clothes, she was neatly groomed, with buffed nails and shining hair locked into place. Her perfume lightened the air, and I saw Banich's shoulders relax at her approach. Maybe her signature scent had special pheromones blended in.

"I did take baked goods to the station for Deputy Sheriff James Robert Vandenhauter and Assistant Deputy Colin Elijah Jung to enjoy." Karina lingered by the breakfast bar, where she surveyed the fruit bowl nestled between containers of cooling jelly beans. Audrey put down her spoon. "But those muffins and whatnot came straight from my home kitchen, not my shop." Karina picked up a banana and pulled the peel away in long, slow strips. "There wasn't anything questionable about or in them, other than a bit of wishful thinking. And the unfortunate honey."

Karina took a bite of the banana, and Banich's cheeks went red. He stammered something about procedure and needing to avoid even the appearance of impropriety.

"So that's how the deputy sheriff and his assistant got sick," Max interrupted. "But I never gave the professor enough of the honey to truly hurt him. I swear it. I was extremely careful with it."

"Ah, yes, about that." Catesby offered a sheepish smile only I could see. "It's entirely possible that was my fault. It was such delicious honey, you see."

"Max, did Catesby know where you kept the honey supply?" I asked. "Other than the squeeze bottle you carried in your bag?"

"It was locked up in the lab, with a warning label on the cabinet." Realization dawned on Max's face. "But the professor sometimes borrowed my keys when he'd misplaced his own and locked himself out of his office."

"That happened once," Catesby protested. "Twice at most. But my young protégé is correct. I effectively purloined young Max's honey supply for the trip to Grady. Max was always so stingy with it, though now I understand why. The stuff has an exquisite taste, and I didn't want to be forced to go without. I had little idea how long we would be gone from campus." He paused. "I didn't realize it would be a permanent departure."

"Always so dramatic." Trey rolled his eyes at Catesby, then leaned down to waggle his ghostly fingers for Simba's entertainment. "You died, dude. Get over it."

"I guess it's like Karina said." Max slumped in their seat. "The professor must have secreted the full jar out of the lab and brought it here to satisfy his sweet tooth."

"Oh, you don't even know." Karina gesticulated with her half-eaten banana, the peel flopping about. "Every time you stepped out of sight, he slathered more of that stuff on his toast, muffins, whatever."

"So he hid it in that big suitcase of his. I swear, I just wanted him to feel sick enough to back off," Max said. "So I could try to catch up on my own research. But even with everything he did, none of that justifies murder."

"Assuming the coroner's report lines up with oleander poison, and that the other details of your story can be confirmed, manslaughter is the more likely charge," Banich said. "But I need to know what happened to the squeeze bottle of honey. Ms. Mudge said you kept it in your satchel?"

Max looked at the floor. "I got rid of it. When Suri was visiting Jim in the hospital, I slipped it into medical waste. I didn't want anyone to accidentally use it."

I could have kicked myself. I should have noticed the honey bottle's absence after we returned from Seaside, when Max emptied their bag onto the dining table to offer me a stack of sticky notes. "Max, how did it never occur to you that the oleander honey killed Catesby and made everyone sick?" I asked, too bewildered to give into anger. "Why didn't you say something sooner? Maybe people still would have gotten sick, but we could have helped them right away."

"How could I have known?" Max started to cry again. "I thought I had the only supply in that squeeze bottle. And I controlled it. But that's why I kept running so many tests, I guess. I just didn't want it to be possible. I can't believe it all went so wrong. I can't believe I did this. I'm so very sorry."

"I'm not unsympathetic to your plight, young person." Banich looked genuinely touched by Max's remorse. "I'll ask the Duniway County DA to take into account your efforts to identify the poison for the benefit of the community, even if it pointed the finger at you in the process. And that you turned yourself in."

"Thank you," Max, Catesby, and I murmured in unison.

Banich read Max their rights while Catesby stood by and tried to argue Max's innocence to law officers who couldn't hear him. Trey conveyed as much to Catesby, then told the professor to shove it—more precisely, Trey instructed Catesby in the fine art of "blowing his yammering condescension out [his] lower sphincter." I'm not sure what went on between them while they were trapped in the treasure box, but my guess was they were not now afterlife best buddies.

Max instructed Assistant Deputy Davis in the safe packing and transport of their notes and equipment, along with the treasure box and the jug of tainted honey. I hoped such diligent cooperation would count in Max's favor, too.

"So that's it, then?" Audrey asked. "Colin will be okay? And no one else will get sick?"

"That about wraps up the mystery poisonings, yes," Banich replied. But there was still an open murder case to solve, and Banich's grim expression let me know he hadn't forgotten.

"Suri?" The ghost of Ravi King hovered by the dining table. "I don't think I had any of the honey."

CHAPTER FOURTEEN

Monday morning. Valentine's Day.

I awoke with a killer headache. Not a migraine, but an intense tension headache that gripped my neck and shoulders and made me feel like I was wearing a tight elastic band across my forehead.

Audrey would spend the day with Colin, who had been discharged from the hospital and was recuperating at home, thank goodness. She'd baked a few plain breads and other easily digestible goodies and made batches of soup that his stomach could tolerate as he healed. I'd overheard her on the phone with him making plans to catch up on streaming sci-fi movies in between long naps.

I assumed Karina was similarly tending to Jim, though maybe without the sci-fi. At least with the poison identified and appropriate treatment administered, Jim's prognosis was excellent. He was out of danger.

The people of Grady were also on the mend, but whoever killed Ravi King was still unknown and at large. Remembering those traced letters in the foggy teahouse window made me shudder. But Ravi's ghost had no leads for me to follow. He was confused and upset, and unable to focus. Finding his murderer was Chris Banich's job, anyway.

I didn't know what, if anything, I could do to help Max.

The witch bottle in my wardrobe remained a mystery, but I was back in my cottage and the ghost of Thomas Catesby was making himself scarce. This time, I welcomed Trey's oversight. Knowing I wasn't completely alone, even when I couldn't see him, was a comfort. My sleep Sunday night was deep and dreamless.

I greeted Monday morning in rumpled pajamas and with even more rumpled hair. Valentine's or not, it was another cold, gray day at the coast. Light rain tapped against the windows and roof.

I puttered around my kitchen, closing cupboard doors with too much force, while I made myself a dry cereal breakfast and waited for the microwave to heat water for my tea. I was startled by a light rapping on my ocean-front window.

Eddie stood on the other side of the glass. Outfitted head to foot in winter gear, he looked ready to embark on a week-long wilderness adventure. His smile was bright and cheerful—the complete opposite of the weather—and I felt lighter at the sight of him.

"Get dressed," he said as I opened the door and ushered him inside. "We're going for a hike."

I pulled my robe tight against the cold air and closed the door. I told him he had to be kidding. He reminded me of the overlook his buddies at Coastal Fire and Rescue had spotted in Rock Coast State Park, and suggested that getting some fresh air into my lungs would be a healthy distraction from the horrible week I'd had.

"Plus, I have the day off, and the Tea Reader is still closed, right?" he added.

"Way to rub it in." I padded around the breakfast bar to retrieve my mug from the microwave. "You want some tea?"

"Suri, you can't sit inside all day and ruminate," he said.

"Watch me," I replied, but my crankiness was fast turning into flirting.

"If you stay put, you run the risk of getting dragged into more drama," he said. "Come out with me. Let's have some easy, active fun."

Eddie was smiling at me again, and my resistance was an ice cube left out in the sunshine. Against my better judgment, I got dressed. I poured my tea into an insulated thermos and tied the laces of the hiking boots I'd gotten from Loki.

"IT SHOULDN'T BE TOO MUCH FARTHER," Eddie said to reassure me. I hadn't been complaining, though I probably groaned a couple of times as we trudged uphill through occasional mud bogs and around big rocks. "Maybe another mile to the overlook."

It was a cool morning, not enough to worry about ice on the rocks we scrambled over, but sufficiently cold to freeze our breath on the air. And, yes, it was also raining, but it was a light rain that pattered on the evergreen fronds high overhead and created a pleasant mist nearer the ground.

Here I was, hiking in the woods, voluntarily, in winter. Jim wouldn't have believed it. I scarcely believed it myself, but I was having fun.

We hiked steadily upward, taking a few sharp switchbacks and following the meandering and damp pine-needle covered trail. I kept pace with Eddie, but I could tell from his gait that he was moving slower to accommodate me and allow for conversation.

"Thanks for getting me out," I said for at least the third time. "I didn't know how much I needed this. Thanks for the push." It felt good to draw brisk, fresh air into my lungs. It was invigorating to feel my heart pound in my chest and know it wasn't because I was having a panic attack.

Eddie squeezed my arm. "Spending time in the woods is always a good idea."

We hiked a few more minutes in active, companionable silence. I reached beyond the sound of my huffing and puffing and listened for birdsong and croaking frogs. Even in winter, the forest was alive. All I had to do was notice.

"There's something I've wanted to ask you about," Eddie said. "And you can tell me to go to hell, if it's none of my business."

"Now I'm intrigued," I replied, keeping my tone light.

"I'd like to know more about your history with Jim Vandenhauter."

I made an effort to keep my pace steady. "What do you want to know?"

"I know you used to date, but there's more to it, right? A lot more."

I took a deep breath. Eddie stopped walking. "Do you want to sit down?" he asked. "Take a break?"

"No, I want to keep moving." I swallowed hard, but the lump in my throat wasn't as stubborn as expected. The stirring in my chest wasn't the usual tightness of stress or anxiety, either. Maybe my body was responding to the rich, oxygenated air of the forest, or maybe it was the company.

Eddie fell into step beside me.

"It was a long time ago now," I began. "Jim and I were together in Oregon City, back when he was a new trainee and I was working at the local library. It was around that time that I . . ." I took another breath. "When I started seeing ghosts."

"So that wasn't something that began when you were a child?"

"No. And maybe I'd be better at it or more comfortable if I'd always been this way," I said. "For me, it happened in my twenties. It was kind of abrupt, from what I remember." I paused. "But that's not what you're asking."

Eddie remained quiet as we continued along the trail. I listened to the birds again and to something scurrying, unseen, in the shadows of the forest.

"I'd gotten a warning," I said. "From a former librarian."

"From a librarian who had died."

"Mmm." A cold drop of rain fell on the back of my neck, found the gap between my skin and my coat, and ran down my spine. It was not unlike the sensation I'd felt when the ghost of Marjorie Greer appeared to me after closing at the library, hovering by the reference shelves of encyclopedias and atlases.

"I hadn't met her in life," I said, but I'd recognized her from the portrait hanging in the library's public conference room. She'd been the branch's head librarian in the 1970s and 1980s. When I saw her, she wore the same gray blouse, its modest ruffle complementing her silver bob and setting off the short strand of pearls around her neck.

"I tried to ignore her," I continued. "I assumed I was hallucinating, or that I wasn't getting enough sleep. But she kept showing up, three nights in a row, with the same message, growing more urgent with each repetition."

"She was trying to help," Eddie said.

"She warned me about a troubled patron who was planning an attack. Pete Hanney. He'd been banned from the branch for harassing one of the younger library aides." I ducked under a low branch that Eddie held up for me. "I didn't know what to do. Was I seeing things? Should I believe her? Who would believe me?"

"Jim did," Eddie said.

"Jim did."

We walked on, Eddie waiting for the rest of the story while I figured out how to tell it.

"He tried to tell his boss, the chief in Oregon City," I said.

"But Jim was the new guy, and it must have sounded like a crazy story. They just laughed at him, though one detective looked into it and said the patron wasn't a threat. But you know Jim."

"I have an idea," Eddie said.

"He was with me in the library when it happened." I didn't remember what I'd had for breakfast that day, or what I was wearing. Was it sunny or gray outside? I couldn't tell you. But those twenty-two minutes in the library branch were seared into my brain.

"It was his day off, too," I continued. "But he wanted to be sure I was safe, and that everyone in the library was safe. It was a normal day, and I worried I'd gotten Jim and myself worked up over nothing. Then Hanney came in with a semi-automatic weapon." I came to an abrupt stop on the trail. I closed my eyes and tilted my face upward so I could feel the rain on my skin. So I could be reminded of where I was, and where and when I wasn't.

Eddie rested a hand on my shoulder, grounding me. "I don't want to upset you. You can tell me another time."

I opened my eyes. "It's okay. You deserve to know." I continued forward, stooping beneath a tree limb that hung over the narrowing trail. Eddie had to crouch to clear it. "The second Hanney pulled out his gun, Jim shot him in the arm, but it wasn't enough. Hanney shot seven people before Jim could hit him again, in the neck."

I listened to the rain and the birds instead of the echoing gunfire and terrified screams in my memory. On a long inhale, I breathed in clean air instead of the sulphur smell of gunpowder. I took off my left glove and trailed my bare fingers over the damp bark of the tree trunks we passed.

"He shot Jim, too. Five people died." I'd known them all on sight. Alice Crabtree and her toddler son, Alex, arriving early for story time. Teenager Mike Lopez, who was checking out four recent graphic novels. Noreen Williams, returning a massive stack of large print mystery novels. And Alta Murray, the librarian who'd had Hanney banned from the branch. "Two others, including the young woman Hanney had harassed, ended up in the hospital, but they survived. And then Jim was in critical care for weeks. There was an infection."

Eddie stepped ahead of me and lifted another low branch so I could pass. "So you feel responsible for him. Or guilty about what happened."

"More or less," I said. "Less now, I think. There's more to it. But." I shrugged.

"It's okay. I think I understand." Eddie stretched his long arms over his head and heaved a hearty sigh. "I want to say a few things. First, if you hadn't listened to the ghost . . . Yes, maybe Jim wouldn't have gotten hurt, but so many more people could have died, including you. Both you and Jim did the right thing. If no one told you that before, I'm telling you now."

"Okay." I hoped the rain on my face disguised the fact that I was trying not to cry.

"And next . . . You know, Suri, I think this thing between you and me could go somewhere real. I think you think so, too. And I think my main flaw, in your eyes, is that I'm not Jim."

He let his words hang in the air. I sucked in a slow breath. I didn't know how to respond. He wasn't wrong, but I didn't want to admit that out loud.

"Of course," he continued, "I also think one of my primary positive attributes, for you, is that I'm not Jim."

"Eddie." I stopped, and he turned to face me. I laughed. "I think you're absolutely right."

There, in the gloomy forest on a cold, rainy February morning, Eddie Cortés gave me a smile that outshone the brightest sun.

That's when we heard the screaming.

∿

WE RACED BACK DOWN to the trail, looking for a lesser-used fork we'd passed earlier. Eddie was on his phone, trying to get more information from the Coastal Fire and Rescue dispatcher. Whoever was in trouble had called emergency services, but Eddie and I were closer.

"How far off the trail did the caller say he was?" Eddie held the phone in front of him as we dodged wet branches and scrambled over slick rocks. "We should be able to get to him before the rescue crew, and at least assess the situation."

"Here's the turn!" I shouted as I slid off a slippery rock and hit the ground. The screaming coming from deeper in the woods was a fair indication we were getting closer.

We took the fork. The trail was easy to lose as we pushed through the overgrowth of ferns, trees, and tall prickly weeds. The ground underfoot was uneven, with plenty of stones and roots to trip over.

"They're about twenty minutes out from your location," the dispatcher said on speakerphone. It sounded like Luke, one of the few of Eddie's co-workers I'd met. "Maybe longer, given the terrain. Be advised of wildlife on the scene."

"Wildlife?" I asked Eddie just before a wet evergreen frond smacked me in the face. I wiped what I hoped was mud off my cheek. "Like squirrels or a raccoon?"

"More like a mountain lion." Eddie helped me over a fallen tree trunk. "I'd send you back to the car, but I don't want you out here by yourself."

"It's okay. I want to help." I was slowing him down, and the screaming was getting louder and more frantic. "Go on ahead. I'll catch up."

Eddie gave me a hard look of concern, then nodded and pushed forward. I narrowly avoided another wet frond slap to the face.

"Suri!" a voice exclaimed beside me. Startled, I tumbled into a thorny bramble of dead blackberry. "Suri! Bud's in trouble! You have to help!"

I looked up and saw the ghost of Ravi King on the shabby trail. He shimmered as raindrops passed through him. "Ravi? What are you doing out here?"

"It's Bud!" The ghost looked genuinely afraid. "He's in a tree, and he's hurt."

"Bud's in a tree?" I asked. It took a full minute to extract myself from the blackberry vines. It was winter and the vines were dry and brittle, but the thorns were still sharp and they clung to my coat and pants.

"Come on, Suri!" Ravi's urgency, plus the idea of "possible wildlife" spooked me. Suddenly, I wasn't keen on the idea of Eddie sprinting ahead without me. I blundered forward and lost the trail entirely as I followed Ravi deeper into the woods.

"Hurry!" Ravi cried. "He's up this way!" The screams were getting louder, so I had to be headed in the right direction, with or without a path. I wanted to ask the ghost why Bud would be out in the woods in the freezing rain, but he was probably treasure hunting, this time without his partner. Bud was alone, and whatever trouble he'd landed himself in sounded dire.

"Help! For the love of God, please help!" Bud's voice came from dead ahead. I stumbled through a tangle of what looked like honeysuckle and more dead blackberry vines, and found myself in a small clearing.

Bud was about fifteen feet off the ground, hugging the branch of a massive cedar tree and screaming for help. His left leg was torn up and dripping blood onto the wet earth below.

I was about to call up to him, to let him know he wasn't alone anymore and to ask what he was doing up in a tree, when Eddie entered from the other side of the clearing and motioned for me to stay back and be quiet. I shot him a quizzical look, and he pointed to the big cat who came out from behind the broad trunk, circling the cedar tree.

She was sleek and graceful, the dark spots on her golden coat rippling above lean muscles with every step. Blue-green eyes, sharp with intelligent focus, briefly took in both me and Eddie before turning back to her prize in the tree.

That wasn't any mountain lion. The apex predator at the base of the tree looked like a leopard, and she had a taste for Bud Barlow.

~

"WHATEVER YOU DO, Suri, don't make any sudden movements." Eddie's voice was calm on the other side of the clearing, as if he encountered a wild, clawed and fanged predator circling a man in a tree every week.

The leopard growled and rumbled complaints deep in her throat as she circled the tree, twigs snapping under her massive feet. Every movement was fluid, terrifying grace. She sniffed at the fresh blood on the ground, then looked up at Bud and licked her lips.

Eddie needn't have worried. Even with the ghost of Ravi King shouting in my ear to *do something* to help Bud—who was screaming in the tree and dripping blood—my unexpected proximity to a large, carnivorous feline was enough to keep me rooted to the spot.

"Why doesn't she just climb the tree?" I whispered to no one in particular. Not that I wanted to give the leopard any ideas about how to more quickly and efficiently dispatch the terrified human clinging to the branch. But she was a cat, right?

"Toying with her food," came the unexpected reply.

I clapped my hand over my mouth to muffle my startled shriek. Per usual, Loki had appeared out of nowhere, or maybe he'd snuck up on me again. Eddie shot me a quick glance to make sure I was okay. Eyes wide, I nodded back and watched him creep along the perimeter of the clearing.

"Your friend won't have much luck trying to corral the cat that way. She's too clever for that." Loki's impassiveness was the most unsettling part of having a front-row seat to a potentially fatal mauling. Dressed in his customary black—even his outer-wear—Loki perched on a wet rock and leaned back into a thick clump of ferns.

"Have you got a better suggestion?" I hissed, hoping he actu-ally would have a better suggestion. In an Eddie-versus-leopard cage match, I didn't think Eddie had particularly good odds. "Or maybe you could, I don't know, *help*?"

Loki cocked his head as if to say, *"What would be the fun in that?"* and went back to observing the scene from Wild Animal Safari Live.

"Can't you see he's hurt?!" Ravi's image wavered in front of me in distress. "Help him!"

Bud's screaming coalesced into discernible sentences, now that other people were on the scene. He didn't appear to have much hope of survival as he clung to the cedar branch, his muti-lated leg hanging limp and leaking red. Below him, the big cat breathed in the blood in the air and whipped her spotted tail in excitement.

"This is it!" Bud bellowed. "This is how it ends! It's karma coming for me, just like the horoscope said. I shouldn't have done it!"

The leopard made a performative leap to swat the air inches from Bud's face, and Bud shrieked as he nearly lost his grip on the branch. Back on all fours, the leopard glanced briefly at Eddie, Loki, and me. She looked amused and intent, and her jaw dropped open as if to laugh. Unnerved by the cat's piercing eyes, I lost my footing and tripped backward into another blackberry thicket. The leopard turned her gaze up to Bud and appeared to smile.

Her paws were the size of saucers. Her thick rope of a tail looked powerful enough to knock a man off his feet. And Eddie was still moving in his slow circle, trying to get around behind her.

"Eddie? Maybe we should just wait?" I didn't need to whisper. The cat's full attention was on her bloody prey in the tree. I pulled my phone out of my pocket and tried to figure out who to call.

"The animal's healthy as far as I can see. Looks well-fed. Has to be from the sanctuary." Eddie stepped behind a half-buried boulder in his path and vanished from sight. "Oof!" Eddie grunted. "Found a hole. Some tools, too."

Loki sat up tall and tried to spot Eddie. "Is there anything else of note in that hole, Mr. Cortés? Perhaps a wooden chest?"

The leopard growled, followed by a grunting sound that was somewhere between a meow and a belch before she licked up more of Bud's blood from the moss and dirt.

"It's going to kill me!" Bud screeched. "Ravi, I'm sorry! I should have listened to you. I was selfish. I shouldn't have tried to steal Cyndi, when it turns out she doesn't like me, anyway. Joke's on me!" Bud's nervous laughter dissolved into wailing sobs as the leopard stretched her long forelegs on the tree trunk, took a moment to sharpen her claws, then started to climb. "I shouldn't have tried to steal the treasure. And I shouldn't have killed you! You were my friend, and I killed you. I didn't think it through. It didn't seem real, until it was. I took the greedy coward's path, and my punishment is coming for me."

"Bud killed Ravi?" I watched in horror as the leopard scaled the tree with ease and reached Bud's branch. She lowered her head and snarled at him.

Ravi flickered beside me, his expression blank as he looked up at his friend howling in the tree. "Bud? It was you?"

Face to face with the leopard, Bud shrieked and scooted farther out on the branch, dragging his injured leg and smearing blood across the bark in an attempt to delay the inevitable. "Ravi,

I'll see you soon, partner. And you can kick my ass right to hell, where I belong."

My heart pounded in my ears. My feet locked in place. I didn't know what to do. Should I charge at the tree, yelling and waving my arms, and try to distract the leopard? Then she would just come after me, or Eddie or Loki. She was fast and strong and could make a quick snack of any of us. But she had chosen her quarry. The leopard advanced slowly on Bud, paw over paw, a perfect predator.

Immediately below, the ghost of Ravi King looked up in horrified disbelief. "How could you, Bud? We're *friends*. Partners. How could you just kill me?"

Loki hopped down from atop his boulder and stepped into the clearing, looking like he'd nearly missed his cue. "Ah. Well. Here, kitty kitty?"

Eddie reappeared from behind the rocks, streaked with dirt and mud, and called after Loki. "Mister, I wouldn't do that if I were you."

The leopard paused and glanced down at Loki. She looked annoyed.

"Do you have any idea what it was like to die like that?" Ravi shouted, with no one but me to hear him. "The *pain*, Bud! And the terror, because I didn't know what was happening. And you chose that for me? Because of an old box we found in the woods? Because you couldn't have Cyndi? You know what? Getting eaten alive by a wild animal is too good for you."

"That's quite enough," Loki called up to the leopard. His voice was the only source of steadiness in the vicinity, and I tried to latch onto that. "You've had your fun and done your job. Come on down from there, now."

The leopard glanced again at Bud, growled, and gave him another near-miss swipe that seemed more frustrated commentary than threat. She leapt down from the tree, making a graceful but heavy thud of a landing that I felt in my bones. The leopard stood a few meters in front of Loki, and I was only half that much farther behind him.

"Our situation has not improved," I said, surprised I had any voice at all and that my knees hadn't given out. I edged toward Eddie as he answered his phone.

"Yeah. Okay, but we've got a leopard here," he told the caller. How could Eddie sound so confident and in control? Bud was still screaming in the tree, even without the imminent threat of mauling. Loki stepped in front of the leopard, motioning her toward him.

"Dude! Stop pretending you're some kind of wizard," Eddie called to Loki. "You're not a wild animal whisperer. You're going to get hurt."

Eddie's mouth hung open as the leopard padded toward Loki. She gave his outstretched hand a sniff, then head-butted his hip, nearly knocking him off balance.

Loki leaned down to speak into the big cat's ear. "Thank you for standing watch. Your steadfast assistance is appreciated."

I didn't think leopards could purr, but I swore that's what I heard as Loki ran a hand down her back. With eyes half-closed, she turned to lick his wrist.

"So maybe he is some kind of wizard or wild animal whisperer," I said as I leaned against Eddie, and he wrapped an arm around me.

"What is this guy's deal?" Eddie whispered. "That is not normal."

We heard the shouts of the approaching rescue squad as they hiked through the woods and tried to locate us. Eddie got back on the phone to give directions to our position.

"It's too late!" Bud bawled in the tree. "It's too late for me. You should just leave me here to die. I deserve it."

"No one's leaving anyone," Eddie called to Bud while keeping an eye on the leopard. There was no guarantee that Loki's pacifying distraction would last.

"I would appreciate if any items unearthed in this area are not turned over to the authorities." Loki stroked the leopard's ears while she rubbed her face against his legs and made a meowing grunting sound that I hoped communicated contentment.

"What?" I peered into the hole Eddie had fallen into. A shovel and pickaxe lay in the dirt. "Bud was looking for more treasure?"

"This is close to where we were digging before." This time, I wasn't startled when Ravi's ghost materialized beside me. There was too much competing chaos for something as simple as a sudden ghost to rattle me. "Bud was trying to protect the site, and maybe find more."

I looked at Loki. "You're after the treasure, too?"

Loki cocked his head and listened as the rescue crew drew near. His lips ticked up into one of his subtle, maddening smiles. Instead of answering my question, Loki gave me a tiny nod before he whispered something to the leopard.

"They're almost here," Eddie called up to Bud. "Hang tight. Just a few more minutes."

"How are they going to deal with the leopard?" I asked Eddie. "Anyone got a big cage and a tranquilizer gun?"

There was no need. When I turned back to the clearing mere seconds later, Loki and the leopard were nowhere to be seen. I heard rustling moving away in the thick brush.

A three-member team from Coastal Fire and Rescue reached our location and went to work helping Bud. One medic scaled the tree to assess Bud's injuries while the others fitted together a metal-framed litter to carry him to safety.

"I can't believe he killed me." Ravi's ghost hovered at the edge of the clearing, wearing an expression of incredulous disappointment. "We were partners. He was my friend. Why would he do that?" Ravi muttered the same question again as he faded from view.

CHAPTER FIFTEEN

The Tea Reader was back in business. Down the street, the Tea and Botanicals Dispensary had also re-opened its doors, but only for a limited time. Just a few hours after Max's arrest for the accidental poisoning of Grady and Standish Beach, Karina announced the TBD's going out of business sale.

I stood inside the TBD's once busy dining room a few minutes after ten on Friday morning and tried to pretend it was just another day in Naghatune Bay. One final customer, a twenty-something in a fleece hoodie and cargo pants, paid for the shop's very last "high tea cake" and gobbled half of it down as they walked out the door.

Karina locked the door behind them. "Well, then," she said with a sigh. "That's it." She turned to me with a smile. "Your teahouse must be full to bursting. Back to your usual numbers by now?"

"Mmm." I gave a curt nod and blamed my reticence on the headache. The pain wasn't all that bad, but the Tea Reader's numbers were abysmal. Even with both sides of the Tea Reader open for business, there seemed to be no way to climb out of the financial hole we were in. The competition from Karina's establishment, then the closure following Ravi's death, had driven the Tea Reader into the ground.

Barbara had delivered the grave news less than an hour earlier as she stood behind the barista counter and watched the teahouse fill to standing room only. If I didn't figure out a way to fill the gap, and fast, Karina's Tea and Botanicals Dispensary wouldn't be the only shop on Grady's Main Street closing its doors for good.

But Karina didn't need to be burdened with any of that.

A knock sounded outside the TBD's door. Chief Deputy Banich gave a terse wave from the other side of the glass.

"What is it now?" Karina groaned as she unlocked the door and let him inside. "Before you ask, we're all out of everything."

"Good. That's what I came to check on," he replied. "No chance there's something left in the back of a freezer somewhere? Something with a little cannabis kick to it?"

"All clear, chief." Karina gave a mock salute, and I felt myself warming toward her. It was too little, and too late. "And your people already scoured the place for any leftovers of Bard's product."

"How did you find out about Bard?" I asked. The "little something extra" that Ravi and Bud reportedly added to their tea had been one of the missing pieces of the puzzle. Unbeknownst to Karina, her assistant manager had been selling his own home-made powder blend of THC, ginseng, and a touch of guarana to customers off the books. Assistant Deputy Davis let it slip to me that the combination was especially potent and supposedly invigorating, but with a mellowing effect. After Karina shot down his new product idea for the TBD kitchen, Bard had sourced the ingredients from leftover cannabis stems in the TBD kitchen and made a pretty penny from his illicit side hustle.

"Too many people making repeat trips up from Standish to make tiny purchases to cover their deals with Mr. Walker," he said. "Like coming to Grady for a single CBD gummy, when they could pick up a pack of ten at their local Plaid Pantry. I would have caught it sooner, but first I had to figure out what kind of traffic was normal for the area. From there, it was a matter of looking at the store receipts and finding patterns. Mr. Walker was always on duty for those purchases."

"Very thorough. You figured it out in a matter of days," I replied. I didn't want to ask how long Bard had been running his side business, right under the nose of local law enforcement. Banich had a low enough opinion of Jim and Colin as it was.

"I still don't buy that you didn't know what he was up to," Banich told Karina, but she was done engaging with him.

"We've been through this," she replied. "I did not know my assistant manager was selling high-test THC powder out of my shop until you told me about it yourself. If you can prove otherwise, I suggest you do so."

Banich sighed and turned to me. "When Mr. Walker got sick, he'd been trying to find the pattern in the poisonings, just like you did with your wall of sticky notes, in case his powder was the culprit. He thought he'd accidentally poisoned himself and was afraid he was dying. That got him talking."

"But you knew his product wasn't making anyone sick," I said. "Right?"

"Lab results from Hattieville came back quick." Banich chuckled. "He didn't know that."

"That's low," I said.

Banich shrugged. "Too bad your call to the health department got tagged as a nuisance complaint. We were already watching Mr. Walker, of course, but the extra ammunition might have helped."

My stomach clenched. I glanced at Karina. If she knew I'd reported her shop to the health department, she didn't let on. Or maybe she simply didn't care anymore. "And Ravi?" I asked Banich. "It really was Bud who killed him?"

"The THC from Mr. Walker's powder complicated the coroner's job a bit," Banich replied. "It really was cardiac arrest, brought on by cyanide, homemade from cherry pits. Bud Barlow snuck it into Ravi King's tea at your teahouse, then deliberately spilled the evidence across the floor as his friend went into convulsions." He sighed and scratched the back of his head. "He hadn't counted on Mr. King dying right in front of him, or that it would be so gruesome."

"The pain," Ravi's ghost had lamented to Bud. "What a horrible way to die," I said.

Banich ignored my comment. "It was Mr. Barlow who ransacked Ms. Coyle's place, too, trying to get his hands on the treasure box. He didn't know Mr. Walker had absconded with it." He gave Karina a sideways glance, and she shook her head. I didn't volunteer that I'd been the one to inadvertently point Bud in Karina's direction.

"So, you're skipping town while your boyfriend is still on the mend?" Banich asked Karina.

She seemed to bristle at the mere sound of his voice. I didn't know why he appeared so intent on aggravating her, or why she was peevish in his presence, but I did know I didn't want to get into the middle of it. Though Karina was leaving town, I'd heard Banich was sticking around, at least until Jim and Colin were back on their feet and back on the job. I didn't want to spend that time on Banich's blacklist.

I made my excuses for a hasty exit, but Karina grabbed my elbow. "If you don't mind? Deputy?"

Banich's left eye twitched. Karina had gotten under his skin and burrowed in like scabies mites. "*Chief* deputy," he muttered as he headed for the door. "Never imagined three arrests in just a few days in such a small town."

Karina locked the door behind him, then turned to me. "I'm sorry about the witch bottle."

My jaw dropped, my earlier suspicions confirmed. "That was you?"

"No, not me." She blew out a long exhale. "It was Bard. Turns out he did the same thing to that former barista I told you about. The one who left? Stacey. Apparently, she found out that he was selling his special powder, so he got even by planting one of those nasty things in her apartment. Her whole life flipped inside out. I don't blame her for leaving." Karina shrugged. "When I confronted him about his side hustle, he admitted he'd broken into your place to plant the bottle, to sow some minor chaos in your life in case you really were psychic and would figure out what he was up to."

"I'm not psychic," I replied. I remembered the lone figure walking along the shore the evening after Ravi died. Had that been Bard? Had he snuck in and planted the witch bottle while Audrey and I were baking?

"He also wanted you occupied to clear the way for me and Jim, so I'd be distracted," Karina continued. "So I wouldn't notice his side business." She laughed. "I know you won't exactly be sorry to see me go, Suri, but I'll miss you all the same. I wish I'd had the chance to get to know you better. Maybe we could have been real friends."

"Even though you're dating my ex?" The question was past my lips before my brain could stop it.

"And even though you're my competition, professionally speaking, because our clientele overlapped." Karina looked wistfully around her empty store. Some of the furniture and fixtures would follow her to Seattle, while the rest would return to the Pot Stop's corporate storage. She sighed. "But I'm not sorry to leave Grady. I'll miss Jim, and I'm glad he'll be okay. It's a shame he's not up for trying the long-distance thing. I think we could have had something really good."

That was news to me, but Karina was on a roll, so I kept my surprise to myself.

"I never knew running a business in a small town would be so complicated and upsetting," she continued. "So, Seattle, for a more stable fresh start. I'll have my own shop again, with more of an R&D focus."

"A fresh start sounds nice. This might help." I reached into my coat's interior pocket and pulled out the copy of *New in Seattle* that Loki had left in one of his mystery boxes.

Karina flipped through the book. "This is perfect! And you say you aren't psychic."

I made my way toward the door. My head was starting to throb, and I needed my morning tea.

"A fresh start for your friend, Audrey, too," Karina replied. "She really boosted my profile with corporate, and they've paid her handsomely for her infused jelly beans recipe. I'd tried for months to get that recipe to work, then she swooped in and completely remade it! Of course, I'm using CBD instead of her herbs and whatnot. I'm calling it Baked Beans. They think I'm a star." Karina laughed.

This was also new information, but there was no doubt Audrey deserved to be rewarded for her efforts, especially since I was going to have to sell my car or a kidney to cover the next month's payroll. The Tea Reader had to close. Maybe Audrey could take a nice vacation with Colin when he was feeling up to it.

I wished Karina well and stepped outside into the icy rain. I really hoped no one would remember it was my birthday.

WITH THE TBD closing its doors, the Tea Reader was packed with customers once again. As a rule, I don't care much for crowds or noise, particularly in enclosed spaces, but it was gratifying to see the teahouse tables filled, with more patrons standing in pairs and trios to laugh and gossip and enjoy their tea and baked goods.

Bypassing the long line at the barista counter, I retrieved an older copy of *The Naghatune Reader* from the floor. With Bobby Jackson recovering from the recent rash of poisonings, it would be a few weeks yet before our weekly paper was back in circulation. The paper was open to the horoscopes, in which Gemini was warned that karma was lying in wait. I put little faith in these weekly predictions, but for Bud at least the forecast had proven true.

When I reached the counter to check in with the teahouse manager, I found Barbara serving pastries and making tea drinks at such a brisk pace that she was breaking a sweat.

"Hey, boss." Barbara squeezed past Taylor at the register to grab the last savory scone from the pastry case and slip it into a bag for Emmaline Kapul. Taylor was back as a teahouse barista after losing his job at the TBD, but we'd already advised the staff to look for other employment options.

"Morning, Suri!" Emmaline exclaimed in cheerful surprise. "We're so glad you're up and running again! And the place is so busy, too! Such a shame about Karina's shop, of course." She leaned closer. "Any chance you might start carrying similar items here?"

I forced a tight smile. "Probably not."

"Ah, well. Doesn't hurt to ask." She shook the pastry bag in her hand. "Taking this over to Murray. Poor man got his new heart medication confused with some tainted gummies when he stopped in at the dispensary to sit and read his paper. That's his story, anyway."

"You're a good neighbor," I replied. "Please tell Murray I hope he's feeling better soon."

Emmaline nodded and disappeared into the crowd.

Barbara called Cyndi out of the kitchen to fill orders, then motioned for me to follow her to the far end of the counter.

"How's it looking?" I asked, but Barbara's grim expression told me everything I needed to know.

"The same. The teas we already had on order came in

Wednesday, to replace everything we had to throw out. That'll last us a while. But we don't have the money to buy any more after that. With payroll, insurance, utilities, and the license renewal waiting to be paid . . ." Barbara grimaced. "I'm sorry to say we may not last through next week. Thank goodness for Audrey baking every night, so we have something to put in the cases."

"We'll need to compensate her for that," I said. "For her time and supplies."

"If we can," Barbara replied. "The hole is just too deep, boss. Unless you've got any magick tricks up your sleeve I should know about."

"I wish." I wondered if Karina might have room in her new shop in Seattle for some of the Tea Reader staff. Barbara wasn't one to exaggerate. If she said that, barring a miracle, the teahouse and bookshop would have to shut down in the coming days, I believed her.

A loud cheer erupted at the front of the teahouse as Eddie and three others from the Coastal Fire and Rescue crew came through the front door. Once again, Eddie and his co-workers were local heroes. The CFR squad had saved Bud's life and distributed the antidote to the oleander poison through Grady and Standish Beach, along with Audrey's magick jelly beans to help the medicine go down. Eddie and his work buddies accepted handshakes and slaps on the back as they made their way through the crowd.

Despite the bleak outlook for my business, I couldn't help the smile on my face. It seemed to appear whenever Eddie did, along with an excited tingle in my chest. Whatever happened with the Tea Reader, I was determined to find a way to remain in Naghatune Bay. I got the feeling Eddie was worth sticking around for.

"Whatever they want is on me!" Earl Greenbauer exclaimed

as he waved toward Eddie and his co-workers. "Hell of a job, saving the town. Keeping us all safe from both man and beast!"

"You and your friends should get some of the credit," Eddie said as he reached me. He towered over me and warmed me with his smile. "With all the work you did to figure out what the poison was."

"That's totally off the record." I grinned up at him, and Barbara went back to filling customer orders. I wanted to ask if Eddie had heard anything more about the escaped leopard. The big cat hadn't been seen since Bud Barlow's dramatic rescue and murder confession. But Eddie leaned toward me and caught me off-guard.

"I've got the night off," he said, his words sounding more like a question.

"Do you now?" I dove into his welcoming brown eyes. It was nice to forget about my financial woes for a minute or two.

He bent closer, dropping his voice. "I could bring dinner, if you want to pick out a movie to watch? Something low-key but special for your birthday."

Before I could answer, Earl Greenbauer slapped Eddie on the back and shoved a frosted cookie into his hand. "A town treasure, I tell you! You treating this boy right, Suri?" Earl laughed and pulled Eddie toward the register, where he ordered half the menu for Eddie and the rest of the rescue squad.

Barbara appeared beside me with a tall mug of steaming hot tea. I inhaled the comforting aroma of black tea, vanilla, nut milk, brown sugar, and cinnamon. The Simply Suri.

"Thought you might need this," Barbara said with a meaningful look.

I slipped through the crowd toward the pass-through doors leading to the bookshop. I needed some space and quiet to try to figure out what to do.

～

THE QUIET BOOKSHOP offered no respite. As soon as I closed the pass-through doors, Loki stepped out from behind one of the bookcases.

"Really?" I couldn't help my exasperated tone. "Now? What could you possibly want from me now?"

He cocked his head toward a medium-sized cardboard box waiting on the sales counter—another mystery box delivery.

"Thanks, I guess," I said. "But you probably already know that we're going out of business." Saying the words aloud nearly knocked the wind out of me. I clutched my big mug of tea with both hands and took a long drink.

"I wouldn't place a substantial wager on that outcome. Not just yet." He offered another of his subtle, enigmatic smiles. At least this time, I didn't want to strangle him. "Nothing is carved in stone." He chuckled at his own obscure humor. "Sometimes, not even what is literally carved in stone."

Yeah, he's hilarious. "What happened to your raccoon and your cat?" I asked. "Your actual cat, the black and orange one?"

"They don't care for the rain." Loki gestured toward the foul weather outside the window.

That wasn't much of an answer. I stepped behind the counter, turned on the little space heater on the floor, and perched atop the tall stool. "Since you're here, you want to explain about the treasure box, and the leopard, and just all of it?"

"I have significant doubts you would believe any explanation I might offer, regardless of completeness or degree of veracity."

"So you don't want to tell the whole truth, then. Fine. What about only some of the truth? Or a few hints?" I took another sip of tea. Getting annoyed with Loki meant I wasn't feeling as defeated by the prospect of the Tea Reader having to close.

"It's a tricky thing." Loki clasped his hands together in front of his chest. "The past is knitting together imperfectly in my memory. It's a bewildering but not entirely unpleasant experience. The memories are there, almost tangible things calling out like a siren on the shore. But it is so much gossamer and shadow when I reach for it."

"All right, but what about Booker and the swartle elves or whatever? And you said it was Frigga's special tea?"

"Brokkr of the Svartálfar," he corrected me.

"Right. That. What about it?" I didn't want to encourage anyone's delusions. Part of me was certain there was no possible way he'd been telling me the truth about the treasure box before, but I had the growing sense there was some factuality to his claims. I felt ridiculous, but this was Naghatune Bay. Loki communing with magickal underground creatures wouldn't be the weirdest thing going on here. "And you seemed chummy with that escaped leopard. Maybe try starting there?"

"An old friend, I believe," he replied. "One I had feared was lost."

"The leopard?"

"You might have heard of her," he replied. "Seshat?"

An ice pick headache shot through my left eyeball. I focused on my breathing until it passed. "Who are you, really?"

Loki met my gaze and smiled. "Perhaps I should ask to study with you, rather than the other way around. It seems my time in your presence may yet bring me back to myself."

Did I want to spend more time hanging out with this cryptic guy who always wore black and had an unnerving habit of stepping out of the shadows? Not especially. But with the Tea Reader gone, I'd need something to fill my time. If nothing else, maybe Loki could give me an idea of what that creepy blob of green mist had been, appearing alongside Trey, Ravi, and Catesby when the treasure box was opened at the rental house.

"Suri?"

I turned to find the ghost of Trey taking shape in the air just inside the bookshop's front door. The ghosts of my acquaintance had gone quiet after the excitement around Bud's discovery and arrest. It had been a restful break, but I found myself missing Trey. Not that I'd ever tell him.

"I notice the late professor does not accompany you," Loki remarked casually. Did anything rattle this guy? He'd kept his cool and approached an escaped leopard—a wild animal he believed was his friend. I hadn't yet worked out how he could see ghosts. "Has the spirit of Thomas Norman Catesby moved on?"

Trey shot me a wary look. "That's my guess. He kind of wandered off, murmuring to himself about his own genius. Next thing I knew, he was gone."

I hoped Trey was right. I didn't relish the possibility of Catesby's sudden return to pester me about the teahouse's mediocre beverage offerings. Assuming there would be a teahouse to haunt.

"And Ravi?" I asked.

"Haunting Bud in jail." Trey didn't try to conceal his mirth.

"I know you think it's funny," I replied, "but even if there had been gold in that treasure and not just some old tea, I can't imagine murdering a friend over it. What Bud did was unthinkable."

And then there was Max Turner. They hadn't reached out since their arrest, and the sheriff in Hattieville hadn't been keen on allowing visitors or calls from anyone who wasn't their kin or legal representation. Max had been in an awful position with Professor Catesby, and they'd made a terrible series of choices. But if I knew what Max needed, or how I could help, I would have done it.

"It was decidedly more than *just some old tea*." Loki examined the nearest bookcase and seemed amused by the jumbled collection of astronomy guides and books on productivity shelved together with alternate history science fiction. I'd tried separating the books into their respective topics only the week before, but they wanted to be grouped this way instead. Loki ran a finger over the spines. "If memory serves, the cache has accumulated a blood price several times over in the long years since its creation."

For a second, his face shifted into either a wry smile or a grimace. It was tough to tell in the dim bookshop.

"Whatever." Trey rolled his eyes, but I could see that he was unnerved by Loki's words or his presence, or both. He shook it off. "But I still think it's just plain bone-headed for Ravi to voluntarily become a jailhouse ghost. If he otherwise had the opportunity to move on."

"An opportunity which has not yet come your way, I take it." Loki moved to another shelf, where he perused assorted titles on Central American anthropology, social media marketing, and cooking with seaweed.

Trey shot me a look I couldn't read. "No, I haven't. You know something about it?"

Loki didn't respond. I opened his most recent mystery box delivery and pulled out a blood red aromatherapy eye pillow, a cheerful-looking book about going into business with your best friend, a used copy of *The Gate to Women's Country*, and a lava lamp with a gold base and a solidified, blobby column of pink wax inside.

"Groovy." Trey laughed at my irritated smile.

The next item out of the box was a children's book on the big cats of the world. The cover featured drawings of a lion, cheetah, panther, tiger, and leopard chasing each other in a circle around the planet Earth at the center. "Maybe could have used this a week ago."

I turned to Loki. Naturally, he was nowhere to be seen. I hated when he did that.

Trey pointed to Loki's last known location. "That guy, Suri. He is not normal. Are you sure you can trust him?"

I shrugged and went back to unloading the mystery box, which seemed more full than usual. At the bottom were stacks of beach-themed postcards, a collection of Courtney Milan romance novels, and a paperback copy of Tom Wolfe's *The Right Stuff* that looked like it had never been read.

The astronaut book I set aside for Murray Overhill, to keep him company while he recovered. I stacked the other books on the counter and placed a trio of seashell-embroidered tea towels on a table near the front of the store. "Maybe I shouldn't even bother."

"Suri?" Trey asked, but I waved his question away.

"How about you, though?" I asked. "You're looking remarkably calm for a ghost who was trapped in a wardrobe by a witch bottle, then got ensnared by an enchanted treasure box."

Trey groaned and rolled his eyes again. He looked a little rough around the edges and had a kind of beige overtone, but he often bristled when I expressed concern directly. "Eh, I've had it worse."

With little warning, a hail storm erupted outside. Trey and I stood in the quiet bookshop, regarding each other and listening to ice pellets bounce off the window glass.

"Trey, I owe you an apology." Another ice pick headache shot a bolt of pain through my eye, but I gritted my way through it. "I didn't mean to offend you. I'm still trying to figure out how to have a friend who's a ghost, along with the rest of it. But I shouldn't have taken my insecurity or frustration out on you. That wasn't fair."

"I'm sorry, too." Trey looked up at the ceiling as the hail came down harder. "My natural snark can get out of hand when I'm out of my element. You'd think I'd be used to this post-life situation by now, but I honestly couldn't even tell you if I sleep."

Do ghosts sleep? It hadn't occurred to me to ask. "It's only been about four months," I said.

Trey adopted a smug smile. "It took less time than that for me to learn the ropes at Morgan Witter, steal the accounts of my nearest associates, and get myself on the fast track to managing director."

I blinked. "You stole from your friends?"

"Wall Street stuff," he said.

"I've never understood the world of high finance," I replied, raising my voice to be heard over the racket the hail was making on the roof and against the windows. "It sounds complicated and hard."

"Being dead is harder."

"Touché." I closed my eyes. The hail tapered off. There would be more later in the day, and more still in the weeks to come.

I imagined curling up under a thick quilt back at the cottage for a long, dreamless nap while ice plinked and plonked outside. That would be my birthday gift to myself. But I couldn't get Trey's comment out of my head. *Being dead is harder.* All this time I'd spent with the recently deceased, and I had little idea what it was like to be a ghost. Trey had a habit of putting a sarcastic spin on pretty much everything, but that was likely a coping mechanism. It wasn't like death had given him superpowers. He'd gotten stuck in my wardrobe and an old box, and he didn't know whether or not he slept.

The noise of the teahouse crowd flooded in as Audrey opened the pass-through and dashed in. "Suri! Have I got *big* news!" She shut the doors on the cheerful hubbub behind her.

I glanced at Trey as he faded out of view, then forced a smile and turned to Audrey. I wanted my excitement to be genuine, but I worried what her announcement might be.

She stopped short when she saw the look on my face. "Karina already told you? About the money from the Pot Stop Corporation?"

"Sounds like you really impressed the big wigs," I replied. "I imagine they'd be happy to have you, if you wanted to pursue a career there."

"Suri?" Audrey asked. "You're being odd."

"Sorry," I said. "I'm happy for you. I'm just stressed this morning. It's great news! Do you think you'll stay in Grady? Or will we lose you to bigger and better things?"

Audrey looked stunned. "Suri, I wouldn't leave Grady for the world. You're here. Colin's here. And everything's just so weird that I don't feel out of place."

I laughed, and it felt good. "Whatever you decide to do, I'm sure it will be a wonderful adventure. It just probably won't be here at the Tea Reader." I felt guilty about casting a shadow over her good fortune.

"Yeah, I heard about that," she said. "I think everyone has. You know gossip in Grady."

"Great." I hid my face behind my mug and took a massive gulp of tea.

"So, here's the thing. I have an idea. And it's not about kombucha, although we really should revisit that sometime." Audrey's brows furrowed and her mouth twisted to one side as she ran a finger over the spines of the books I'd stacked on the counter. Her expression lightened as she pulled out one title and held it up for me to see.

"What do you think about this?" she asked.

On the cover, five pairs of smiling cartoon characters— human and otherwise—looked to be running or dancing in place while they held thick bundles of oversized, green paper currency. The title was, *How to Thrive in Business with Your Best Friend*.

"Loki." I didn't know if I wanted to laugh or scream.

"I want to invest, Suri," Audrey said. "You know I believe in the Tea Reader, and in you! But even with Barbara running the teahouse, you're shouldering too much with your headaches and the ghosts. Let me buy into the business. Let me be a proper partner."

"I don't know," I replied, but did I have a choice? Not if I wanted to keep the Tea Reader open. Taking on an investor-partner meant shared risks, shared decision-making, and shared control. I wasn't confident I'd be too good at that. I started to feel itchy and hot under my sweater, and I worried a panic attack was on the rise.

Audrey laid a hand on top of mine. "We'll make it work,

Suri. I promise. Our friendship and the Tea Reader both. I want to do this."

Trey materialized behind Audrey and gave me a raised-eyebrow look that could have been optimism or foreboding. I wanted to stay in Grady. I wanted to keep my friends and my business. I was tired and in pain, and I wasn't sure I had it in me to start over again. Hadn't Loki said something, somewhere along the way, about making the most of the opportunities that presented themselves? Or maybe that was from a musical about livestock or dock workers.

"Okay." I attempted to dispel my doubt with a sharp nod. It didn't work. I pushed forward anyway. "Let's do it."

As if on cue, a cheer arose in the teahouse next-door.

"Yes!" Audrey bobbed with excitement and clapped her hands together. "I promise I can handle as much as you need me to, since I know you'll be busy with all the ghost hunters."

A lead weight dropped in my stomach. "With what?"

Audrey laughed. "You know, the ghost hunters. Barbara got the call from Mayor Phil first thing this morning. *The Ghost Patrol* is coming to town. Happy birthday!"

Leave a Review! I HOPE you enjoyed reading *Tainted Treasure*. To spread the word to other readers and support me as an author, why not post a review with your favorite bookseller? Thanks!

Join Jen's List! FOR BOOK NEWS, freebies, and more, you can sign up for my readers list at Jennifer-Willis.com.

· · ·

WANT to know what happens next? Look for *Sinister Snare*, the fourth book in the Haunted Coast series, in October 2024!

ALARM AND EXCITEMENT greet a team of professional ghost hunters who descend on Grady to document the spectral goings-on in the small coastal hamlet. Not everyone welcomes the media attention on their spooky town, while others are jockeying to make cameo appearances.

As the resident medium who can see and communicate with ghosts, Suri isn't keen to appear as an on-camera expert. But when the site of the paranormal investigation becomes a grisly murder scene, all evidence points to one of Grady's own as the killer. Suri has no choice but to get involved.

Suri can't believe her friend is capable of violence, but the locals have been keeping secrets and the town ghosts have their own scores to settle. Can Suri uncover the killer, even if she doesn't want to face the truth?

SINISTER SNARE IS the fourth book in the Haunted Coast paranormal cozy mystery series, set in the same universe as the Rune Witch urban fantasy books.

RECIPES

Heart-Warmer Scones

Non-cannabis version

Yield:
Makes 8-12 scones

Ingredients:
1 1/2 cups flour
2 teaspoons baking powder
3/4 teaspoon smoked paprika
1 teaspoon salt
3 1/2 Tablespoons unsalted butter, chilled
3/4 cup* grated cheddar cheese, aged if possible
(*or more, if you want cheesier scones)
1 Tablespoon finely chopped sage
1 large egg
2 teaspoons spicy brown mustard
1/2 - 3/4 cup buttermilk

Directions:

- Preheat oven to 400°F.
- Combine flour, baking powder, paprika, and salt in a large bowl.
- Grate in the cold butter and mix into the flour until it resembles fine crumbs.
- Mix in half of the cheese and all of the sage.
- Whisk together the egg, mustard, and 1/2 cup of buttermilk, then pour into the flour mixture. Using a fork, bring together to form a soft dough. Add buttermilk in small amounts as needed.
- On a lightly floured surface, form the dough into a rectangle about 3/4-inch thick. Cut into even triangles and place on a lined baking tray.
- Brush the tops with buttermilk, then sprinkle with the remaining cheese.
- Bake for 10-12 minutes until risen and golden.

Vanilla Shortbread Cookies

Yield:
    Makes two dozen

Ingredients:
    1 1/2 cups salted butter, softened
    3 3/4 cups all-purpose flour
    3 teaspoons pure vanilla extract
    1 cup granulated sugar
    3 Tablespoons coarse or raw sugar, for sprinkling

Directions:

- Preheat oven to 325°F.
- Cream together butter, sugar, and vanilla until fluffy (about 2 minutes).
- Mix in flour, 1/2 at a time, then stir until fully combined and a soft dough forms.
- Turn dough out onto plastic wrap and knead gently until smooth. Form into a disc, wrap, and chill for 30 minutes.
- Line a large baking sheet with parchment paper.
- On a non-stick surface, roll dough into a square, about 1/2-inch thick.
- Cut into 2-inch squares and place onto lined baking sheet, at least 1-inch apart. Sprinkle tops with coarse sugar.
- Bake for 22-25 minutes until the bottoms are lightly golden. Cool briefly on the baking sheet, then remove to a cooling rack.

ALSO BY JENNIFER WILLIS

Rhythm

THE RUNE WITCH SERIES

Moon Dog Magic

Elements of Magic

Black Pool Magic

Raven Magic

Chaos Magic

Twilight Magic

HAUNTED COAST SERIES

Crooked Curse

Fatal Fundraiser

Tainted Treasure

Sinister Snare (October 2024)

Poison Pen (October 2025)

MARS ADVENTURE ROMANCE SERIES (M.A.R.S.)

Mars Ho!

Lovers and Lunatics

Mars Heat

For news of future books, occasional freebies, and other updates, please visit jennifer-willis.com and/or sign up for my readers list.

ACKNOWLEDGMENTS

This book wouldn't have been possible without the assistance and support of many key players.

Tainted Treasure went through a significant revision following feedback from a team of beta and sensitivity readers who offered insightful comments and probing questions to help me improve the story. **Mo Corston-Oliver**, **Richard Doty**, **Danielle Gembala**, **Cory Panshin**, **Stephanie Richardson**, and **Rebecca Stefoff** invested their time and their consideration, and I am grateful for their efforts. Whatever errors remain in the text are my responsibility, not theirs.

Laurel Standley was a last-minute gamma reader for the manuscript and shared her scientific expertise with me both in the planning and polishing of *Tainted Treasure*. Laurel again volunteered as the test baker for the recipes included at the end of the book.

Basically everything I publish warrants a shout-out to the **Masked Hucksters—Dale Ivan Smith**, **Rebecca Stefoff**, and **Wendy N. Wagner**—my infamously awesome writers' group. For the past ten years, these amazing people have shaped my career and my life in meaningful and delightful ways, and I wouldn't have it otherwise.

Steven Novak designed another fitting and fun cover for this third entry in the Haunted Coast series and is always a pleasure to work with.

My partner, **Mike**, always gets a shout-out in the acknowledgments, and this time it is doubly earned. He has accepted and encouraged me for more than fifteen years, and this past summer he went above and beyond in caring for me after major surgery. As I continue to recover and reclaim my stamina, strength, and acuity, I have him to thank for sustaining me.

ABOUT THE AUTHOR

Jennifer Willis loves tales of magickal mayhem, unlikely adventure, and playful intrigue.

An admitted sci-fi nerd and urban fantasy fan, she is the author of the Rune Witch urban fantasy series, the Haunted Coast paranormal cozy mystery series, and the M.A.R.S. science fiction romance books.

Author photograph by Rachel Hadiashar.

She is a columnist for *Sky & Telescope* online and the writer behind *The Oregonian*'s former Northwest Love Stories series. She has a byline in the British Fantasy Award-winning *Women Destroy Science Fiction* from *Lightspeed*, which was named one of NPR's best books in 2014.

An amateur backyard astronomer and avid collector of backpacks, she lives in Oregon with her dude, a giant dog, a tangle of cats, and possibly a family of raccoons residing under the house.

She has had a headache every day since November 2014.

For more information . . .
Jennifer-Willis.com

Milton Keynes UK
Ingram Content Group UK Ltd.
UKHW040948071123
432124UK00001B/58

9 798223 474326